A DEAL WITH THE DEVIL

The Spinster Society
Book 2

By Alyxandra Harvey

ARE YOU SIGNED UP FOR DRAGONBLADE'S BLOG?

You'll get the latest news and information on exclusive giveaways, exclusive excerpts, coming releases, sales, free books, cover reveals and more.

Check out our complete list of authors, too!

No spam, no junk. That's a promise!

Sign Up Here

www.dragonbladepublishing.com

Dearest Reader;

Thank you for your support of a small press. At Dragonblade Publishing, we strive to bring you the highest quality Historical Romance from some of the best authors in the business. Without your support, there is no 'us', so we sincerely hope you adore these stories and find some new favorite authors along the way.

Happy Reading!

CEO, Dragonblade Publishing

Additional Dragonblade books by Author Alyxandra Harvey

The Spinster Society Series
The Scandalous Spinster (Book 1)
A Deal With the Devil (Book 2)

The Dainty Devils Series
The Duchess Games (Book 1)
The Countess Caper (Book 2)
The Husband Heist (Book 3)

The Cinderella Society Series
How to Marry an Earl (Book 1)
How to Marry a Duke (Book 2)
How to Marry a Viscount (Book 3)

CHAPTER ONE

One month earlier...

KITTY CALDECOTT WAS not the kind of woman to be invited to a Devil's Night.

She did not own a single silk ball gown, was not being courted by a fine gentleman in a fine hat, and she did not know how to dance a quadrille.

Also, her father was a very poor gambler.

Very, *very* poor.

Unfortunately, he did not accept this simple fact of nature and insisted that his long overdue Great Win was on the next hand. Or the one after that. Surely the next.

Perhaps understandably, Kitty was not particularly fond of gambling. On a hand of cards or the roll of a die, or whether or not Lord Whatshisname would topple his carriage at the next race through Hyde Park. (He would. They always did. It was a sucker's bet. One her father would surely jump on.)

But Kitty *did* know books.

Especially wicked, salacious ones. Joyful ones.

And the Marquis of Eastbourne had been chosen to host this specific Devil's Night, which was ruled over by Lord Birmingham, also known as Devil. He held the bank and the reins, but he chose an assortment of earls and dukes and marquis to host the event.

Marquises? Marquesses?

Kitty also did not know the correct grammatical forms of address.

Kitty's own father was only a very minor baron, and so she had never really had to learn the more arcane rules of Mayfair Polite Society. To her aunt's very loud and pointed chagrin.

To be fair, almost everything was to her aunt's very loud and pointed chagrin.

She had never been invited either. Which was no great surprise.

But Kitty had. For the one night, dusk until dawn, to provide the best naughty novels and chapbooks to the guests, most especially the new Nightingale chapbook not yet available in shops. A most unique party favor that would also allow her to put aside some money to save her sister.

For that reason, Kitty had many complimentary thoughts about the marquis.

That was before the marquis was hauled away by several of Devil's rather brutal-looking men. Peers fought for the privilege of hosting such a night. Even men who abducted women, apparently.

That was before a lot of things.

The evening was as decadent and debauched as expected. Guests were instructed to wear red, and the sheer volume of rubies flashing and garnets dangling off earlobes and blood-colored silks and velvets was staggering. Kitty wore her best dress, which was yellow and nowhere near stylish enough for a regular ball, never mind a Devil's Night. But she was not a guest, rather part of the entertainment. Staff. Thankfully.

Strawberries floated in champagne; cherries oozed from tiny butter-crust pies. A sculpture of a naked demoness reclined over several gold platters, made of soft cheese dotted with pomegranate seeds. There were dozens of gaming tables, half as many billiards tables felted red instead of green, and a betting book to rival any club in London. Courtesans floated between the players offering encouragement from behind crimson, feathered masquerade masks.

Devil stood apart and aloof, watching from the balcony above like a hawk in a gilded nest. He wore black, not red, and though he did not circulate, did not even bother to greet the many patrons below, they all knew exactly who he was and where he stood for the entire evening. Heads turned in his direction between bad hands of cards and between good.

All of the guests orbited him, sending glimpses into shadows to find him: coy, angry, lustful, jealous, desperate.

He seemed bored but also violently aware of everything going on around him. His eyes had found her once: dark, direct, tracking her every movement as she unpacked a box of books currently banned in London. Also, poetry that was not fit to be read aloud in polite company. Her favorite kind. She had felt his gaze on her even with her back turned to the staircase, and when she turned to look up, something shivered inside her.

Something untoward. Alarming.

Something delicious.

She knew the stories, of course—that a wager made on Devil's Night was subject to the Devil himself. He ensured every player made good on his or her debt, no matter the uniqueness of it or the consequences it might involve. She had heard of a duke who tried to renege and ended up losing his foot in the process. Kitty did not often put much stock in gossip. After all, gossip had her leading women in dark rites in the basement of her shop, where she may or may not also eat the hearts of men raw. There was something about orgies too.

As if there was space for that kind of thing in the basement of a London bookshop.

But in Devil's case, the tales were too easy to believe.

But as she did not wager, she did not expect to come away from a Devil's Night in any way changed, beyond in possession of a heavier purse from selling her wares. Hopefully enough to pay off some of her father's more violent creditors, enough for an order of tea and mutton. One day, enough to secure her sister's future. A dowry. *Options.*

Options were rather scarce on the ground for women in London. Unlike vicars, congregating on her front step and flapping their wings like disgruntled pigeons.

She had not expected the chance to change everything to arrive so swiftly.

Nor in the hands of the dangerously handsome, entirely too-riveting Devil.

More fool her.

That was the point of the Devil, wasn't it? Temptation? Everyone gathered here tonight was tempted.

But there was also an undercurrent of fear to their attention.

Which was not Kitty's concern.

Until he sent a man careening over the balustrade.

Entirely too near to her book table and entirely too near to her person. Books were fragile and not be abused. She did not know the man or what he deserved.

A moment earlier, that man had alternated between shouting and begging, his face red enough to match the décor. When he landed, he broke a side table with curved legs, a ship made entirely of glass, and probably several of his bones. To add insult to injury, a portrait fell off the wall behind him and nearly decapitated him. He groaned, nose crooked and bloody.

Someone screamed. But mostly, the guests watched him with morbid fascination, glad not to be on the receiving end. Just as glad to have a story to tell to those back home.

Devil only leaned on the railing, returning the stares until they all turned away with laughs meant to cover their discomfort.

Except for Kitty.

She continued to watch him, safe in her corner, unnoticed. Curious. Drawn to him despite herself.

The clock behind her was circled in a wreath of gilded laurel leaves, elegant and persistent as it ticked closer and closer to midnight. She felt a bit like Cinderella. Or would have, were she not more like a wicked stepsister in this particular tale.

But she would do anything to save her sister.

Even betray her friend.

Maybe.

Probably.

The clock continued to tick at her mockingly.

The time for betrayal came and went and she did not move. She could not. She had done too much harm already and could not stomach going any further. It had been a stupid, desperate plan anyway.

Not like her current plan.

Which, to be clear, was equally stupid and desperate, but far likelier to bring results.

She was still watching Devil when he slipped a folded piece of paper inside his pocket. She had not managed to figure out where the signed vowels were kept—too many of his men came and went. And then he vanished into the shadows.

Kitty was moving before she realized what she was doing, before she could stop herself.

She stepped over a splatter of blood, barely glanced at the groaning man who was being ignored by his friends and decidedly *not* ignored by Devil's men. She slipped between gaming tables, around throngs of inebriated lords too bored to care that she was a spinster and too drunk to remember her by the time she had passed out of view. The music played by the orchestra continued to pour through the room, adding an edge to every roll of dice, every clack of a ball hitting another ball on the felt billiards table. It motivated her to keep going even though she should most definitely turn back.

Should make better choices.

Which would leave her sister to her fate.

Bollocks to that.

She'd happily climb into hell to save her sister. Or trip into it, as it were.

She quickened her pace, heading for the main formal staircase, which she had no business using as a bookseller hired to provide party favors. She ought to stick to the servant stairs in the back. But since the marquis had just been caught abducting women and hiding them in his cellar, Kitty was not too bothered with whether he considered her an uncouth upstart. More dark entertainment for a Devil's Night.

She darted up the first step, the second, and then crashed right into Devil.

It was like bouncing off a mountain. A handsome, suspicious mountain who smelled very good. She tried to catch herself. She assumed he would be as pampered as the other earls she had seen with calf padding in their stockings and in the shoulders of their coats.

Not quite.

She tumbled, tripping over her own feet with a little more genuineness than she had planned. She half sprawled against the railing, the oak scrollwork digging into her shoulder blades. "I beg your pardon!" she said, rubbing at her elbow that had hit at just the wrong angle and sent painful tingles down her arm.

Devil looked down at her, aloof green eyes cold and distrustful. Knowing. Noticing every detail: her dress, which was her best but still nowhere near good enough, the ink on her fingers, which were gloveless because her gloves itched, her lack of rubies. Down to the mending at the top of her left stocking, which she knew on a rational level that he could not see through her skirts but which her body was entirely convinced was possible.

She had not thought being this close to him would affect her, even though his magnetism was palpable. A reaction to his presence was primal. Lions did not walk among gazelles without effect.

Kitty had never seen a gazelle, but she fancied she knew exactly how they felt.

Devil straightened his coat, checked his pockets. Satisfied that nothing was missing, he nodded at her once. He did not say a word, even as he reached down to grip her arm and pull her up.

And *that* was when she stole from the Devil himself.

Last night…

IT HAD TAKEN Devil nearly a month to find her. Him, a veritable devil, and she, a bookseller.

It was embarrassing.

Infuriating.

He who hosted extravagant evenings across England once a year, with every temptation and entertainment scattered like dandelions in a field. He held the bank and the vowels and no quarter was given on a Devil's Night. No exceptions made. Not for king or duke or beautiful woman. God himself could lose a bet and Devil would find a way to make him pay.

All to one purpose.

Which had nothing to do with gambling or wagering or fortunes. Devil did not even particularly enjoy playing cards. But he did enjoy winning, and he enjoyed power most of all.

Like hell would he see it undone by a redheaded menace.

She had *stolen* from him.

Stealing from the Devil was not something that could be ignored. Admired, perhaps. It begrudgingly.

But not ignored.

Never ignored.

It was not a precedent he could afford to set. Even if the lady in question had snapping gray eyes and a very distracting trail of freckles.

Especially then.

They had exchanged a grand total of three polite sentences at the Devil's Night hosted by the Marquis of Eastbourne, before the marquis was dragged away for keeping ladies in his cellar in order to control their fortunes. It had been both a duty and a true pleasure to help take him down. Though credit was mostly due to Lady Clara Prescott and her retired sea captain. Devil believed in proper credit. And debts paid. He had built his reputation on it. Fearsome, exacting, and without the need to defend it for the past few years, beyond the odd attempt on his life from some desperate gambler in over his head.

And now here he was in the dead of night, skulking through a bookshop that seemed to cater to the kinds of stories that were decidedly frowned upon for the good ladies of the *ton*. Ordinarily, he would have been impressed. Amused.

If he weren't already so damned irritated.

The walls were the blue of a Scottish loch, details of the chipped plasterwork picked out in gold. They were not the only things gleaming in the uncertain light of the lampposts outside.

True to its name, the Golden Griffin Bookshop was full of griffins.

They prowled over the ceiling, curled in the corners, scales shimmering, teeth uncomfortably sharp for a place where the air was fragrant with lingering perfume and tea. And, if he wasn't mistaken, whiskey.

He ducked behind the counter and into the back room, curtained off by drapes secured with enormous gold tassels better suited to the opera stage. She was a dramatic little thing, if nothing else. She liked monsters and naughty fairy tales.

He could be a monster.

She read lurid chapbooks, bit the ends of her pencils, and kept a tin of sugared violets under her desk. She also kept a neat ledger, he discovered, skimming the entrances for discrepancies, bribes, hints that she might be more than she seemed. Only someone with dark connections indeed could manage to steal from him. To pluck a vowel straight from his pocket. Many had attempted the ill-advised feat, but no one had ever succeeded.

Until Miss Caldecott.

It would not stand.

Even if she was exactly as she seemed: a pesky bookseller with an impish grin and a serious lack of self-preservation. Innocent.

It did not signify.

Miss Kitty Caldecott was his now.

Now

KITTY WAS NOT having a good day.

It had not started well, and then it had rapidly proceeded to get much worse.

Much worse.

Really, if she could harness the speed and momentum at which everything disintegrated, she could afford to buy a mansion in Mayfair. Twelve mansions. And then she would not be in the pickle she found herself in.

Through no fault of her own.

Mostly.

Partly.

She was not hopeful it would get better.

She had risen early, which was never a good way to start the day, in her estimation. Mornings were meant to pass by on the other side of her window, cheerful and requiring absolutely no input from her. It had been years since such a thing was possible, of course. But her bleary morning brain would not forget—pots of warmed chocolate brought to her bedside with a basket of cinnamon-dusted pastries were hard to forget. It had only been for one summer, when her father was given his title, and before he had gambled away his fortune.

She could do without new dancing slippers, as invitations to balls were not exactly forthcoming. She could go without the newest style of bonnet or ices from Gunter's or weekly tickets to Vauxhall Gardens. She could do without visiting the modiste. As she had proven, daily, over the last very many years.

But that pot of chocolate proved harder to forgo.

Still, she had her bookshop, which brought her more joy than she could have dreamed. Griffin Bookshop catered to the unique reader: those who gravitated toward gothic romances, salacious novels, and wicked poetry, preferably written by ladies. She carried the regular fare, of course, but she had become known for her secret shelves, stacked with the kinds of stories the newspapers disdained because they were not morally improving. Even before the Devil's Night.

Her wares were, truth be told, downright shocking. Just as she liked it. And it was all her own.

So, nothing to complain about, really.

But people who said there was nothing to complain about had very little imagination.

She did not wish to be the kind of person who whined at every little inconvenience, but when she found herself trapped on the roof of their rented house in her nightdress—in a storm, naturally—perhaps one or two complaints might be lodged with management. Posthaste.

If only *she* weren't the management.

This is what came of mornings.

When dawn poked its sharp, bossy nose through her window, she ought to have pressed a pillow over her head. Instead, she stuffed her feet into her slippers, washed her face, grumbled, swore at a chair when she stubbed her toe, and then went to make breakfast for her younger sister Evie.

Evangeline, beautiful and kind, routinely woke as though butterflies lifted her from her bed—smiling, her hair in perfect waves and gold as the sun. Kitty would have said it was as gold as coins, but she had recently been accused of being sly and mercenary.

As the woman who oversaw the household accounts, however, and knew exactly how much sugar and tea cost, *mercenary* was not the insult it might once have been.

Although "sly" hit a nerve she did not wish to explore.

At any rate, there might not be pots of chocolate of a morning, but there would be honey for toasted bread. And butter. One day. Soon.

"You're grumbling to yourself again," Evie pointed out.

"I'm reciting poetry, if you must know," Kitty lied. She did not want to worry her sister, who was nineteen years old and ought to have been enjoying a truly spectacular come-out, dancing until dawn, gathering posies and truly awful sonnets written about her nose.

"Most poems do not use *those* words, and certainly not in that order," Evie pointed out.

"Well, not the interesting ones, anyway." Kitty stubbed her toe again, a bruise upon a bruise. "Arsemonkeys."

"That's a new one."

"Shut your ears."

"Not on your life," Evie returned cheerfully. She hurried to steady the tray Kitty had brought her, teacup wobbling precariously. "You know you don't have to bring me breakfast, Kitty. I'm perfectly capable of fetching it for myself."

"I have to bring Aunt P her tray anyway." Kitty shrugged and nearly upended the coddled eggs slipping across the plate.

"I can do that too."

"You *have* been doing that," Kitty reminded her. "While I've been at the shop. I just happened to wake up early today." She did not add that it was worry that woke her, as it always did. Lord knew their father did not worry. At least not in any way that was productive. Having Aunt Priscilla peruse the gossip papers and parading Evie up and down Rotten Row every afternoon hoping to catch the attention of a single man of good fortune was not particularly useful.

Last month, the woman had bodily shoved Evie into the path of an earl's oncoming carriage in the hopes that something might come of it. Something like a marriage proposal.

Instead, Evie had turned her knee. She might have died.

"Have the Four Horsemen arrived in London?" Evie asked.

"That's a bit grim, even for you. It's early but hardly the apocalypse." Evie might *look* like an angel, but she had a wicked streak as wide as Kitty's. Everything else about her was softer, though, and so people did not notice. Kitty was not soft. There was no time for softness.

If only she could convince the burning in her esophagus that she had everything in hand.

"When Kitty Caldecott willingly rises before the sun, it is dark days indeed." Evie snorted. "Literally and metaphorically."

Kitty could not argue with that.

"Have you taken Papa his breakfast yet?"

"No, it's still in the hall." As she had lovely daydreams of upending the lot over his head, she had opted to wait. Anyway, Evie did not deserve cold, congealed eggs but he certainly did.

It occurred to Kitty, not the first time, that she was not the forgiving sort.

"I'll do it." Evie shrugged into her wrapper. Her long, honey-hued curls fell in a delightful tangle down her back. It hardly needed saying that Kitty had woken to a bird's nest on top of her own head.

"You did it yesterday. And the day before that. Not to mention you have been waiting on Aunt Priscilla, and that is unjust punishment."

"She gets cross when her tea is tepid."

"Her tea could be made with the burning coals of hellfire and she would still find it tepid enough to be cross over."

Taking Aunt Priscilla her morning tray should not have been a harrowing experience. And yet Kitty had drunk an entire pot of strong tea down in the kitchen just to wake herself up enough to manage carrying it up the stairs, never mind dealing with her aunt. Neither was at their best before noon and avoided each other by tacit agreement. Actually, it was more of a peace treaty brokered by Evie for the good of the rest of the household. And the state of the crockery. Her aunt tended to throw things when she was vexed. As had Kitty's mother before she died, only they had never noticed the loss of objects then. They were always cleaned up and replaced as though by magic. Her father still had his fortune then.

Alas.

"I'll take it," Kitty sighed. "I deserve it." She muttered the last, but Evie heard her.

"Bloody bollocks to that, Kitty Caldecott."

Kitty feigned shock, mostly so she could not be pressed to explain herself. "Where did you even learn such words?"

"From you, of course."

"Shocking lies."

Absolute truth.

She had not known that word, or any interesting ones really, when she was nineteen years old.

Also untrue.

She had absolutely known them, only she had never spoken them aloud where someone might hear her. She certainly would not have dared to lecture a country vicar in his late seventies on the etymology of such words, as she had done just yesterday.

Sometimes, being a spinster had its advantages.

Rarely, it had to be said. But still. One took one's entertainment where one could. And if such a man felt at ease to come into her shop to lecture her on her supposedly loose morals, she could lecture him right back. Especially as he had not purchased a single item.

Flinging his toupee into the muddy street may have been taking things a touch too far.

But she would do it again. He had insisted women should be silent. So she had been silent. Mostly. She might leave off the slightly maniacal laugh next time. Oh, who was she fooling? The laugh was what made self-righteous curmudgeons who insisted on marching into her shop in high dudgeon sweat. It was her bread and butter. Especially now that they could not always afford bread *or* butter.

It wasn't her shop accounts or the disdain of the clergy or even the state of their household ledger that sent a bolt of cold dread down her spine.

It wasn't her secrets, her bad decisions, the prospect of what Evie would think of her.

Of the consequences surely chasing her, even now.

It was none of those things.

It was a simple knock at the door, too early in the morning.

Especially when their father answered it with a nervous, falsely jovial laugh. "Lord Portsmouth, how good to see you."

Evie froze. Kitty met her gaze.

"Bollocks," they said in unison.

CHAPTER TWO

KITTY PEERED OUT of the window down to the street below and cursed.

Deeply.

Blasphemously.

The vicar would have fainted at her feet before she even plucked the badger-fur toupee from his head.

Evie's eyes widened. "I shall have to remember *that* one."

"Best not. We can only afford one family disgrace," Kitty said wryly, despite her heart beating in her throat where it had no business being. "Find your own scandal."

Evie snorted a laugh even though there was no time for it. But they always managed to find a way to make each other laugh. Kitty had made a game of their dispossession all those years ago.

Evie frowned through the glass. "That's odd. Why did Lord Portsmouth bring a second carriage?"

Kitty's heart thrummed again, momentarily choking her. She swallowed down the fear, shoving it out of the way so she could breathe. So she could *think*. "I believe he has forgone the courtship altogether."

Evie shivered. "What does that mean?"

"It means that it is your trunk I see being carried out by his outrider." A flutter in Kitty's chest, this time mostly fueled by rage. An improvement. She could do many more impossible things with rage.

"Who has that many outriders while in London?" Evie said slowly.

"Those intending on traveling all the way to Gretna Green, if I were to hazard a guess." Outriders were used for trips into the country where any manner of inconvenience might be found, from highwaymen to broken carriage wheels.

Evie sucked in a breath. "Father is letting him abduct me to Scotland? For an anvil wedding? Surely not."

"Definitely Aunt P's idea. So that your reputation will be ruined before you even arrive and you will have no choice." If Kitty was mercenary, her aunt was downright ruthless. And their father capitulated, as always.

Kitty had never truly hated her family before, not really. She was perilously close at the moment.

Another reason she was nowhere near as good as her sister. But let her sister be the kind one, the good one. In the meantime, Kitty would set both carriages on fire.

Gleefully.

"I won't marry him," Evie said quietly.

"Too right, you won't," Kitty agreed. "For one thing, I have every intention of committing murder before that ever happens."

"Perhaps we might start with running away," Evie said with the same dry tone she had learned from Kitty. She pulled a small valise form under her bed.

"How long have you had that packed?" Kitty asked, pride shoving her heart back down into her chest where it belonged. Evie was not a little girl anymore. And she was so much more astute than anyone gave her credit for.

"Since Aunt P pushed me in front of that carriage."

They exchanged a grim smile. "Well done, you," Kitty said, shoving down the guilt and frustration over not doing a better job at protecting her sister. The anger she felt at her father for not being stronger, her aunt kinder. "Hurry."

Evie might be kind and beautiful, with a voice soft as kitten feet, but she was also the untidiest person Kitty had ever met. She had seen overturned carts in Covent Garden that were better organized.

In this case, it at least offered a cloak draped over a plant slowly suffocating under the resulting lack of sunlight. There were no longer any housemaids to tidy up after them. There had not been for a couple of years now. Though Kitty had made a reasonable success of her grandmother's bookshop, despite her mother's insistence that their history in trade was something to sweep under the rug posthaste, it was still not enough to allow them the same luxuries as their previous fortune had briefly done. When their mother died, their father had no one to temper his gambling.

And as it turned out, he was not particularly good at it. He was too trusting. Too desperate.

The bookshop was the only thing that had saved them from outright ruin. Along with selling everything they owned of any value. Except for the diamonds and pearls that Aunt P hid from creditors and gaming hell thugs in places Kitty had no wish to consider.

"Put this on." Kitty shoved the thick velvet at Evie. She could practically hear the plant gasping for breath as it was freed. "There's no time for you to get dressed." Not with two carriages waiting outside. And not with their father employing that particular laugh before nine o'clock in the morning. The one that clearly heralded he was in over his head. Floundering.

Her blood chilled.

"You'll have to go out the window."

"Not again." Evie hastened to tie the cloak ribbons around the neck.

"Aunt P has already found all of our hiding spots," Kitty replied. Evie darted away in the opposite direction of the window. "Hurry!"

"I can't leave Galahad behind. She will never remember to feed him. Especially not crickets—she thinks it's disgusting."

"It's a little disgusting," Kitty allowed. They crunched. She always felt sorry for them. "I'll feed your pincushion."

"You're always at the shop," Evie replied stubbornly. "I'm not leaving him behind."

Which was how Kitty ended up shoving her baby sister and a confused hedgehog in a gold cage out of a top-floor window.

As far as escape routes went, it was not ideal. Even before it started to rain.

But it was better than the alternative.

The alternative being Lord Portsmouth.

THE WINDOW WAS safely shut and Kitty was hurrying across the carpet when their aunt appeared in the doorway. Aunt Priscilla was a tiny, imposing woman with fair hair streaked silver. It was clear which side of the family Evie had inherited her delicate bone structure and glowing skin. Kitty's red hair and freckles came from their father's side.

Aunt Priscilla might be no bigger than a minute, but she was all teeth. All of the time.

"Kitty, what are you doing in here?" No one stood against Mrs. Priscilla Bartley for long, annuity or not.

Except for Kitty.

"I was bringing Evie her breakfast, Aunt P."

Aunt Priscilla narrowed her eyes. Kitty held her gaze, raising one eyebrow. An entire battle of wills occurred during that one silent moment, complete with bloodshed and betrayal. But never surrender. Never that.

"Lord Portsmouth is here for your sister."

"It's barely nine in the morning."

"I didn't ask you for the time. Get your sister."

"It's rather gauche, such an early call, don't you think?" She only said it to needle her aunt.

Aunt P's right eye twitched. Direct hit. "Don't keep him waiting."

"She's not here," Kitty said.

"I beg your pardon?" Her aunt's voice was sharper than Galahad's spikes.

"Evie is not here," Kitty repeated.

"Where the devil is she?"

"I'm sure I don't know. I came in and she was gone."

"A likely story. There's a devil here, and it's you."

"I'm not the one trying to shove her into that blackguard's carriage."

"Hush, you silly chit. He'll hear you."

"Good. Because you cannot be serious. He's *vile*."

"He's an *earl*." As if that forgave anything. Everything. For her aunt, it did. "And don't call me Aunt P—it's vulgar."

"He's had three wives who all died within a year of the wedding!"

Kitty was quite serious about burning down those carriages. She would prefer to wait until Lord Portsmouth was inside, but she would also happily go out and do it right now and save everyone the bother.

Her aunt caught her arm, painfully digging nails into her skin. "You are not Evangeline's guardian."

"I wish I was. I would never sell her."

"Don't be so dramatic. Rumors, gossip. It means nothing. The lower classes always talk."

Coming from a woman who wielded gossip like a sword. And had come from the very same lower classes.

"*Three* dead wives is not idle chatter."

"Childbirth is dangerous."

"One of them drowned."

"So is swimming."

"She drowned in a *very shallow* pond." Kitty wanted to scream.

"We need him, Kitty," Aunt P said. "He does not care about her lack of dowry and has offered us a proper townhouse in St. James's Square. *St. James's Square.* And he has been nothing but courteous to your sister. And to me. He thinks she is beautiful.

Angelic."

"We don't need him," Kitty said stubbornly.

"The only gold we have left to our name is your sister's hair."

"Evie deserves better."

"We all do," Aunt P said bitterly. "Tell that to your father and his debts."

"It doesn't matter, does it?" Kitty asked as the rain tapped at the window. "She's not here."

She could not wait much longer to follow Evie. The roof would turn slippery, and Evie's knee was still healing. By the end of most days she needed a cane to support herself, despite their aunt shrieking about it interfering with the line of her gowns. Evie had wrapped it with white silk roses in a kind of compromise. Kitty made a note to take it from where it was poking out from under the bed. Galahad liked to bat at the flowers, and he was stronger than a little ball of spikes had any right to be. Kitty had once found the cane halfway down the stairs by tripping over it and nearly breaking her entire body. Perhaps that might work on Lord Portsmouth.

"I shall find an excuse," Aunt Priscilla hissed. *"While you find your sister."*

"Of course, Aunt P."

Her aunt narrowed her eyes, clearly suspicious.

Fair enough.

Kitty wouldn't have believed her either.

Devil ought to have sent one of his men to do this work.

He did not often break into shops or skulk through early morning gardens. Anymore, that was.

But Miss Caldecott intrigued him.

Even if the gold paint from one of her bloody griffins had already proven impossible to scrub out of his cuff. His valet would make that noise in the back of his throat, like a peacock caught in a storm.

And now here Devil was, leaning against a tree, rain dripping all around him.

He could be wrapped in silk sheets and softer skin, awake because he'd had too good a time to sleep—not awake because he was hunting a sly fox of a woman.

He refused to acknowledge the fact that this gray morning was already proving to be more interesting than his usual pursuits. That there was a shot of excitement he had not felt in too long. Opulence, risks, beauty. He had gorged on it.

This was something else.

Curiosity and another twinge of some emotion he could not—or would not—name kept him where he was.

Watching her.

Hunting.

He paused. Cursed.

Why was the bloody woman on the roof?

CHAPTER THREE

KITTY WAS ON the wet, miserable rooftop because her sister was on the wet, miserable rooftop.

It was as simple as that.

Not that Devil would understand that, were she to imagine him watching her from the lilac bushes across the street. Which she would not. Because she was not that fanciful. Or insane.

In any case, she had bigger things to worry about. Like not plummeting to her death. All while steadying her sister with the bad knee and the birdcage full of annoyed hedgehog.

With any luck, were Kitty to roll right off the shingles, she would land on Lord Portsmouth and break his neck. Obviously, she would prefer other means of stopping him, but beggars couldn't be choosers. And she *was* trying to be a better person. Despite recent evidence to the contrary.

Evie was quite right—running away was suddenly a perfectly reasonable option. Although crawling away was perhaps a better description. Inching, even.

The rain fell like silver needles, and then blew sideways so as to inflict maximum turmoil. It dripped from her eyelashes and soaked into her nightdress. She hadn't had time to change into something more suitable, had not even had time to find anything more than a shawl Evie had tried to knit before realizing she could not knit. It resembled nothing so much as a confused fishing net in red yarn. Not subtle and not particularly helpful. Two terms to perfectly describe her morning, really.

The last month.

Year.

Never mind. That was a problem to be dealt with under considerably drier circumstances. With a pot of tea. Or a bottle of whiskey. An entire strawberry cake.

The wind gusted most disobligingly.

Evie's slippers skidded on the wet shingles. Kitty made a grab for her and they teetered, dangerously close to the edge. She could have sworn someone shouted something unflattering about mad girls from across the street, but it was likely a coachman cursing his own now-wet state. There was no earthly reason for anyone to look up or even be able to see them through the sheets of rain. "Slowly," Kitty gritted from between clenched teeth. "Slowly."

"On the bright side, if I tumble to my death, I won't have to marry Portsmouth."

"You're not going to fall," Kitty said. "But if you should, make sure to use him as a landing spot."

"I should have brought my cane. I could have skewered him on impact."

Kitty snorted. "I will hire someone to paint it as a portrait. We can hang it in the foyer."

"We can't afford portraits anymore."

"Oh, right."

"*I* could paint him."

"You are an atrocious painter. He'll look like he's part badger. Or like he's melting."

"All the better."

"True."

If you couldn't jest with your sister on a rooftop with lightning flashing disconcertingly close to your heads, what was even the point in having a sister?

"Perhaps I should maim myself a little," Evie said in a tone that was too considering and too even for Kitty's peace of mind. "If I had a scar or a crooked nose, he would not find me beautiful anymore."

"You'd still be the most beautiful girl in England. It's disgusting, really."

"Not to Portsmouth. He's not the type."

Because she was quite correct, Kitty only said, "Let's save that for a last resort, shall we?"

"We can't stay up here all day." Evie had to shout over the sudden burst of wind.

"I have a plan!" Kitty shouted back.

"That's what I'm afraid of!"

There was very little time left for talking or jesting after that. It took considerable concentration to cross the rooftop, the chill numbing her fingertips. The roof of the adjoining house was in much better repair and considerably less steep. Which was a comfort, as Kitty had made the mistake of looking down.

"Everything is so much less daunting from up here," Evie said. "More like a dollhouse city."

Kitty jerked back from the edge, feeling slightly queasy. She had not given nearly enough consideration to the matter of getting back down to the ground.

The glorious, stable ground.

Currently, very, *very* far away.

"Are you well?" Evie shouted. "You've gone funny."

Kitty tried to smile—to mixed results, if Evie's reaction was any indication. Her sister visibly recoiled.

"I don't know what you are doing to your face," Evie said. "But I demand you stop it immediately." She held the hedgehog in his golden wire palace out of reach. "And don't cast up your accounts on poor Galahad."

"Let's just get down." Kitty's teeth chattered even though it was not quite *that* cold.

"Two more houses," Evie said encouragingly. "Sir Reginald spent all that money on new balconies and trellises, remember?

It's quite sturdy."

Kitty would have preferred a ladder. Or an actual staircase.

"You're a very interesting color," Evie pointed out conversationally. "A bit green, a bit chartreuse."

"Not at all fashionable of me."

"You'd be thrown out of Almack's."

For so many reasons. Even if one of the patronesses routinely and with near-religious fanaticism came to her shop to purchase the very books she looked down her nose at Kitty for selling.

Thunder rumbled, and Kitty felt it under her feet. Lightning flashed. It was getting dangerous, and not just because the way down was several stories of wet trellis and hopping from balcony to balcony. The next ripple of thunder came with a flash of lightning Kitty swore she felt in her teeth. She jumped with a loud, strangled yelp.

And promptly lost her footing.

Evie was too far away and her hands were full of hedgehog.

Kitty sprawled and slid down the roof, too slippery to stop herself, too rough not to hurt all the way down. She caught herself on the edge by wedging her heel into the eavestrough. Rain pelted her, running in her eyes and her mouth as her pulse bolted like a spooked horse.

"Kitty!" Evie reached her, grabbing her arm. She was suddenly pale, teeth chattering. "Don't you dare die and leave me alone."

"I wouldn't dream of it," Kitty croaked. Her knees felt like stewed celery. "Isn't Sir Reginald away? Something about the seaside?"

Evie nodded. "He invited me to go with him."

Kitty was momentarily distracted. "He's eighty-three years old."

"I don't think he *meant* it to be indecorous."

"Hmm. Either way, he likes you. I'm sure he won't mind if we go through his house. He's always wanting to show you his new décor."

"I'm not sure this is what he had in mind."

Kitty was too busy twisting to point to the window behind them that was relatively easy to access. Evie helped her to her feet, which were still not quite as steady as she would have liked. "It's unlocked," she announced. She wondered if weeping with relief was going a bit too far. Maybe her aunt was right. She *was* dramatic.

"Housebreaking is a hanging offense," Evie said, reclaiming Galahad's cage from where she had wedged it in order to reach her sister.

"Not for someone as pretty as you," Kitty said. "Me they will hang with all alacrity."

"You're pretty!"

"Aunt P says I have the devil's hair."

"Aunt P *is* the devil," Evie muttered.

The door led to the attic, and a narrow-crooked staircase. "Hello?" Kitty called out. "Sir Reginald? Anyone?" She winced at the wet footprints they left behind. Not very surreptitious of them.

The silence peculiar to an empty house greeted them.

As did a small, dry parlor entirely decorated with cabbages. "Gah."

"That is…a great many cabbages."

"What do we do now?" Evie asked. "We can't hide out here forever. Sir Reginald might return today for all we know."

"We're going to hide you until I can fix this," Kitty said, using a table runner embroidered with pink and green cabbages to sop up some of the water dripping from her hair into her face.

"Where?"

"Where no one would think to look for you."

The safest place she knew.

And the very last place she wished to go.

THE SPINSTER SOCIETY was located in a large, well-appointed house on the edge of Hyde Park. It shared back gardens and greenhouses with the house next door, which belonged to Lady Priya Langdon. She had purchased it for the additional greenhouses for her horticultural pursuits but opened the house to a peculiar kind of ladies' society.

It was whispered about from one end of Mayfair to the other. The society left calling cards in ladies' retiring rooms at balls held in the very best houses—warnings to fortune hunters, of men with all of the power and consequence but generally without any *actual* consequences. Men like Lord Portsmouth.

Oh, how it infuriated men like him. They could not get to Lady Priya, or her army of spinsters.

Kitty did not have the occasion to frequent many balls—even before their father's disgrace, barons were only invited to the most peripheral of social gatherings. She did not cross paths with dukes and earls often. She knew their wives from selling them naughty books and treatises on the position of women in modern Britain. Also ancient Sparta, where women could own property and inherit fortunes.

Books on ancient Sparta were very popular.

All to say that Kitty knew about the Spinster Society through other means. Mostly because she had a friend who was a member.

A friend she had betrayed.

And Priya knew everyone's secrets. Dukes, dowagers—even the prime minster was not immune. The king himself likely had secrets he did not even know, but for certain Priya knew them.

That was how Kitty knew Priya was perfectly aware of her transgressions.

She would not blame the woman for slamming the door in her face. As long as she did not slam it in Evie's.

"Where are we?" Evie asked. The rain had lessened but not cleared completely. They had run all the way here through the streets of London in their nightdresses. They could not stop now.

Not yet.

"Just keep going," Kitty said, ducking onto the path that led between the houses through hedges trimmed to resemble leaping fish and alcoves of sweet-smelling lilacs. The risk of being spotted was too great to knock on the front door. Two women soaked to the bone in their nightdresses were hard to miss. And honestly, Kitty was not sure of the etiquette in this situation. They were not servants or tradesmen, but also not ladies of high rank. They were supplicants. The side door seemed safest.

Kitty would beg if she had to.

The sun peeked out from behind the clouds, shining on the road, on the carriages and the street sweepers darting out of their hiding places. On pedestrians emerging from their houses, umbrellas in hand. "Don't stop," Kitty urged her sister on.

"Galahad's caught!"

"I've got him." Kitty stopped to attend to the gold cage snarled in a lilac branch. "*Go*. Knock three times, then once more." She'd been given the secret code before she had made the choices she had made. She would not waste the chance it gave her sister at a happy life. One that did not end broken at the bottom of Lord Portsmouth's staircase or floating facedown in his picturesque pond.

Galahad, woken from slumber, carted through rain and thunder, jostled about and then finally dangled from a tree, did not seem terribly impressed.

Neither did the shadow of a man emerging from the nearby alcove of greenery.

"Miss Caldecott."

Kitty froze, recognizing those dark, languid tones.

The Devil himself.

"I've been looking for you."

She was doomed.

Chapter Four

S HE DID NOT know the Devil personally. Despite her aunt's opinion on the matter. Or the fact that she had picked his pocket.

He was lean, black haired, fierce jawed. He exuded dark patience, calm and unhurried, but with the sense of leashed power you knew instinctively you did not want turned on you. You did not want his attention.

Should not want it.

Craved it nonetheless.

And now here she was, caught in the lilac bushes in her wet nightdress. It did not exactly inspire confidence in her ability to take him on. She would, though. And she would win.

Because she had to.

"You have something of mine," he said in that soft, dangerous voice. She nearly had to lean forward to hear him. That was his gift, surely. You stepped toward the fire instead of running away like any sensible person. She had heard men threaten and yell, pound at her father's door, smash porcelain on the floor, shatter windows.

None of it as effective as that soft, dangerous voice.

Effective in several different ways, a great many of which were not remotely appropriate to the matter at hand. She shifted from one foot to the other, looked him in the eye. Which was not as easy as it sounded in this close proximity, considering he was tall and she was…not.

"I'm sure I don't know what you mean."

She knew *exactly* what he meant.

"Everyone has a tell, my little thief," he murmured. She could smell rain and roses and Devil: smoke and amber, dark like a forest. Otherworldly like his moss-green eyes. "Tell me, Miss Caldecott, are you planning to defy me?"

"Yes." She blurted it out before thinking better of it. Her options at present were to brazen it out, play the innocent. Run.

Running did not seem feasible. He was too close, too big. Too clever.

His laugh was a surprise to her—and, it seemed, to him as well. "People who are caught stealing from me don't often defy me as well. It isn't healthy."

"That must be dull for you." She did not know where she found her courage, her sass. Only that when you were drowning anyway, you may as well do it with fervor. Whiskey would drown you as quick as water, but at least it was more fun. Possibly running through a storm was not good for the mind. Or any sense of self-preservation.

"Hand it over and perhaps we can pretend it never happened."

She did not think he offered that often. If ever. It was tempting.

But not tempting enough. She needed it more than he did.

"I have nothing of yours," she said.

His eyes narrowed under those strong brows, sharp and cutting as any knife. "Is that so?"

"I don't even know who you are, sir."

"Don't play games you can't win, Miss Caldecott." He was getting closer still, pressing one hand to the trunk of the twisted tree at her back. Her mouth went dry. "I don't give second chances."

"I don't require one." She was mad—she had to be. Standing

about in a wet dress had addlepated her entirely. She was *taunting* the Devil. When he was in the right and she was very much in the wrong.

"I think you do," he said quietly. "And it's too late now. You'll beg like all the others."

She narrowed her eyes even as her breath caught in the back of her throat. Why was her body reacting as though it were an offer and not a vaguely threatening statement? Warmth fluttered low in her belly.

Outrageous. She was Kitty Caldecott, purveyor of filth.

She straightened her spine. "No."

"No?" His voice wrapped around her, tightening like silver chains.

"Certainly not." She did not sound quite as firm as she would have liked. It was distracting to have one's blood rushing all through one's body as though some dam had broken under her skin. Thinking of chains in a way she really ought not be considering. Not now. Not here.

His boot edged between her feet, leg pressing gently between hers. Another temptation, a promise. A warning.

And then he blinked.

Utterly befuddled.

If nothing else, she could go to her grave knowing she had befuddled the Devil. She did not imagine it was an easy thing to accomplish.

"Your feet…are bare."

She followed his gaze and blinked herself. "Yes." She'd forgotten. He was definitely more accustomed to fawning and flattery from beautiful ladies than he was to a woman with all the dignity of a bedraggled cat, with bare, muddy toes peeking out from the dirty hem of her nightdress.

Clearly any possibility of distracting him from her teeny-tiny theft by seducing him with her elegance and grace was entirely off the table.

It was resignation she felt. Triumph, even, at this befuddlement. *Not* disappointment, thank you very much.

It would be so much easier if he were not so desperately attractive. It was more than the collection of his features: strong but also almost delicate. Impossible to look away from.

It was something else, something primal. Mysterious.

And then Lady Priya stormed around the side of the house, gardening apron streaked with dirt, trowel in hand.

Kitty was relieved at the interruption. Of course she was.

The gold bangles around Priya's wrist made a merry sound when she pointed the trowel at Devil as though it were a sword. "*You.*"

"Lady Priya." He barely looked away from Kitty. As if he couldn't. It did something to her insides.

Something unhelpful. Distracting. Not to be trusted.

She was not a woman for a man like Devil. Even for a moment in a garden full of rain and lilacs. She was a thief. A *problem.*

Priya looked like a fairy queen, flower petals caught in her black hair, murder in her eyes. "Lord Birmingham."

"Devil."

"I'm not calling you by that ridiculous nickname," she sniffed. Her spine must be made entirely of steel. "Since I am not permitted at your Devil's Night, you are not permitted on my property. Shoo."

Devil straightened, expression mocking and hard. "Shoo?"

"Shoo."

"Don't make me shoot you, mate," an Irishman said calmly from the other end of the path.

"Gallagher."

"Birmingham."

The swords, though nowhere to be found, were drawn. Despite the mild way they greeted each other, everything was suddenly sharp. Menacing.

Devil's gaze found Kitty again, and she felt entirely too much like a moth pinned to a board. Not a butterfly, fluttering and colorful. A moth, all paper wings and darkness. He smiled slightly, and it was not the least bit reassuring. "Until we meet again, Miss Caldecott."

"No, thank you." She didn't know what prompted her to keep poking at him.

He paused at the end of the lane, tone dark and whip-sharp, before stepping back into the damp and shining bustle of London.

"Get her some damned shoes."

CHAPTER FIVE

S PINSTER HOUSE WAS welcoming, bursting with flowers and the scents of tea and warm currant scones wafting from one of the drawing rooms.

Priya did *not* lead Kitty to the drawing room.

Instead, they climbed the stairs to Priya's study, where Evie waited. The walls were painted with dramatic red dahlias, and there were gold candlesticks and gilded pots filled with orchids and jasmine. It smelled like earth and leaves and the tea cooling on the mahogany table: cinnamon and cardamom and other spices Kitty could not name. There were ledgers stacked on the windowsill behind her and a small statue of a cheerful man with an elephant's head.

Someone had brought Evie a towel, for which Kitty was grateful. Evie was using it to wring water from her hair. "Kitty! There you are. Thank you for rescuing Galahad."

Kitty set down the cage as Priya sat in a chair carved with lilies. Mr. Gallagher shut the door behind him and leaned against it, very much at his ease and also clearly very much her protector.

"Where's the bloody knife I gave you?" he asked calmly, his Irish lilt soft. His blue eyes were not at all soft, though they *were* fond. Kitty was quite certain no one had ever looked at her that way in the whole of her life. Something too akin to envy prickled through her.

"I have this." Priya held up one of the many gardening tools tucked into her thick apron. A clod of dirt fell directly on a sugared scone sitting on a painted porcelain plate that likely cost more than Kitty's entire wardrobe. Priya did not notice.

"That's a trowel, love," Mr. Gallagher pointed out, amused. Mostly amused. *Somewhat* amused.

"It worked, didn't it?" She stabbed at an imaginary enemy. "I do not care for that man." Not so imaginary, then.

"Don't worry, you have ten times more secrets in your little finger then he can even dream of," he assured her.

She preened for a moment, a glimpse into her true self, before Lady Priya, director of the Spinster Society took hold again. Her posture changed, the tilt of her head. "Miss Kitty Caldecott."

Kitty was getting tired of the way people said her name—suspicious, faintly derisive.

Even if she deserved it.

She nodded once, biting back every sharp comment she no longer had any right to make. This was a mess of her own making. She would take her just deserts. For Evie.

And because she was truly sorry, though no one was likely to believe her. And it changed nothing, not really.

"Is Clara here?" Kitty asked quietly.

"Clara is in Scotland on her honeymoon," Priya said. "You'll have to wait to apologize to her."

Kitty had already apologized. But she was happy to do so again. As many times as it took. She missed her friend.

Evie frowned. "Why does she have to apologize?"

Kitty's smile felt strained and desperate on her face. "Evie, please. Let it be."

Evie did not stop frowning. If anything, she resorted to an outright scowl. "All my sister does is work at her shop selling books, where she has to put up with appallingly rude behavior. I assure you, she does not have time to do anything else, certainly nothing requiring an apology."

If only that were true.

Priya, thankfully, only looked impressed. Some of the roiling panic in Kitty's chest abated. Evie would not suffer for her mistakes.

"Evie," Kitty said, "Lady Priya is quite right. I do owe some-one an apology." She looked at Priya pleadingly. "But I was told it would not affect the help my sister needs." They could not wait for Clara to return from Scotland. That could take *weeks*. They did not have *minutes* even to spare.

After a considering moment, Priya sighed. "That is correct."

Relief made Kitty's exhalation loud and shaky. She swallowed it back. "Thank you." Evie was still scowling. Kitty shook her head once, pleading. "My sister has drawn the unfortunate attention of Lord Portsmouth."

Priya's eyes narrowed. Mr. Gallagher swore under his breath. Evie started to look truly nervous, abruptly aware that her sister had not been overreacting.

"He came to our house at dawn with a carriage bound for Gretna Green."

"He planned to abduct her."

It was not a question. Kitty answered anyway. "Yes. With my aunt's assistance. And my father's."

Priya's expression was a terrifying thing. It was also a comfort that reached into Kitty's chest and pried some of the thorns free. "That is unacceptable."

"Our father owes money to many men, most of them just like Portsmouth," Kitty forced herself to say. "But most of all to Lord Portsmouth."

"Ah."

"I don't know where else to hide her while we consider our options." It did not need pointing out that the difference in their social standing was vast. Insurmountable.

"We crawled out the window and over the rooftop," Evie said, passing the towel to Kitty.

"Without shoes," Priya said. She had heard the command Devil threw at her. "That, at least, we can remedy straightaway.

And find you proper clothing."

"Thank you. Can Evie stay here?" Kitty did quick calculations in her head as to how many books she would have to sell to cover the cost of meals and anything else Evie might require. She would have to part with her prized edition of *The Mysteries of Udolpho* that had once belonged to her author Ann Radcliffe herself. There was a collector who had been coveting it for months.

"Of course she can," Priya said as though that had never been in question. "That's why we're here. Because men like Portsmouth have the run of Society and they don't deserve it."

"Did he really murder all three of his wives?" Evie asked in a small voice.

"Yes," Priya said bluntly. "But he shan't have *you*."

Evie and Kitty were shown the library, parlors, and a room built over a large pool of water for swimming. Kitty had never seen anything like it. She had not known such things even existed. There were plants everywhere, giant, soft ferns, spikes of lilies that scented the air, delicate orchids, lemon trees and hibiscus from India.

They were introduced to the other ladies in the house: Ladies Emmeline and Matilda, and a Miss Cunningham, who was being taught how to wield a sword in the ballroom. Kitty wondered if they would lend her a sword. Perhaps if she poked Lord Portsmouth with it enough times he would bugger off.

Unlikely.

And she did not like the idea of passing the problem on to some other woman, some other older sister.

Finally they were taken to a small bedroom on the third floor, with a yellow-striped coverlet on the bed and a lovely view of Hyde Park through the window. There was a chair in the corner, a writing desk, and an armoire filled with dresses for women of every size. Evie was clearly not the first girl to be hidden in this room.

"This one should fit you well enough." Evie handed Kitty a

deep rose walking dress trimmed with ribbons and silver buttons.

"I can't wear that."

"It will flatter you."

"It's meant for a lady," Kitty pointed out. "Furthermore, for a lady who is about to promenade or dance a quadrille, or whatever it is proper ladies do. I will stain it with ink and dust and God knows what within ten minutes of being at the shop. Especially if that sour old Mrs. Battersea keeps throwing rotten eggs at the door." It was a lovely fabric, though, a thin muslin so soft Kitty could not help but stroke it once. Then she reached for a perfectly presentable dress in a dark blue with white stripes. "This will do well enough."

"There's not a single ruffle to that."

"I'm too short for ruffles."

"Too stubborn, you mean. You know I have a better eye for these things."

"Why are we arguing about ruffles?"

She knew she ought to tell her sister what she had done to Clara, but then Evie would insist on taking on some of the culpability, feeling as though it were her fault because Kitty did what she did in her determination to protect her. But it was Kitty's fault entirely.

Well, perhaps her father and her aunt could shoulder a *little* blame for putting them in this blasted predicament in the first place.

"Aunt Priscilla will eviscerate you," Evie said as Kitty washed her feet in a basin and changed into the dress and a pair of walking boots more comfortable than any pair she had every owned. "Perhaps you ought to hide here as well."

"I can handle Aunt Priscilla."

"I'm not sure the entirety of the British Royal Navy could handle her." Evie's tone was wry, but she sat on the edge of the bed, looking lost, clutching Galahad's gold cage to her chest.

"Try not to worry," Kitty said. "No one would think to look for you here. And I shall sort it out."

"How?"

"I have a few ideas up my sleeve."

She had *no* ideas up her sleeve. None. Not a single blasted one.

She smiled. Comfortingly.

Evie grimaced. "Not that smile again. You'll scare Galahad."

Kitty kissed the top of her head. "There is a library here, and that pool for swimming. The ballroom is full of weapons. I'm quite envious."

"Do you think Priya would let me help with the gardens?"

"I don't see why not." Kitty hugged her hard. Galahad made a sleepy sound of protest when the cage tilted. "No letters. Don't tell anyone where you are, not even your friends."

"I won't."

"Promise?"

"I promise."

PRIYA WAS WAITING at the bottom of the stairs, gold gleaming at her ears and wrists. She cut a half-wilted bud off a peony plant with brutal efficiency. "Miss Caldecott, a moment, if you please."

Kitty nodded and followed her down the hall and out into the greenhouse, warm and smelling of dark mud and green leaves and every kind of bright flower. With Hyde Park hulking behind, you would never guess London also waited beyond, full of coal smoke and the stinking Thames heating up under the summer sun.

Priya moved to a bank of lily of the valley, examining the leaves for Kitty knew not what. She seemed well satisfied, though, and moved on to a lemon tree in a clay urn. "Clara warned me you might seek our help for your sister," she said. "And we will help, as I said. Of course we will. Just as we would help *you*, though I am thoroughly cross with you."

"I deserve it."

Priya watched her through narrowed eyes for a long moment before sighing. "You're taking all the fun out of my righteous indignation."

Kitty nearly smiled. "I'm sorry."

"Stop that."

"Sor—" She cut herself off.

Priya did smile, though briefly. "I remember you, you know."

Kitty was surprised. "You do?"

"You send women our way more than anyone else."

"Ah." Kitty nodded. "It's the shop, you see. The kinds of books I sell. Ladies either see me as someone who is dangerous or someone who is safe."

"And you have chosen safe."

She winced. "Mostly."

"Yes. That business with Clara."

"Yes." Kitty rubbed at her breastbone.

Priya sighed again, thoroughly disgruntled. "Clara says she has forgiven you, so I suppose I ought to as well."

"I will regret it every day." Kitty had lost a true friend. Not *lost*—tossed away. Betrayed.

"To be fair," Priya continued, "had I a sister, there is nothing I would not also do to keep her from Portsmouth. And I would also have done the same for any of my friends to be quite honest."

"Thank you."

"Do stop being so polite—it's disconcerting."

Kitty relaxed her very stiff, very proper posture. A little.

Priya nodded at her thoughtfully. "You are not out in Society, I gather?"

"My father is barely a baron, and mostly by chance. He invented something no one will discuss that the king and his men found useful in the war. But he is now thoroughly paupered," Kitty replied drily. "So, no."

"Good."

"Good?"

"You are not missing much. And anyway, you are far more useful to me if you are *not* a debutante."

"A spinster, more like."

"Even better." Priya grinned.

Kitty smiled back. "I suppose so."

"You could stay here, you know. With your sister. You would be safer."

"I would," Kitty agreed. "But she wouldn't."

"Oh dear."

"What is it?"

"I'm beginning to like you. That won't do at all."

"I did think about running," Kitty admitted. "But we'd never be able to stop, and I don't have the funds to keep us safe on the road for more than a week at most. We could ruin her, of course, demolish her reputation, but Portsmouth…"

"Would still have his revenge." Priya tucked a sprig of rosemary into her apron. Kitty had never seen rosemary grow to the size of a small tree before. "I'm afraid you're quite correct on that score. He has already told half of Mayfair that he is marrying your sister. That alone is enough to guarantee the outcome in his mind."

Kitty swore. He would never let them get away now. Not with his pride so thoroughly in the mix.

"I wish I had more to offer," Priya muttered. "We have been trying to find proper evidence to damn him, but there's nothing so far. I do so hate it when they are clever. I can tell you that his last wife is not officially dead—she is missing."

Kitty perked up. "Really?" If she could find Lady Portsmouth, Evie would be safe. The House of Lords and Parliament did not look favorably upon bigamy. Murder, they turned a blind eye to.

"There's not much to go on. Lady Caroline Portsmouth has done an excellent job of disappearing, for which I applaud her."

"Unless Portsmouth is behind it."

"Unless that, yes. And he is great friends with the Marquis of Eastbourne. They are thick as thieves, which I cannot like."

The same marquis who had imprisoned several women in his cellars in order to control their fortunes.

Kitty was in over her head.

"I won't send you in unarmed," Priya murmured.

A small thrill of excitement snuck through Kitty's anxiety-tensed muscles. "I would love a weapon. Something pointy."

"Matilda will sort you out. In the meantime, I suggest you stay far away from this house. I'm not certain Portsmouth wouldn't think to have us watched. We are not popular with Eastbourne's friends. We make them nervous," Priya said smugly. "You cannot be seen anywhere nearby."

"I understand." Kitty was in no less dire circumstances, but she did feel less tossed about, less hopeless. She understood a little better now the way Clara had spoken about the society, and about Priya.

"I do wish I could do more, but my Spinsters are spread very thin at the moment and our newest member is far too green to go up against someone like Portsmouth. Oh, and Kitty?"

She paused in the doorway. "Yes?"

"How well do you know Lord Birmingham?"

"Devil? As well as you'd expect, which is not at all."

"Careful there."

When Lady Priya Langdon, Keeper of the Secrets of the Most Powerful People in England, told you to be careful—you'd best be careful.

CHAPTER SIX

T HE GOLDEN GRIFFIN Bookshop and Circulating Library was Kitty's refuge.

It was small and narrow, next to a teashop that always smelled delicious and across the street from a shop that sold enameled snuffboxes. Her mother's family had run it since her grandmother's mother was just a girl. They had sold plays, mostly Shakespeare then, with a brief foray into political tracts and travelogues.

Kitty was the one who had decided to focus on novels, especially those penned by women. With a secret side business of naughtier works readers would have been too mortified to ask for at the Temple of the Muses bookshop. The Temple might have several floors of tomes and novels and journals, more than Kitty could ever aspire to, as well as a very distinguished clientele, but she was fairly certain they did not have *that*.

Pity for them. It was great fun and paid her rent. And why shouldn't women have their own amusements? She had no intention of floating through life like an angel or trapped high on a pedestal. People on pedestals could not save their sisters.

And they were not handed mysterious packages from the Spinster Society of "everything you might need for necessary mischief and mayhem." With a farewell that consisted of a cheerful "Take no prisoners!"

She let the soothing, familiar smell of paper dust and vanilla soothe her. It was shadowy and quiet—a holy silence like inside a church, even as carriages jostled for space on the other side of the window and peddlers shouted of their wares, anything from baked potatoes to shoe polish and Pears soap. Here, she was safe. Here, anything was possible. Fae kings, dragons, krakens.

Freedom.

The shop was not particularly spacious, but there was a small reading room and she had painted everything a moody gray-blue and attacked every bit of trim with gold paint. When the candles were lit and the rain was at the window, it positively glowed. Gold griffins prowled over the ceiling, lurked in the back of bookshelves, peered from over the door like the friendly guardians she considered them to be.

Every time a pinched lady of the *Ton* or a vicar on a crusade decried the declining moral standards of the shop and of women in general, Kitty painted another griffin. When her own grandfather threw slimy vegetables at the window, she added a huge griffin on the outside wall, complete with his enormous walrus mustache. He took deep offense at how she handled the family business. But her grandmother had given it to *her*. Just as it had been left to her by her own mother, his very stubborn wife who chortled every time he bemoaned the fact that Kitty sold filth. No matter the strain in the relationship, the shouting or the disdain, the Griffin bookshop belonged to the Griffin women.

Her father deeply disapproved of Kitty being in trade, as a daughter to a baron, despite the fact that he had been granted a barony on the grounds of a bit of secret business gone fantastically—and accidentally—well.

And since that very same baron had squandered all of their money, he could keep his disapproval to himself. It would not buy tea. Or fish for supper.

Kitty pulled the curtains to let in the daylight and fell into the familiar, quiet bustle of the day. She sold the usual number of Byron's poems, a steady supply of *Pride and Prejudice* by A Lady, and three copies of Mary Wollstonecraft's *A Vindication of the Rights of Women* even after twenty-four years of being in print. She sold several more copies of Maria Edgeworth's *Letters for Literary Ladies* because it was one of her favorites and she would not stop recommending it, along with the same writer's novel *Belinda*.

After which three young ladies circled her desk, whispering to each other, eyes wide. Kitty waited, long used to the pattern. Another circumambulation of the shop, which did not take long. One of them opened a caramel sweet from the teashop next door for fortification. "Have you…" she whispered. She had a beauty mark at the edge of her mouth. "That is…"

Her friend huffed out a breath and puffed up her chest as though she was very brave indeed. Her blonde ringlets positively quivered with courage. "Oh, let me. We've come for the Nightingale stories." Her tone was strident, her cheeks red.

"They are great fun. Come with me, if you please."

They followed Kitty behind a bookcase set parallel to her counter. Behind was a cozy reading room, and the circulating library. Also, books in open trunks that could be locked at a moment's notice. It was safer for her customers this way. Some of her more risqué books existed in a hazy unknown legality. She did not technically sell them. She left them out and a customer bought a sketch of a gold griffin instead. It was not a perfect system, but it had kept her relatively safe thus far. She had only been questioned once by a constable, and she had blinked at him innocently without a shred of comprehension until his own stammered explanations made him so uncomfortable that he left and never returned.

She'd added three griffins to the ceiling that day.

But Clara's publishers offered a great deal of bribes to various members of Parliament and the courts to be considered merely "frivolous ladies' novels." It had allowed the Nightingale to become extremely popular. One still did not flaunt *Ravished by the Rakehell*, but it was safe enough to purchase, safe enough to sell or lend through the circulating library. Aside from that, Kitty also carried the widest selection of Minerva Press novels.

Kitty left her customers to peruse and whisper together. It was some time later when one of her regulars floated into the shop. There was no other word for how Lady Winthorpe entered any space—she *meandered*. She could have been on fire and Kitty was fairly certain she would still meander like a bit of dandelion fluff.

"Good afternoon, Lady Winthorpe," Kitty greeted her.

"Miss Caldecott, good afternoon to you." Lady Winthorpe had blue eyes like faded flowers and a disconcertingly direct gaze, plus moon-white hair. And a great love of racy novels. And gossip. "Any news, dear?"

"I'm afraid not." *I almost fell to my death off a roof this morning. My father tried to sell my sister. I stole from the very last man in all of Britain one should steal from, including the king and all of his dukes.*

Lady Winthorpe frowned at the sound of other customers invading her little corner. She had brought her own padded stool and insisted on keeping it there so she could peruse comfortably. "How long will they be?"

"Not much longer, I shouldn't think." There was no way of knowing with new and nervous customers. "Would you care for some biscuits?"

"I always care for biscuits." Which was precisely why Kitty always had them on hand—lavender-sprinkled crescents, wafers dipped in chocolate, butter biscuits topped with strawberry meringue. She offered Lady Winthorpe the plate as her footman backed out to wait on the sidewalk. "Thank you, dear. Has that nasty vicar been back?"

"Which one?" Kitty asked drily.

"Oh dear, there is that pack of them, isn't there?"

"I'm afraid so."

"And the Ladies' Society Against Any Kind of Amusement Whatsoever." More usually known as the Ladies' Society for Moral Standards. She shook her head, looking terribly dismayed.

"They must lead very dull lives indeed."

She glanced at the corner again and let out a mournful sigh, followed by a much more irritated one for good measure. Kitty bit the inside of her cheek against a laugh. She knew what was coming: a hurricane of soft hints and gentle threats. No one stood against Lady Winthorpe. Mostly because she so often wandered away when one tried to fight back.

"Dears, I should like to sit down." She settled herself like a partridge, if partridges wore bonnets trimmed with roses and what looked like a cabbage made of emeralds. Perhaps Kitty ought to introduce her to Sir Reginald. "Oh no," she continued breathily. "You don't want that one—that man has clearly never touched a woman. Try this one. And this one. And don't forget my favorite!"

Honestly, she was better at this than Kitty was. The ladies were gently banished with their pile of books so that Lady Winthorpe could browse without interruption. They paid for their purchases and left, the one with the beauty mark lingering. She swallowed awkwardly, toying with her glove. She had the haunted and hunted shock that Evie had had when Priya confirmed that Kitty was not overreacting over Portsmouth's cruelty. "I heard…" She trailed off.

Kitty waited. She knew from experience that if she said the wrong thing, or even the right thing too fast or too forcefully, the girl would bolt.

"I… Someone said you knew how to…run. Where to go."

Kitty wanted to ask a hundred questions. "Yes. Are you in trouble?"

She nodded mutely.

"Do you need a safe place or a safe doctor or something else entirely?"

"I don't know. You must think me silly."

Kitty shook her head. "Definitely not. You can go to the Spinster Society," she added. "On Bolton Row. Believe me, they will help." She did not mention any of the Spinsters by name.

"The Spinster Society? In Mayfair? Oh, I couldn't. I'm not a fine lady."

"They would still help you. But I understand." Priya was equipped to handle the peerage and their particular types of power. Shop girls and innkeeper's daughters did not always have the same problems. Though power was always at the rotten root. "There's another house in Covent Garden—"

The door burst open, slamming into the wall.

The girl jumped like a scalded cat.

"Depravity!" Vicar Andover shouted. He huffed angrily, like a bull—or like an old, portly man who had walked too fast.

His wife slipped in beside him, just as starched and vinegary as if she had come from a pantomime. Mrs. Andover's tightly pinned hair did not detract from her beauty, all chiseled bone structure. But her eyes were shrewd, hungry. She was a devoted—and very loud—member of the Ladies' Society for Moral Standards. She attended weekly meetings to learn how to best harass those she thought were contributing to the downfall of society. Kitty knew because the woman had started shouting it at her on a regular basis over the past couple of weeks.

It made Kitty tired just to look at her.

Also vexed. So very vexed.

Sweat beaded the vicar's upper lip. He pointed to the girl, who looked as though she was ready to vanish into the floorboards. "Run! Run from this sinful place!"

The girl fled.

Kitty could have cheerfully murdered him. There was no telling when or if the girl would find the courage or simply the opportunity to come back for the information she clearly needed.

The vicar and his wife stared at Kitty, who raised an eyebrow. "Have you come for the latest issue of *Harris's List of Covent Garden Ladies*?" The list was a guide to the prostitutes of Covent Garden and their...specialties. Kitty did not actually have any copies on hand—they were mostly purchased by the men of the *Ton*, who did not often frequent her shop.

But the offer made the vicar and his wife choke. He sputtered, looking as though he might faint. His wife was made of sterner stuff. "This is no good work for a spinster," she said in strident tones.

Kitty's shopkeeper smile did not falter, mostly because she knew it infuriated them. "As the only spinster here, I'll be the judge of that, thank you very much."

The vicar sucked in an offended breath. And then he gagged.

He had just remembered he was holding a bag of eggs. Anyone could see they were not fresh.

Kitty tensed. If the contents of that bag even grazed any of her books, especially the rarer ones, she absolutely *would* murder him. The damage would be impossible to fix.

The moment grew brittle. Mrs. Andover's eyes went positively gleeful with violently righteous indignation.

And then Lady Winthorpe toddled out from her corner with a handful of books. She blinked at the vicar. He blinked back at her. "Sir, there is something wrong with your eggs," she said.

"Erm." It was the best response he could muster when faced with a dowager countess. Even Mrs. Andover froze for a moment before stiffening her spine. She elbowed her husband in the midsection. Hard. Kitty saw the exact moment when they thought they had a new weapon in his arsenal.

She leaned back and ate a lavender biscuit. It tasted like a garden. She should have gone for the chocolate wafer. "Your ladyship, you cannot know this, but you have stumbled into a den of iniquity," she said. "Or was it depravity? I can never remember."

"Goodness," Lady Winthorpe said mildly. "I could see how your luncheon might make one think that. You really ought not to eat those eggs." She waved over his shoulder, summoning her footman. "Miss Caldecott, if you could wrap up my books. I would rather not get that odor in my new bonnet ribbons. *Not* elegant in the least."

Mrs. Andover did not take that well. Her lips puckered.

"Of course, Lady Winthorpe." Kitty wrapped them in her best paper, adding a ribbon tied in a large bow. The vicar's eyes bulged out of his head the entire time. Mrs. Andover continued to vibrate with outrage.

Lady Winthorpe's footman paid Kitty, without even hinting for credit, which she appreciated more than just about anything at the moment. Getting even the wealthiest members of the *Ton* to actually *pay* for their purchases could be somewhat of a challenge. Just ask her father.

Lady Winthorpe wrinkled her nose. "Do take those away, vicar. They are making my eyes itchy." Her footman loomed, perfectly able to project ominousness even with the old-fashioned uniform and curled wig his employer required of him.

But it was her lady's maid who thoroughly discombobulated the already discombobulated Mr. and Mrs. Andover. She entered the shop, took one sniff and one look at them, and her spine turned to steel in a way that Mrs. Andover would surely envy for the rest of the day. "Absolutely not," she snapped at him. "Get out this instant. That is a *countess*."

Flustered, the vicar turned on his heel and left. His wife lingered, curled her hands into fists, and eventually stalked out.

Kitty ate another biscuit. "Well done, Beth."

"Hmph. That one will be back."

"Of that, I have no doubt."

"And I told your ladyship not to come in here," Beth scolded the dowager countess. "I know perfectly well what you read and could have shopped for you."

"And ruin my fun? I think not." Lady Winthorpe patted her maid's arm distractedly and meandered away without a farewell.

It was quiet for the rest of the afternoon, until evening began to fall, the light turning blue, then gray. Kitty still felt a tiny bit smug that the Andovers had been sent running.

Until she stepped outside.

They had clearly returned while she was in the back room. And they had done more than throw eggs. They must have had help. The Ladies' Tiresome Society for Moral Standards and Double Standards, no doubt.

Kitty kept two brooms for this very reason. One to sweep the dust and mud from boots off the floor and one for the splatters of truly disgusting things she found on her doorstep on a regular basis. Moldy lettuce, old fish, rotten fruit. Potatoes that had turned deeply noxious. Green things dragged from the Thames that she had no interest in further classifying.

Bookselling was not for the weak of stomach.

Not that she imagined for one moment that the other bookshops in London had to deal with any such thing. Irate customers, theft, spills of tea, certainly. But not this. No one kept eggs in a basket until they turned rancid in time for a visit to the Temple of Muses. Even Mrs. Andover would not dare.

Actually, she might.

Kitty indulged in a cross sigh, making sure no one saw her. She did not know if the Andovers or the Ladies' Society or any of her other critics lurked about to watch her get upset, but they would go away disappointed every time. Every. Single. Time. It was a point of pride.

And honestly, at this rate, she was used to it.

It barely registered as a problem when one's sister had been sold into marriage to a murderer in exchange for forgiving a gambling debt.

Light the lamps, pull the curtains, tidy the shop. Scrub the front step, scrape paint off the window, tally the ledgers. Order more chapbooks. Wash refuse from the door. It was all part of her day at this point.

Anyway, she had a system. A bucket of sand, a broom, and sometimes an extra sixpence for one of the street-sweeping boys if she simply was not feeling up to the mess. Fortunately, this evening's offering looked to be nothing but regular produce, malodorous but nothing like a basket of old fish after a sunny day at market. Another sigh, and she got to sweeping. It left smears on the pavement. Eggshells cracked under her shoes.

"What the hell is this?"

Kitty jumped. The shop window reflected Devil standing behind her, summoned as if from the darkest depths. Those intense, arrogant eyes that saw everything. His scowl was evident, even in the murky glass. She would have to wash it as well. The window, not Devil.

Washing Devil. Suddenly all she could think about was hot, soapy water, a bare chest, that half-smile.

He made her stupid.

Unfortunate, but true.

She turned, her heart thumping in her chest in that way only he seemed capable of eliciting. Hopefully he chalked it up to fear or guilt, which he was no doubt accustomed to. Not lust. Which he was also accustomed to.

Never mind that, Kitty Caldecott.

She was a clever, red-haired spinster who was accused of being fierce and immoral and an upstart. She ought to bloody well act like it. "Can I help you?" she asked as calmly as her body would allow.

"You're wearing shoes, which is an improvement," he replied. "But you are standing in… What is that, exactly?"

She glanced down. "Cabbage and rotten strawberries. Someone must have been giving it away from a stall at Covent Garden. Definitely eggs. And that might be a fish bone. By your left boot."

He moved his foot and narrowed one eye at her as if he did not know what to say.

Twice now she had flummoxed the Devil. She felt more than a little bit proud about that.

"My mistake—it's an eggshell."

"Powerful smell," he said.

She couldn't argue with that. And she refused to consider the kinds of expensive perfumes the women he knew would wear, ensnaring him with subtle amber or lilac or gardenia.

Kitty Caldecott and her *Eau of Rotten Cabbage. Parfum de Poisson.*

"Why exactly are you painting the sidewalk with this mess?" he asked when she stood there staring at him like a startled frog on a log. He did not touch her, but his voice did—it wrapped around her arms, her waist, her throat. It was sharp, dark. Seething. "Did someone do this to your shop?"

She shrugged one shoulder. "The hazards of a bookshop."

"I highly doubt that."

"Fine, the hazards of *my* bookshop, then."

"That, I can more easily believe. Why exactly this mess?"

"Oh, you know. Books written by women sold to women by a woman? Moral corruption, lewdness, etcetera." She sounded bored, even to her own ears. It had taken her some time and effort to develop that particular trick, she did not mind admitting.

"Ah yes," he said. "I am familiar. I am particularly fond of being called *licentious*. It has a certain flair."

Kitty would not smile. This was not a moment. This was a soft attack, a first volley.

"You probably should not be seen here," she added, much more cheerfully. "Can't be good for your reputation. Good day, Lord Birmingham."

"Nice try," he returned mildly. "Inside. *Now*, Catherine."

How did he know her real name was Catherine? She rarely used it. And why did the sound of it in his mouth shiver through her? Her thighs actually trembled.

Unacceptable.

Thrilling, but unacceptable.

And then Devil took a step closer, and another, a tall, sinfully handsome earl who could command the king himself, closing in on her until she was being backed into her own shop without even realizing it. Past the shelves, under the gold griffins, over the crooked, uneven floorboards. And right into the edge of her desk. She gasped a little, without meaning to. His gaze dropped to her mouth at the sound, then lifted again. "You have something of mine."

CHAPTER SEVEN

"I'M SURE I don't know what you mean." She sounded sharp, stern. Like a proper spinster.

She knew it wouldn't be enough to deter a man like Devil. She wasn't a complete idiot. Despite the fact that she found the moss-green flash of his eyes distracting, the slightly too perfect shape of his mouth fascinating.

He was every inch the fallen angel: beautiful, tempting, burning with an unholy power. With that strangely delicate curl to the side of his lips when he almost smiled.

Possibly she was reading too many novels.

This was a man who always got what he wanted and who was at this very moment trying to intimidate her. He hadn't threatened her yet, but it was surely the very next thing on his agenda.

The fact that he smelled delicious made no difference to her.

She hadn't even noticed.

Much.

She refused to take a deep breath to figure out if it was cedar or pine. Or frankincense? Definitely incense: sweet, spicy, smoky.

To a church she had never been to, where devils were angels. Where fire did not burn—it merely led you home.

"Kitty." It was clearly not the first time he had said her name. His half-smile was devastating. "Am I boring you, Miss

Caldecott?"

She swallowed. "Not at all. But we're closed for the day." She moved slightly, trying to slip past him.

His hands closed around the edge of the desk on either side of her. There was no violence or anger to the movement, only finality. He wanted her caged and so she was caged. "I don't think so."

"Goodness, I had no idea you were so obsessed with literature," she said, deciding to brazen it out. "I suppose I could sell you some poetry. Byron? Or perhaps *A Vindication of the Rights of Women*? I always keep it in stock."

He leaned a little closer, just enough that she could not see anything but him. Gone was the bookshop, the light darkening at the window behind him. There was only Devil. "I've already read it."

"You…have?"

"And I'm not here to discuss literature or political tracts, Miss Caldecott. You've taken something from me and I'll have it back."

"Egregious accusation."

Also: entirely true. Kitty was desperate enough to try anything. It would save her sister. Lord knew, her other plans had not.

And now here she was.

"I imagine you have already searched my shop," she said. It had taken him a few weeks to find her, after all.

He inclined his head.

"Arrogant jackass," she muttered.

"What was that?" The question was smooth, a challenge. She felt the press of his knee against her, the brush of his arm. Her breath stuttered, just a little.

"You broke into my shop, didn't you?" she accused.

"Well, you did steal from me."

"I can't imagine why you think so, as you've found not a shred of evidence."

"I'm not done searching."

"Oh? I assure you, you'll find nothing untoward on my person." She lifted the hem of her borrowed dress, past the plain stockings where they were tied with ribbon at her knee. He tracked her fingers, the bare skin of her thigh.

Stop taunting him, Kitty.

Instead, she tugged the pocket free from where it was tied around her waist over her stays and opened it. "See? Empty?"

If her voice was a little husky, she absolutely would not admit to it.

"I doubt very much you had my vowel on hand when you ran across the rooftops this morning in order to later hide in your borrowed dress."

How did he know it was borrowed? How did he notice *every* little detail? It was infuriating. Then again, this borrowed dress was much finer than anything she had in her own trunks and just a little too long for her. She dropped the hem, once again refusing to consider the silks and satins and embroidered ribbons he was no doubt accustomed to seeing on powdered, pampered ladies. And nary a paper cut from book pages or ink stains from ledger calculations.

He'd already told her this morning that this was not a game she could win.

She straightened, the weight of the day back on her shoulders. Her collarbones ached. She was suddenly exhausted. Playing at being a temptress was ridiculous. Futile.

"Fine," she admitted. "I stole from you."

He retreated just slightly, as if she'd surprised him.

"But it's mine now and I'm not giving it back," she added.

"Oh, aren't you?"

She lifted her chin mutinously. "I need it."

"I need it more."

"I find that doubtful."

"Do you, now?" He was still as a blade, shining and sharp.

"Are *you* being forced to marry Lord Portsmouth?" she

snapped.

"No, thank Christ."

"Well, my sister is."

"A pity, but I fail to see how that is my problem." Every word was a dark promise of retribution, a tightened bowstring. A sword leaving the scabbard, ringing with only one purpose: to cut down the enemy.

"I need every weapon at my disposal," Kitty said. "Including the debt vowel belonging to Lord Worthing."

"Belonging to *me*."

"To *me*, actually."

He huffed a brief, incredulous laugh. More of a complicated exhale. She did not imagine he laughed often. "There are men who have lost limbs for less."

"I am not a man."

"I've noticed." There was a purr to his voice suddenly, a charm that made every nerve ending below her navel shimmer to life. The scoundrel.

His mouth was near her ear, his breath soft, calling up a trail of goosebumps as though they belonged to him. Heat washed through her when his lips brushed against her.

"You're trying to seduce me," she said as flatly as she could, which was a struggle, as all of the blood in her body was suddenly flinging itself about with wild abandon. That his ploy was working was something he did not have to know. Could not know. Ever.

"Believe me, you'll enjoy it more than my other tactics."

Of *that*, she had no doubt. Especially as there was that particularly harrowing story of a duke missing a foot after crossing Devil. He had not been jesting about the missing limbs. Probably.

She liked to think it was a rumor, an exaggeration.

She was fairly certain it was not.

She flattened her palms over his chest, the muscles firm under her touch. Was he strong all over? Hard and powerful?

Not now, Kitty Caldecott.

"I don't think so," she said.

He paused. "Pardon?"

She nearly laughed. He had not been denied in a very long time. But she would only disappoint, and anyway, it would not get her what she needed.

What she *wanted*, almost certainly. Not what she *needed*.

What her *sister* needed.

"I won't be seduced." Even if she suddenly really, *really* wanted to be. Rather desperately, it had to be said. She knew her cheeks were pink, the skin below her collarbones. She always blushed at the worst times. No delicate pink wash, just an angry red. "And I have freckles."

Now why had she said *that*?

Devil blinked, his mouth caught between a smirk and a promise of something darker and more delicious. "Pardon?" he said again.

She refused to repeat herself. Bad enough to be an idiot once.

"I happen to like freckles," he murmured.

She shot him a look. There were no fewer than three advertising sandwich boards being carried about by peddlers across the street at this very moment, all selling various concoctions promising to eradicate bothersome freckles forever. Arsenic washes. Lead paste. Lemon water—which she knew from experience the summer she was twelve years old did not work and only broke her out in an itchy rash.

Devil did not take her seriously. She could hardly blame him. She'd acted a breathless ninny ever since he backed her into her own shop. And before that he had seen her stumble across a rooftop, run through London barefoot, and wrestle a hedgehog in a gold cage out of a tree. She was not precisely daunting, as far as adversaries went.

Yet…

She was a bookseller. She knew account books and costs and percentages. Profit. The value of a thing.

"I have something you want," she said.

"Yes." There were threads glittering through his tone that she could not decipher. "Though I can do without Worthing's stable of horses."

"But still, it's what was promised to you. I imagine if I went about showing the *Ton* how easy it was to steal from the Devil, that would cause problems for you."

"Careful." It was a quiet growl, no less effective for its softness.

She swallowed. "Yes, well, as I said, I have something you want. And *you* have something I need."

"I'm gratified to hear it."

She rolled her eyes. "Not that."

It was clear no one had rolled their eyes at him in a very long time either.

She was out of her depth.

Oh well. Sink or swim.

"I will give you the vowel," she said.

"I know."

She frowned at him. "You are vexing."

"Believe me, the feeling is mutual."

"You also think you are vexing?" she asked with feigned innocence. "I don't blame you."

That almost-laugh again. Crossed with another…growl?

Why did she feel that sound in her thighs?

Not the point.

"I will give you the vowel," she repeated pointedly. "After you help me rid my sister of Lord Portsmouth."

"I am not in the habit of murdering earls," he said. "Though I could."

"Not murder." She paused. "Well, not *yet*, anyway."

That time he definitely smiled. "And why exactly do you think I can help do away with an unwanted suitor?"

"Don't be tiresome. You're *Devil*."

"I am."

"You have power and money."

"I do.

"And don't you think if I had either of those things I would have already freed my sister? Mayfair runs on those two things like water runs a millwheel."

"And reputation."

"Fine, that too. Yours is rather fearsome."

"I was beginning to think you hadn't noticed," he said drily.

"Don't be daft. It's very useful to me."

"I am, of course, delighted to be of service." The sarcasm to the slight bow of the head was thick enough to choke on. "Why don't you just marry your sister off to someone else?"

She sighed, more than a little annoyed. "Yes, because kind men who overlook no dowry whatsoever and a father-in-law in debt grow on trees in London. Or better yet, I'll just order one from the shop next door, shall I? Perhaps they'll throw in a meringue."

"Kindness? That's what you want?"

"For my sister, yes. And enough money to live comfortably."

"And for you?"

"For me?"

"What do *you* want, Miss Caldecott?"

He pressed closer, and she realized her hands were flattened against his very nice chest. She dropped them hastily. The tingle she felt was imaginary. Obviously. "Immaterial."

"Is it?"

"Entirely." Why was it so warm in here? She should have opened a window. Was she sweating? That was hardly ladylike. Or appealing. Not that it mattered.

"Hmm."

"What does *that* mean?" she demanded. She was blotchy, she just knew it. Pink and red and freckled and *shiny*.

"Nothing."

"Liar."

"You are very brave." He said it calmly—detached, even. As though she couldn't see a flash of something dark and furious in his face before he wrestled it away. "To steal from the Devil and then call him a liar."

She shrugged because anything she might have said tangled in her throat. Had she pushed him too far? She was no gambler. Clearly, the lack of talent ran in the blood.

"Very well, then," he said softly, dark eyes snaring hers as easily as if she were a rabbit and he a wolf. "You have yourself a deal."

Relief made her feel lightheaded. She held out her hand to shake. He glanced down, amused, then predatory. Alarm bells rang inside her skull.

"Oaths used to be sealed with a kiss to make them legal. And you're in bed with the Devil now, my little thief."

CHAPTER EIGHT

S TEALING FROM DEVIL had seemed like a good idea at the time.

Very well, it was always a *bad* idea, but anything was better than Portsmouth marrying her sister and then murdering her when he grew tired of her. Or keeping her locked up if she gave him sons enough to secure his lineage.

But Kitty had not imagined stealing a scrap of paper would make things *worse*. She was the last kind of woman a man like Devil would notice. He had beauties falling at his feet, elegant women, charming men, all begging for his attention. Kitty would have much preferred to disappear, thank you very much.

Too late for that now, alas.

And none of it mattered, not as long as Evie was safe.

"Oaths haven't been sealed with a kiss since Henry VI," she blurted out. "Since the Black Plague."

Why did she keep saying things out loud? With her mouth?

"Fascinating," Devil said, and it mostly did not sound like an insult. "Let me guess, you read about it in a book?"

He had no idea the kinds of books she read.

"At least that is a travesty we can rectify. History must be preserved, after all. We owe it to king and country."

She knew what he was doing. He did not really want to kiss her. He only wanted her flustered. Confused. Vulnerable.

Well, she would show him.

She curled her fingers into the fine material of his coat and yanked him forward. Taken off guard, he let her. It was the only explanation, seeing as she was a good foot shorter than he was and several stone lighter, even soft as she was. He was all muscle and sin and taunts you knew you should not answer, no matter how tempting they were.

He thought she would flinch away if he kissed her.

So she would kiss *him*.

It had been some time. She did not fool herself into thinking a single kiss from a short bookseller with old lettuce on her shoes would turn his world upside down. She had stolen kisses as a girl and a great deal more since then—she was a spinster; she wasn't *dead*. But there was no time for a dalliance when your father was busy ruining the family. And lately the men she met were more interested in throwing rotten vegetables at her door. It was not exactly flattering.

No matter. This kiss was not about allure or desire. It was merely a battle in the war. A surprise attack.

Which did not mean she could not enjoy it.

She would be an absolute idiot not to. Such chances did not come along every day. For Devil, they no doubt did, but for her?

Never.

She pushed up on her tiptoes before she lost her nerve. She kissed him lightly, teasingly, with a tiny lick over his bottom lip. But also haltingly, because part of her was waiting for him to shove her away, to laugh. To do anything but kiss her back.

He froze for a brief moment that nearly demolished her resolve, not to mention any shred of self-confidence.

And then he kissed her back.

Oh, how he kissed her back.

She'd already thought she was in over her head. There was no doubt about it now. Not with his clever hands in her hair, tightening, tugging her head back to hold her where he wanted her. Finding just the right angle to take her mouth like it belonged to him. He kissed her as if he had all the time in the world, so deeply and so thoroughly, her knees actually went soft. She had thought they only did that in the books she read.

When he tangled his tongue with hers, licking deep, she made a tiny sound, a whimper that would have embarrassed her if she were not already desperate for more. More of his mouth, more of his hands tight in her hair keeping her still when the world buffeted her from every side. More of *him*.

She had known he would be good at this. Objectively.

But she had not realized how it would affect her. How it would start fires in her belly, soften the muscles of her inner thighs, send heat streaking throughout her whole body, even the parts he was not touching. Why wasn't he touching them? All of her? Everywhere. Anywhere.

He controlled the moment, her responses. The kiss she had started was his to finish. She was used to being the one who started everything and ended everything. Opening the shop in the morning, emptying the hearth at night. Hiding her sister from creditors and bullies and earls.

For one long, blessed moment there was nothing to do but give in.

Nothing to do but chase pleasure. Not even chase it, only meet it when it was given to her. She did not know what she had expected from Devil: expertise definitely, but also smugness. Maybe boredom with her, nonchalance. Power.

But there was only hunger and need and the way their bodies met, even with the layers of clothing between them. He was hot and hard and demanded every single bit of her attention. She gave it gladly, catching her breath when she remembered breathing was necessary, resenting it for breaking the tangle of their tongues. He nipped at her lower lip, and she felt it in her nipples and all the way down into her womb.

He grasped her chin, forcing her to meet his gaze. His eyes glittered in the blue light of dusk. For a wild, beautiful moment, it was all that mattered. There was no theft, no debt, no sister hiding in a house in Mayfair.

"We have a deal, Miss Caldecott," Devil said. "Don't forget it."

As if she could. She was more likely to forget her own name.

KITTY CALDECOTT HAD kissed the Devil. What was more, he had kissed her back.

It was embarrassingly difficult to concentrate on the mundane tasks of getting on with her day, but the Ladies' Novel Society met once a month come hell or high water.

Come vicar or Devil.

Kitty was quite sure the society would break down the door were she not there to answer it. It had become tradition.

And at the moment, she could not afford to break tradition. Both literally and figuratively.

And she could not relive the feel of Devil's mouth on hers forever. The slide of his tongue. She ought to have known he would kiss like that. *Devilishly.*

She had work to do. She would start with opening a window, because why was it so warm in here?

The front door opened, the bells jingling cheerfully. The sound door anchored her to the moment: her shop, her favorite books, readers who were as invested as she was in the lives of fictional characters. This mattered too.

First to arrive was Miss Peridot, elderly and rotund. "Why is it so cold in here?" She was eating a raw onion, as usual. Someone had told her when she was very young that onions kept the mind sharp. Miss Peridot very much liked her brain. She knew too many people her age who became addled or confused. And her age was none of your concern, thank you kindly.

Miss Cecelia Xavier and Miss Anne Sutcliffe followed, friends who had debuted together years ago and found each other much more amusing than any of their gentleman prospects. Lady Susanna, whose husband was very dashing and escorted her to the shop, greeted everyone with a tip of his hat and returned to collect her when she was ready to go home. Miss Hastings hid furtively under her cloak, which was not unusual for new members. Her hair was lightly powdered, turning it an undistinguishable color.

Kitty had hoped that the woman the Andovers had chased away might come back.

On the bright side, no one else returned with questionable cabbages or noxious eggs.

This was home for Kitty. Truly home. All that was missing was Evie sitting next to her with her needlework, making wry comments that always took people by surprise.

"Where's Galahad?" Cecelia asked, pulling her knitting from her basket.

Galahad was also a treasured member of the circle. More than once it had been suggested that he be the president. As the actual president, Kitty decided not to take offense. It was difficult to compete with a hedgehog who rolled into a ball, leaving only his tiny nose poking out.

"And Miss Evangeline, of course."

Kitty grinned when Victoria snorted. Everyone loved Evie, but even she could not compete with her hedgehog.

"She's feeling a bit under the weather," Kitty said.

"She needs raw onions in vinegar," Miss Peridot announced. "I'll leave you one."

"That's very kind."

"Bah."

As Kitty wasn't sure how to respond to that, she offered everyone biscuits topped with strawberry jam. The book they had borrowed from her circulating library sat on a small table, well read. Kitty sincerely hoped it did not smell like onions.

"I admit, I fancied Lord Buchanan," Miss Xavier said.

"Cecilia, he's a villain!"

"He's simply misunderstood," Cecilia insisted stubbornly.

"He stabbed a man."

"One time."

"Twice!"

"But he did that...bare chested." Cecilia dropped her voice reverently. "And because that other chap disrespected his love."

"But she does not love him back."

"Of course she does," Miss Peridot said. "She's not an idiot. Merely a little slow."

Kitty exchanged a grin with Victoria. This was her favorite part—when everyone grew heated, forgetting these characters only existed in a book. But that wasn't strictly true, was it? They existed here, in this moment, in their imaginations. They became a part of their lives and of the stories they told themselves.

"That heroine is a cabbagehead," Victoria declared, mostly because she enjoyed the way Lady Susanna turned faintly purple when she disagreed.

"She is young," Lady Susanna said. "She'll find her courage."

"Let us hope she does so before Lord Buchanan razes a village to the ground. I do love a grumpy laird."

"I prefer the stable lad, at any rate," Miss Peridot announced. "He has burly thighs."

Miss Hastings blinked. She was not accustomed to literary salons mentioning thighs, burly or otherwise.

"I hope someone writes about a Viking hero soon." Victoria winked. "Because I also prefer burly thighs."

Miss Hastings made a strangled sound that may or may not have been a giggle.

"Still not as delicious as Lord Drake," Victoria continued.

"Not the vampire again," Miss Sutcliffe said. "I don't care for heroes who cannot have a picnic in the sunshine."

"It's England." Lady Susanna shrugged. "There's never any sunshine anyway."

"Perfect for a vampire," Kitty agreed. *The Vampire and His Lady* was not nearly as racy as the chapbooks that it had inspired. But it was so popular, it paid her shop assistant's salary. It was so popular, in fact, that even a year after it was first published, Kitty regularly gave sold-out walking tours of the places in London featured in the story.

"But imagine all the history he has seen!" Lady Susanna replied. "The stories he would have."

"I'm more interested in his thighs," Victoria said. "Miss Peridot?"

"Definitely." Miss Peridot grinned. "And think of the many years he has had to practice."

That strangled sound from Miss Hastings again.

"Have we shocked you?" Kitty asked quietly. Invitations were required for this particular salon, but Kitty did not remember her. She must have been recommended by another member.

Miss Hastings shook her head. "I haven't read *The Vampire and his Lady* yet."

A truly shocked silence greeted that pronouncement. The kind of shock not elicited by burly thighs or ravishing rakehells or even that one book with the sea monster.

"You haven't?" Cecilia ceased knitting immediately, as though an emergency was occurring right under her nose. "Truly?"

Miss Hastings shook her head.

"Well, that won't do," Miss Peridot said. "I'll lend you my copy."

"Do you mean the copy you have yet to return to the circulating library?" Victoria asked smoothly. "Thereby making the circulating bit rather difficult."

"Bah. You have three more copies."

As they bickered fondly and Miss Peridot promised Miss Hastings that her life was about to change forever, Lady Susanna's husband came to collect his wife just before fisticuffs threatened to break out between the others over who was more fierce, Lord Buchanan or Lord Drake.

Kitty sat back in her chair, feeling hopeful for the first time that day. Let the Temple of Muses keep its treatises and tracts and biographies of well-traveled men. She would choose this every time.

Naughty books and naughty ladies.

She was still not quite ready to go home and face her aunt by the time the salon had dispersed, and so she dragged the box of gold paint and brushes out to the pavement. The side wall could use another griffin to join the one she had painted with her grandfather's enormous and affronted mustache. After her visit from the vicar and his indignant wife, she deserved another griffin.

Perhaps it was a silly tradition, but it made her feel better. Heartened. Marking the battles she refused to lose and the sense of humor she refused to sacrifice to sad people with no sense of whimsy and an abhorrent lack of tolerance. She could whine and worry and nurse her wounds, or she could paint a griffin.

She chose the griffin, as always.

She also liked to keep the shop surreptitiously open late at least one night of the week. Those who needed help came to know what it meant when she lit that particular candle in that particular window. Safety. Secrecy. A referral to the Spinster Society or the house just outside Covent Garden. A place to hide, if only for an hour.

She was proud of her little shop and the community that had gathered around it, however furtively. She would not see it fall to placards and moldy potatoes thrown from carriages. She knew what it felt like to be without options. After her father lost his fortune as suddenly as he made it, and before her grandmother passed the shop to her, Kitty had spent too many sleepless nights trying to find a way to protect her sister. To hide her from the creditors, to feed her more than once a day. To fend off Evie's first marriage proposal at the age of fifteen.

She'd hidden Evie in the back cupboard of the shop and then hidden all of her father's snuffboxes (which he believed were lucky) for good measure until he refused the offer.

She'd painted her first griffin that day, on the floor in front of the cupboard. Her grandmother had taken one long, hard, searching look at her and then promptly announced she was moving to the seaside and Kitty was in charge.

Kitty propped her small ladder against the wall, smiling. That first month had been a whirlwind of ten-page letters (cross-hatched twice and nearly impossible to decipher) sent almost daily to her from her grandmother, full of advice and threats. Kitty had kept them all, even though she had spent more time at the shop than at home and already knew every corner of the business.

She added gold paint in a thick layer, trying not to dwell on the last time she had done this. Clara had helped her, and they drank too much truly awful wine and stale cake the shop next door could not sell and shouted about books until the very early hours of the morning.

Tonight, it was her and the griffin, who was slightly cross-eyed. For some reason, all of her griffins turned out slightly cross-eyed.

Her, the griffin, and a young man running in her direction.

His coat was askew, there was a bruise on his face and blood on his collar points. He was panting, trying to keep running but not having much success. From her vantage point, Kitty saw the three other men chasing him, shouting. One of them waved a bottle of port. They had the air of indulged firstborn sons.

"Duck into the alley," Kitty said to the gentleman they were chasing, even though his buttons were gold and he'd likely never set foot in an alley in his entire life. "Back door of the bookshop is open."

He glanced at her, sweat and blood staining his intricate cravat. He wheezed something that might have been "thank you" before stumbling into the alley.

"Where did he go?" the first of his pursuers shouted. None of the other pedestrians did much except for getting out of their way. When the Mayfair lords came looking for trouble, the rest of the neighborhood knew to turn a blind eye and hope they were not the next target. No one here could afford to go up against an enraged duke or a bored marquis's son.

"Can't be far, the ponce."

"I don't care who his brother is; we're dumping him in the Thames. I knew he frequented that molly house."

They were drunk, wealthy, privileged. Cruel.

All of her least favorite things.

They thundered toward her. Her ladder shook, not the sturdiest at the best of times. Pity.

It took barely a nudge for the pot of gold paint to tumble off the step. Right onto their heads.

The howling was exquisite.

She climbed down to a safer height in case they came for her, and then gasped. Rather theatrically, if she had to be honest. She did not think she had much of a career waiting for her on Drury Lane. She was, however, very accustomed to facing off against bullies, as a woman who was both overlooked and besieged. Somehow at the same time.

Also as a spinster.

She widened her eyes and teetered dangerously. "Oh!"

Gold paint dripped off a patrician nose. Landed on a polished boot that cost more than half her circulating library stock put together. Was spat onto the pavement.

It was all of the paint she had and was going to cost a fortune to replace. Someone across the street laughed. "You scared me!" Kitty said before the trio could react to the laugh, which in her experience never improved matters.

"You little—" The taller one took a threatening step closer, then wobbled, too much port in his system and too much paint in his left eye.

"I'm so sorry." Kitty fluttered her hands helplessly. "You ran into me!"

"Where is he?"

"Who? Oh dear, here let me help you." She waved a rag soaked with spirit of turpentine, which she used to clean her brushes right under their noses. They recoiled as one.

The taller one gagged. "Get off."

"It will get the paint off your face." And it would burn like hell. Serve them right.

"Never mind her—let's go, before this stains my coat." Too late.

"It's in my hair."

They hurried away, and Kitty watched them until they were out of view. Her startled, concerned expression turned sharp. "Mayfair jackasses."

"I couldn't have said it better myself." Their victim hovered in the mouth of the alley, wielding a broken plank from a packing box. His left eye was already swelling and roughly the color of a boiled beet. The wall was holding most of his weight. "Thank you."

"You're welcome," Kitty said. "Come inside and we'll get you cleaned up."

"I couldn't…"

"They might double back. I would not put their getting lost past them in their state."

He winced, lowering his makeshift weapon. "True."

Kitty helped him inside to the corner by the coal grate, where she kept supplies for just this sort of thing: comfrey for poultices, bandages, vinegar. A small bottle of gin that tasted remarkably like the vinegar.

He sat with a groan. "Aren't you going to ask my name?"

"Not as a rule, no," she replied, pouring water into a dish and handing it to him with a clean strip of cloth. "Here, it will hurt less if you wash the blood off by yourself." She turned him toward the cracked mirror.

He wiped at his face, poking at the mess of colors blooming above his eye. "I've heard of this place," he said, quietly. "I didn't know if you'd be open so late."

"Sometimes I am."

"You heard what they said about me."

She lifted her chin. "Makes no difference to me whom you love, and it says more about them than about you."

He blinked. "That's it?"

"That's it. You are not the first to find his way here for that reason."

"You can't just go about dumping paint on Mayfair lords like that."

"Can and shall. Anyway, to see you leaving a molly house would place him at the molly house too, wouldn't it?"

He opened his mouth, shut it. "You ought to be a barrister. Better yet, a judge." His smile turned sly. "But really, the molly house part is less what got under his skin. It's more that I also stole his lady's attention last week." He flinched, working his jaw. "Goddamn it, that hurts."

"I draw the line at pulling teeth," Kitty informed him. Not only would she likely cast up her accounts, but he was in good enough spirits and seemed the type to prefer a joke over a pat on the head. He wasn't in dire straits and could certainly afford to pay for a dentist. She had been a convenient port in the storm and was glad for that. It made everything else bearable.

"Thank you," he said again. "Truly."

"I'm happy to help."

AN HOUR LATER and Kitty had probably avoided going home long enough. Her still slightly-inebriated but at least no-longer-bleeding-all-over-himself guest had left, and she had put away the ladder and her brushes. There was nothing left to do except walk home.

And relive every moment of that blasted kiss now that there was nothing left to distract her.

The feel of Devil pressed up against her. His breath in her mouth, his fingers gripping the back of her neck, keeping her still for his taking.

What was locking the money box, and then walking down the street now crowded with more young men getting ready to carouse? What was *any* of it compared to the thrill of being kissed by Devil?

She was being a goose. A kiss did not change anything, not

really. It secured her aid. It got Devil what he wanted: the wager she had safely hidden in the jar with her paintbrushes. She moved it daily: in the sugar canister, now mostly empty, under the plant in the back parlor, inside Galahad's bag of carrots when he was not satisfied with the bugs hunted in the commons. Inside her best Christmas hat. Inside her shoe, more often than not.

She would keep the kiss the same way: a memory that moved around too fast for reality to touch. A small thing just for her.

She allowed herself to feel his mouth claiming hers again, to relish the strength of his crowding her against the table, the hitch in his breath. It was hers the whole length of her walk home.

And then she was Kitty Caldecott again. Sister, daughter, niece. Embarrassment to the family.

In a house drafty in the winter with lack of coal for the grates, with most of the rooms empty of furniture that had been sold and faded squares on the walls where paintings had been taken down. Except for a seascape that covered the damage left by a man who stopped by to collect money owed to his gaming hell.

They had one small parlor left for use, because her father still fancied himself a baron with a baron's lifestyle, still gentry enough to be called upon by wealthy merchants if not the aristocracy proper. And because Aunt Priscilla was determined to act as though she were a duchess until someone made it so. They both sat by the window, only two candles burning for light when once there was a forest of beeswax tapers with little notice to the cost.

"Where is your sister?" Aunt Priscilla demanded as soon as she saw Kitty. Her cheeks were red, a clear indication that she was in high dudgeon and had been for some time.

"Isn't she here?" Kitty asked innocently.

"Don't play the fool with me."

The trouble was that Aunt Priscilla was also so much more clever than Kitty's father. She could spot a lie, a weakness, inside a mere hesitation. And she descended on it like a hawk on its supper. There would be blood and feathers in the parlor before bedtime.

"Are you listening to me?" Aunt Priscilla seethed. "We need her back in this house this instant!"

"No." Kitty did not know what else to say that had not already been said. "Father is the one with the debt—he can pay the price. Not Evie."

Her father, soft, gentle, and often bewildered, looked as though he might cry. He sniffled once. Kitty could not let it soften her. He was always sorry. Genuinely sorry. For a little while.

And it never made a difference. Not really.

There was always another wager, another debt. The only reason the bookshop was still running was because her grandmother technically still owned it. She was in a seaside cottage, not dead—as she liked to remind everyone, usually through summons to visit her and odd packages of pulled taffy and seashell art sent as gifts. Kitty missed her fiercely. Granny demanded the accounts be sent to her so that she had something good to read, along with every story written by the Nightingale.

"These aren't like the others," her father said miserably. "These are not gentlemen, poppet."

The man who had punched a hole through their wall had not been a gentleman either. He had looked at Evie as though she were chattel to be bartered or taken. That was when Kitty had first started to find hiding holes for her sister. The *gentlemen* that followed suit, it had to be said, were no better. Not one whit.

"Evie is not coming home," Kitty said firmly. "Find another way."

"There is no other way," Aunt Priscilla said with all the resonance of a funeral bell. "Don't you think I've tried?"

"I'll find one." Kitty rubbed at her breastbone. She wished she were back at the shop—back on the rooftops, even. Anywhere but here. She'd considered convincing her grandmother to sell the shop, but she knew even if they sold every single book and tract and every shelf down to the fastenings, it would not be nearly enough. And her father had other debts that needed paying.

Kitty wanted to scream.

Followed by a strong cup of tea and an entire strawberry cake. And wine.

Instead, a knock sounded at the door.

She gave very serious consideration to crawling under the settee and staying there until whoever it was went away. They never did. She knew that from long experience.

As they did not have a butler, nor a housekeeper, Kitty answered the summons, the usual anxiety swirling in her stomach. Another collector? Someone more violent than the last? What story could she spin to buy them time? What promise? What lie?

But it was worse than a debt collector with a smug smile and an iron pipe in hand.

It was Lord Portsmouth.

She would take the iron pipe over the perfumed pomade, the entitled ennui, the cold entitlement in his eyes. An iron pipe might be reasoned with, might be bought off, eventually.

Kitty tried to smile like a woman who was not hiding her little sister. "Lord Portsmouth."

He looked down his nose at her. There was cruelty under the cold beauty, an utter disregard of consequences because he had never had to grapple with them. "Miss Caldecott."

When she did not immediately move out of his way, nor invite him inside, his mouth tightened with annoyance. The kind of noble annoyance that razed a village because it blocked the view of the river from the ancestral manor. His dead ancestors all rolled in their graves at once over her insolence.

"Kitty, for heaven's sake," Aunt Priscilla snapped, followed by her best smile in Lord Portsmouth's direction. "Let the earl in. Where are your manners?"

Kitty stepped aside.

"Would you care for some tea?" Aunt Priscilla led the way to the parlor. "Kitty, ring the bell," she added, even though there was no one to ring the bell for.

"Claret," Lord Portsmouth demanded. "I'm on my way to my club," he said to Kitty's father, who had risen with a jovial, if nervous, smile. All his smiles had been nervous since Kitty's mother had succumbed to that winter fever. "Where is your daughter? I don't like having my plans disregarded. We ought to be married already."

"Of course, of course," the baron agreed. Sweat gathered at his hairline.

Aunt Priscilla shot him an irritated glare before turning back to the earl. "I do apologize, my lord. You know how girls get. Evangeline wanted everything to be perfect."

"Where is she?"

Aunt Priscilla glanced at Kitty, who stayed silent. Her aunt forced a laugh. "The little minx has gone to Paris, can you believe it?"

"I beg your pardon?"

Surely Lord Portsmouth was aware that they could not afford a trip to the other end of London, never mind *Paris*. Evie had no dowry, for heaven's sake.

"She wanted a trousseau fit for a countess," Aunt Priscilla pressed on. "Something *you* would be proud of. She won't be but a fortnight."

A *trousseau*? Evie had a single hedgehog to her name.

"I don't care to wait a fortnight."

"It will give us time to plan something lovely—a ceremony in the local church, perhaps?" Lord Portsmouth's local church was St. George's. Shopkeeper's daughters did not marry at St. George's. Despite the very fine lineages of their grooms.

If Lord Portsmouth's posture got any straighter, his spine would snap in two. A woman could dream.

"What game is this?" he snapped.

"No game, no game," Kitty's father rushed in to assure him. "Just a girl with nerves, nothing to worry about."

"We had an agreement."

"Yes, of course."

"I don't care to be kept waiting."

"If you cannot wait, Portsmouth," Kitty's father said hopeful-ly, "I do have another daughter."

Lord Portsmouth barely glanced at Kitty. "Don't be ridicu-lous. She's far too old."

She was ten years older than her sister, true. Which still made her fifteen years younger than he was. She did not point it out. Nor did she point out the fact that she would rather swim naked in the Thames in August than marry him. She bit her tongue so hard she tasted blood.

"Two weeks," Lord Portsmouth said, "or I take everything and have them toss you in debtor's prison. Your daughters too. And your widow of a sister."

Her father would not survive debtor's prison.

The earl stormed out, fuming.

Aunt Priscilla turned on Kitty. "Now do you see what you've done?"

CHAPTER NINE

K ITTY DID NOT sleep well.

Hardly a surprise.

She had a feeling that the man lurking across the street was there under Lord Portsmouth's orders. He knew very well that Evie was not in Paris. He was loathsome, but he wasn't an idiot. Pity. She would have preferred that to the cruelty that showed through his shining smile. It soured the blood.

She would have to carry on as she always did. Work at the shop, lead tours, consult with collectors and writers. Do everything as though she were not hiding her sister in a house not so far away.

Lord Portsmouth did not like being contravened in any way. He had chosen Evie, and in his mind, that was that.

Over Kitty's dead body.

She let the curtain fall back into place. A dog barked from somewhere. A warning. She read for an hour or so, then tossed and turned in her bed, which might as well have been made entirely of thorns and iron nails.

She woke in a beastly temper.

She snuck out of the house, deciding that discretion was the better part of valor. She might actually get into a physical tussle with her aunt or her father, were she to come across them in the hall. Not a particularly refined aspect of her character, but there you had it.

The streets were mostly filled with servants rushing back from the markets and people like her getting ready for the day. It would be a few hours yet before the peerage were ready to shop or even wander about for their own amusement.

Kitty let herself in, inhaling the comforting and familiar scents, enjoying the way the soft light fell on her books. The Golden Griffin Bookshop was a balm. A port in the storm.

Also, it would seem, under attack.

Across the street, the same man from earlier appeared to be watching her. Watching her watch him watch her. When he headed her way, Kitty fumbled to lock the door and pull the curtain.

Just in time.

The handle turned under her fingers. She stepped back when the door rattled ominously. "I know you're in there," the man barked. "Let me in."

It was foolish maybe to pretend she was not there when he had clearly seen her, but Kitty refused to grace him with a response. Partly because her heart was thundering and she was very afraid her voice would come out reedy and thin.

"Lord Portsmouth wants a word."

She considered dragging a bookcase across the door but would never be able to manage it.

"Just tell him where your sister is—that's all he wants to know."

She went hot, then cold. Her skin prickled painfully. There was just enough fury to temper the fear. "She's in Paris," she said.

"Don't lie to the earl. It doesn't go well for girls like you."

"We're closed," she shot back with false sweetness. "If you're looking to buy a novel about the torrid love affair between a sea monster and a pirate, you'll have to come back."

Confused silence.

Another rattle of the door while her breath caught in her throat.

It was another quarter of an hour before she opened the curtain. The traffic on the road had increased, blocking her view. If he was still out there, she could not see him. She did not for one moment believe he had given up so easily.

She snuck out the back door and popped through the cramped kitchen of the adjoining teahouse. She could not afford the cup of very strong tea nor the macaron with chocolate shavings, but sometimes such things were a necessity. She drank her tea and let the warmth settle through her. She drank two full pots before she felt equipped to return to the shop.

Mostly out of pride. And because she could not hide out forever.

She even went to the front, but that was spite more than pride. She found them both very useful when things turned sour.

And the Golden Griffin Bookshop was hers. She would not let anyone take it from her. Not a bully sent by an earl or a bully sent by the Ladies' Association for Moral Standards.

Because her week did not appear to be improving apace, the front windows were covered in slimy rhubarb compote and what looked like the innards of a steak-and-kidney pie. She would have loved to have blamed it on the stranger sent by Portsmouth, but she knew better. Such a wealth of bullies for her to choose from.

Kitty wrinkled her nose and muttered curses that would have made a hardened criminal blush, but did not lose her bored, placid expression. They did not deserve her reaction.

They deserved a great deal worse.

She reached for the broom tucked into the doorway. No one ever tried to steal it. It would be a nightmare to clean.

"Again?" Devil asked from behind her.

She would have liked to say that she jumped or squeaked like an adorable mouse.

She did not.

She shrieked. Then she proceeded to choke spectacularly on said shriek and finally cough out a strangled giggle. Her eyes watered in protest.

Devil merely watched her, one eyebrow raised. "Are you quite finished?"

She thumped her chest to make sure her heart still knew what to do. "You scared me."

"Evidently."

He was so polished, so confident. It made her want to flummox him again.

It made her want to do other things, too. A great many other things that made her toes curl just from her thinking about it. And were much more enjoyable to contemplate than the rest of her day.

Devil was clearly not overcome with manfully controlled desire for the shrieking redheaded spinster standing in what could only be described as the world's most disgusting soup. He frowned at the mess. "How often does this happen?"

"Once a week. Twice." She sighed. Just a little. "Often."

"No."

"No?"

"No."

She wasn't sure how to respond. It wasn't that he didn't believe her or was arguing with the facts; he simply did not care for them. At all.

He gestured subtly, not even turning his head. Kitty *did* turn her head but could not see whom he was summoning until they were suddenly right there—two tall blond men who could only be brothers and who also resembled enormous Vikings lost on a raid, about a thousand years too late. Kitty had to crane her neck to take them all in. "Hello."

They inclined their heads in unison. They were very polite for marauders.

"Set up shifts," Devil ordered them. "Overnight as well."

"Yes, Devil," they chorused.

Kitty frowned. "What's going on here?"

"I'll tell you what is no longer going on—no one is tossing produce at you, rotten or otherwise."

Kitty had read more than her fair share of poetry. Some of it romantic, much of it filthy. None of it compared to his steely, cold offense. On *her* behalf.

She went warm right down to her toes even as she tried not to. She had to remind herself that she was not the swooning type. "But...you don't like me." He probably did not need reminding of that. "I should think you would enjoy seeing me get my just deserts."

"If anyone will be serving you just deserts, it will be me."

Goodness.

Once again, her body interpreted his threats as delicious promises. She nearly squirmed under his hard, knowing gaze. She licked her lower lip. His eyes followed the movement, flashed.

"Give them your broom."

She handed over the broom with embarrassingly quick compliance. "That's very kind of you," she said to the nearest Viking brother.

"I'm the one telling them to clean it up," Devil muttered.

"Yes, but they're the ones actually doing it, and believe me, it's not pleasant work." She smiled at them again. "Would you like some tea? Maybe a slice of cake?" She did not have cake and could not afford it.

"No, thank you, your ladyship."

Kitty snorted as she turned back inside. "I'm not one of his aristo ladies. Kitty will do fine."

"Miss Caldecott will do fine," Devil told them. "And don't look at her like that. She's not the damned cake."

Kitty poked her head outside, positively beaming. "Someone thinks I'm cake?"

Devil almost looked amused. *Almost.* He landed somewhere between exasperated and tolerant. She would have argued for the pleasure of arguing, but that would have also meant cleaning up the soupy mess on the front step. No, thank you. She was too tired for that sort of nonsense.

And she was most definitely too tired for the mess that greeted her inside the shop. Someone had broken in while she drank two pots of tea and tried not feel as though she were drowning.

Someone with very little regard for books. Fury and fear chased each other up her spine, like cats with their claws out. "Bollocks."

It was all she had time to say before Devil yanked her right off her feet, shoving her behind him. "Outside."

"I doubt anyone is lingering."

"*Outside*," he ordered her. "Godric," he added to one of the brothers, "check the back alley. Wulf, keep an eye on Miss Caldecott."

Kitty was abruptly standing on the stoop with her very own gigantic Northman shield. London was immediately wilder, darker. Parasols and footmen and little white dogs on diamond leashes may as well have been on the moon. This was the purview of footpads and housebreakers and men who lurked in the shadows.

"Clear," Devil called, and some of the tingling apprehension pumping through her bloodstream abated. She shivered.

"Thank you, Wulf," she managed before marching back into her shop.

The view had not improved. One shelf was pushed over. Her teapot was in shards, her inkwell turned over on the desk. Books lay scattered everywhere, delicate pages in disarray. The rage she felt could have rivalled the sun. To throw fruit or fish bones was one thing. Insults scrawled in paint she could handle. Lectures, disdain. They were nothing.

These were her *books*.

"Are you crying?" Devil sounded just as hard as he usually did, but also concerned. Un-devilish.

"I am *furious*," Kitty said through her teeth as she wiped her eyes. "Tears do not quite cover the bloodthirsty vengeance I mean to have."

"Good girl."

She nearly punched him. She also nearly purred. It was very

confusing. Chalk it up to the events of the last few days.

Then she decided she might quite like to punch him after all. He caught her first before it could connect—of course he did.

"Don't patronize me," she said. She was breathless. Entirely because of the anger, of course. It could not possibly be for any other reason.

"I assure you, I wasn't. I meant every word."

She honestly didn't know if that was better or worse. He was still holding her fist. She was quite sure he was more accustomed to kissing the back of ladies' knuckles, not catching wild swings at his pretty face. Why was he so blasted pretty?

"Has this happened before?" he asked quietly.

There was a first-edition book by his boot. She made a tiny sound of horror. Monsters had been here. There was no other explanation.

"Kitty?"

"What? *That's a seventeenth-century book.*"

He released her in order to crouch down to save the book. It was *The School of Women* and, naturally, had fallen open at a page with a drawing of ladies shopping for toys of a phallic nature. Kitty would not blush or squirm. She was not some young miss, sheltered and sweet.

"I asked if this kind of thing has happened before," Devil said.

She shook her head. "No. It's usually vegetables and diatribes. Lettuce and lectures. I could start my own penny dreadful series, all alliterative poetry." She rubbed at her breastbone. "Nothing like this."

"Then you're not going to like what you find in the back room," he said.

She met his gaze, her bones already sparking with outrage. She launched herself toward the back room, where she kept her overstock and her little table for tea and muffins for the Ladies' Novel Society.

The contents of several boxes were tossed about. Books, periodicals, journals. Inkwells, quills, random bits and bobs from lots she had purchased from an estate sale before her entire life had been upended, much like her shop.

She cursed. A lot.

"You *are* vicious," Devil remarked.

"Not like your duke's daughters, I know." Her hands were balled into fists again, on her hips.

"If you think that, you really have not met much of the aristocracy."

"My father is barely a baron," she reminded him. "And he lost his fortune some time ago. Some of it to you, I am sure."

"Very likely." He was not bothered. "At any rate, I happen to like vicious. I trust it far more than a swoon or a simper." He slid her a sidelong glance. "Just don't punch me again."

"No promises."

The easy repartee between them was surprising. Even more surprising was how it put her at ease, even with everything in literal shambles around her. She dropped into the chair, fatigue blurring the edges of everything. "What am I going to do?" She hadn't meant to ask it out loud, and she certainly would not have expected a response of any kind, not from Devil. It was more a whisper to herself.

"We're going to get it all sorted," he said darkly. "And then I'm going to find who did this."

She blinked up at him. "You will?"

"Yes."

"Why?" She knew better than to look a gift horse in the mouth, but the question popped out before she could stop it. If her father were here, he would have flapped his hands with the strain of it and then walked away. Her aunt would have refused to get her gloves dusty. Her grandfather would have said, "Good riddance," followed by the many reasons she deserved the break-in.

No one she knew, aside from her sister, would have even considered getting even. Would have already assessed what needed doing and called for Wulf through the back door to send him for whiskey and hot tea with biscuits, after which he and his brother could put the bookshelves back up where they belonged.

Kitty bit her lip very hard to stop more tears from forming. This was not the time for crying. Not for that reason, anyway—just because someone else was making the decisions for a moment. Just a moment. And they were *kind* decisions.

"Was anything taken?" Devil asked her.

"I don't know." She swallowed, forcing herself to stop staring at him. It was a very pleasant pastime, but no good would come of it. The way his hair curled lightly over the back of his cravat, as if he'd just been standing on the windy moors, would not get her books back on the shelves. "I have an inventory for the shop, of course, but these books were bought from an estate sale. I haven't had time to really go through them."

Devil frowned at them. Suspiciously.

"I don't think a thief hid inside one of those boxes for the past week, just waiting for this moment to strike," she pointed out.

"Fair enough. Do you often buy from estates?"

She shrugged one shoulder. "Sometimes. It's not what I specialize in."

"I know what you specialize in."

"Everyone does."

"Your detractors could easily have done this."

"Maybe," she said. "But it's not the way they usually operate. And if most of my books were tossed about instead of stolen and my money box is still intact, why bother rifling it in the first place?"

"A very good question."

"Just to punish me, I suppose?" She sounded mournful even to her own ears. That would not do.

He glowered at that.

The tip of the knife she used to spread butter on the muffins she bought from the cart outside was impaled in the wall. It was vaguely menacing. But mostly puzzling. "As a threat, that needs work," she decided.

"It's threatening enough."

"It's unclear and not very informative."

"I'm sorry, are you finding fault with how you've been at-tacked?"

"I'm used to better, if I'm honest."

"I don't think you realize just how terrifying that is." He tilted her chin up, searching her face. "But at least you've color back in your cheeks."

"This kind of thing usually makes me splotchy, not pale. Curse of the redheads." Why had she said that? "I didn't sleep well." And why had she added *that*? He didn't care. And it didn't matter.

Honestly. A little break-in was no reason to abandon all of her wits.

Tell that to those very addled wits, currently fleeing the scene of the crime.

She made a small tower of books rescued from the floor, to give herself something to do that was not chattering. Or tearing up. Or wondering what he would do if she just leaned over and bit him. Just a little. Right there on his sullen bottom lip.

She was *absolutely witless*.

She gathered up a trinket box and a knot of the kind of rib-bons people used as bookmarks sometimes, thick and velvet and clamped with gold beads. A stack of lace doilies. A book with a false cover: *Etiquette and Decorum*. Underneath: *Ravished by the Rakehell* by the Nightingale. Clara's nom de plume.

It would take hours to set everything back to rights.

"This will take all day," she said. "I am quite certain you have better things to do."

CHAPTER TEN

WHAT THE HELL was he doing?

Devil was lingering, and he never lingered.

Lingering usually meant tears or threats, begging or blustering, depending on the person. Assassination attempts more than once. There was a reason he traveled with his own men. Dodging bullets and blades became tiresome after a while.

But here he was, demanding filth be cleaned off shop windows and tea fetched for its owner, who might herself breathe fire if given half a chance. He did not hold good odds for whoever had broken into her shop. She would eviscerate them.

What was left of them, at any rate.

And it would be his pleasure to watch.

Anyone could see that Kitty would put herself between anyone who needed her and danger. He'd heard the stories of the Golden Griffin, not just the kinds of literature she sold to those bold enough to ask for it, but the fact that women who needed help tended to find their way to her. The ladies of Mayfair might have the Spinster Society, but there were others not fine enough to be able to march up to the front door of a London townhouse. Lady Priya would let them in, of that he had no doubt. But they were more comfortable coming round the back door of that odd little bookshop north of Mayfair.

Lady Priya collected secrets; Devil collected debts. Kitty collected strays.

She had been doing so long before their paths had crossed. Before she stole from him.

She knew how to take care of herself. She didn't need him. He shouldn't even be here. Especially not without his reclaimed vowel back in his hand. But he hadn't been able to stop picturing her sliding across a rooftop at a dangerous speed. Or the way she had leapt between her and her sister in Priya's side garden. That ridiculous hedgehog in a gold cage.

It was enough to addle any man.

It should not have been enough to addle *him*. He had seen too much, knew too much.

And yet she insisted on taking him by surprise.

Not to mention the way her lips parted when he claimed her mouth. The heat of her soft body. He was well past the age where a pretty face and a tart tongue should lead him in circles. Tell that to the rest of his body. There was a hunger searing through him such as he had never known.

He was a man of four and thirty. It was embarrassing, really.

Courtesans and debutantes and widows were constantly throwing themselves into his path, all perfumed breasts and salacious whispers, and he barely noticed anymore. But when Kitty tripped right into his life he was suddenly a poet? Thinking about her freckles like they were constellations of rare stars. Comparing the taste of her to oranges and spices from faraway lands.

Preposterous. He didn't have a poetic bone in his body. Ask any of the numerous men who attempted to weasel their way out of a debt owed to him.

Devil watched Kitty for one more moment, not understanding why he was loath to leave. Finally, he bowed his head abruptly in farewell and stalked out the front door, feeling like an ass.

With poetry on the brain.

He was not ten feet from the door, between a lady with a

ruffled parasol and a gentleman walking a small dog, when MacLeod joined him. "Trouble at the Sins," he said. He was a short man in his late thirties, with a lightning-fast punch, a ready smile, and ladies constantly trailing him. Also a ragged scar across his throat from where a sword had nearly decapitated him. Men who returned home from the war were not safe, even in the fine streets of London.

"There's always trouble somewhere," Devil remarked. "How did you find me?"

MacLeod snorted. Fair enough. It was an insulting question. He might be the third son of a viscount, but he was also Devil's first lieutenant, for lack of a better title now that they were no longer in the army. He knew the gaming tables and the aristocracy almost as well as Devil did. And liked them even less. "You're up early," he said.

Devil did not answer.

MacLeod glanced over his shoulder, spotted Godric at the bookshop door. "That's a new position. Is it part of the standard rotation now?"

"Yes."

"Why?"

Devil, once again, did not answer. MacLeod smiled, slowly. The kind of smile that was just asking to be punched. "Shut it."

"What about the Sins?"

"I'll take care of it."

WHEN DEVIL LEFT the bookshop, the ensuing silence had a different quality, as if it too knew what was suddenly missing. As if it remembered him, taking up all of the space without even trying. The smell of incense. The air crackling the way it did before a storm. The cup in Kitty's hand was warm, the tea a comforting aroma.

He had sent for tea. For her.

She did not understand him.

Her fingers tightened on the glazed clay. It was sweetened

with milk and sugar. She had not had both milk and sugar together in her tea for months, including her two pots guzzled just that morning. A small thing considering the state of, well, everything. But an important thing. Because *he* had thought of it.

She was very close to smiling into the tea. She was simpering over hot water and leaves. She set it down with a decisive thud. Picked it up for one more sip. Back down.

Time to get to work.

Sorting books was soothing. Cataloguing damage to books was infuriating. The combination was exhausting. Still, it kept her from fretting about Evie. A little.

Barely.

She was very good at doing several things at once. She could juggle three disasters at the same time. If only it were a merchantable skill. She got the shop back to rights and then tackled the mess of the last estate sale purchase. She often hired a Mr. Mayhew to purchase on her behalf. He traveled more easily, not being tied to a shop or a sister. And he was a man. As a woman, she was sometimes not even allowed inside the auction house. And when she *was*, she had to spend most of her time dodging sales tactics and suggestive smirks. "Accidental" brushes against her backside.

It was a good lot: mostly books, with very few knickknacks. She still had a collection of glass ferrets from the time that lady had refused to part with her dead aunt's book collection unless Kitty also took her ferret collection. They were rather disconcerting, with eyes that followed you everywhere and teeth made of bone. When Aunt Priscilla was being particularly...well, *herself*, Kitty hid them in her bedroom as a little surprise.

Sometimes revenge was a glass menagerie with painted eyeballs, strategically placed on a bedside table. Inside the chamber pot.

Kitty was particularly proud of that one. Aunt Priscilla's shriek had echoed down the hallway. As she had just pushed Evie in front of a carriage, it was the very least Kitty could do.

Kitty crouched under the table to rescue a book shoved at a precarious angle against the tipped-over kettle. A small spill of water soaked into her sleeve, but thankfully, it had not reached the book. She backed out and flipped through the thin pages to be sure. *Desires of the Duchess*, volume two. A beloved staple for most of Kitty's collection. Racy, courageous. Deeply and deliciously wicked.

Also defaced.

Someone had written in the book. It was clearly not by the thieves, who had broken in and then proceeded to not actually steal anything. The handwriting was bold, feminine. Slightly smudged, as though rushed, like the book had been shut tight before the ink was fully dried. A hasty scrawl, a note curious to find in the margins. Kitty was accustomed to notes in nature guides correcting the author's translation of the botanical Latin (a surprisingly common occurrence), but it was less common in novels women hid under their beds. This was personal. Desperate.

I do not think it long now. I'll be at the oak tree but have a care. We are none of us safe now.

No name from the writer or the intended reader, but when she shut the book, she recognized the name embossed on the cloth cover. Lady Caroline Portsmouth.

Lord Portsmouth's third wife, missing and only *presumed* dead.

THE SEVEN DEADLY Sins was going to be a pleasure hall like no other.

Vauxhall Gardens had thousands of lamps and fireworks, supper boxes and the Rotunda, but it also struggled with the miasma of the Thames on hot summer days and rain on every other day.

The Sins was entirely contained in a Mayfair mansion Devil had confiscated in a wager on which a marquis had tried to renege.

There was no reneging on wagers placed during a Devil's Night, and not at the Sins either. Every deadly sin would be represented: fine foods, willing companions, a boxing ring in the basement, roulette wheels and billiards tables above. Gluttony, Lust, Wrath, Greed, Envy, Sloth, Pride. None of it would be off-limits. Not at the Sins.

Just as soon as things stopped going wrong.

Which was not going to be today, clearly.

Devil's brother Tom was in the foyer, bleary eyed with the hazards of too much wine or whiskey or both. And something else. "What the bloody hell happened to your face?" Devil demanded.

Tom winced. "Why are you shouting?"

"Why are you bleeding on my new floor?"

Tom blinked at his feet. "That's not blood, that's wine. I think."

"And your face?"

"I was born handsome. You're just jealous."

Devil scrubbed a hand over his jaw. His brother could talk in circles like no one he had ever known. And he was a man grown at twenty and four, but also an idiot. Apparently. "We talked about this."

"I'm fine."

"You don't look fine."

"Well, that's rude." Tom flinched when someone started hammering just behind him. "Bloody damn hell."

"Serves you right," Devil said dispassionately. His brother looked the worse for wear but not in any immediate danger. "Learn to hold your drink."

"I hold it fine," Tom muttered. "Why are you here?"

"It's my club. Why are *you* here?"

"I wanted to make sure the mirrors were hung up properly," he said, squinting. "But they are too bright. My teeth hurt."

Devil sighed. "Go up to Sloth and lie down. The upholstered settees came in yesterday. And don't throw up on anything," he added. "Or I'll kill you myself."

"Yes, yes," Tom mumbled.

Devil walked through the many rooms that comprised the Sins, noting what had been done and what still needed doing. The main attraction was Greed: the largest gaming hell in London, and inside a pleasure hall to boot. It took up the entire ballroom and the rest of the rooms on that level. He'd had billiards table hand carved and felted with ruby red. The roulette wheels gleamed invitingly. The card tables were arranged so it would be easy for servants to circulate with drinks and food on platters, encouraging players to stay longer, wager more. Lose more. The dice were stacked and the cards were marked.

But not all of them.

Temptation only kept a person's attention so long as expectations were occasionally met, just enough to whet the appetite, never enough to satisfy it completely. That was the promise of the Sins: more, more, and more.

He was beginning to know the process more intimately than he cared to. Cards did not tempt him, nor dice. He did not care for gambling or pugilism. Women were lovely, of course, but did not turn his head for long.

Until Kitty Caldecott.

She was a dangerous one. Even before he realized she was a madwoman nearly pitching off the rooftop and then running through town in her bare feet. He honestly did not know whether to laugh or curse. A novelty for him.

He knew what he *ought* to do. Crush her. Without mercy.

Instead, he had been abruptly obsessed with getting shoes on her feet and a shawl that was made of more than red tatters around her. To warm her up. Before he stripped her down.

Sudden and unexpected desire was not so strange a thing. It would not distract him. He would not let it. She should know that nothing distracted him.

He remembered her from the Eastbourne estate, diligently working below the balcony where he oversaw Devil's Night. He remembered the flash of her gray eyes, the clumsy tumble that had sent her crashing into him.

Not accidental, that tumble. As it happened.

It should not make him want to smile. *Nothing* made him want to smile.

He jerked his hand through his hair as the workmen paused to nod to him, the air thick with furniture polish and sawdust. He forwent Gluttony, the lavish banquet hall that only needed more tables with the carved lion's heads, and Envy, the ballroom reserved for dancing, for those who wanted to be seen while pretending not to want it. Who wanted the jealousy and the attention of the other guests.

But in the end, the Sins would be the only thing holding their attention.

The pleasure hall held a purpose beyond pleasure, and Devil would not see it eclipsed. Not for duke or marquis. Not for the king himself.

Not even for a tart-tongued bookseller with golden freckles.

Wrath was in the lowest level, a boxing ring with sawdust to soak up the blood and tiered benches all around. It smelled like damp stone and sweat and wine. Just as it should.

Brutus stood in the ring, his hair shorn close to his head, leaning on his walking stick. He was easily twice the size of the fighters he was training and could still beat them into the ground, even with the knee that had never healed quite right on the Continent. He glanced over at Devil and murmured directions to his men before ducking under the ropes. They rushed to obey even though he had spoken as softly as a nursemaid to a babe. A man of his size did not need to raise his voice.

"You're up and about early," he said. "Is it that girl?"

"What girl?"

Brutus smiled. He was easy with his smiles. "MacLeod mentioned a girl."

"MacLeod gossips like an old granny."

"Don't let my old granny hear you say that."

"I don't have a death wish, Brutus," Devil said drily. Everyone in the family was roughly the size of a horse. Granny Brutus, as she was known, was in fact sitting in the corner with a cup of tea and her knitting.

"You're pulling your punches!" she shouted at the prizefighters. "Don't make me come in there and show you how it's done."

Devil inclined his head in her direction, all lordly courtesy. Because he wasn't an idiot. "Granny Brutus."

"Why, it's the very Devil himself." She grinned. "Have you brought me any stories?"

"He's sweet on a girl," Brutus supplied.

"I will take out your other kneecap," Devil muttered.

"Oi, if she's focused on you, she's not focused on me." Brutus shrugged as if he did not adore his grandmother. He only liked to see everyone squirm when she crooked her gnarled finger at them imperiously. Even Devil came when she summoned him, to his men's great delight.

Until she turned on them, of course.

"Who's this girl?" she demanded. Her hair was still thick and braided in a white crown on her head. Queen of the Rings. The lines around her eyes were deep grooves, put there by decades of grins and glares.

"There's no girl." Kitty was a woman. It wasn't entirely a lie.

"There *should* be a girl." Granny Brutus scowled. "I need help to keep you lot in line."

Devil kissed her papery cheek. "You manage just fine on your own."

"She's not one of those debutantes, is she? Too young to know better and drowning in perfume?"

"No."

"Hah, so there *is* a girl."

Devil did smile that time. "Your younger fighter just let his guard down. He drops his elbow."

It was the only thing likely to distract her, and it worked. She stood up, jabbing her knitting needle in the direction of the ring.

"Oi, you wet noodle. Where's your center?"

Brutus shook his head, grinning. "Sacrificing the young, are we?"

"It worked, didn't it?"

Granny Brutus marched inside the ring, jabbing her elbows and punching the younger fighter hard enough to crack his nose. Brutus winced. "Granny, go easy."

"Ha!"

Devil shook his head. "If they survive, there'll be none stronger. Or wilier." The second prizefighter—as yet undefeated—landed on his backside when Granny went for his kneecaps. "MacLeod said there was trouble?"

Brutus nodded. "Back door was off its hinges this morning. And the shipment of liquor was stolen before it even got here. Footpads."

"Footpads taking on a cart bound for the Sins?"

"Could be a coincidence. Ordinary hazards."

"Could be."

"But you don't think it is."

"I never do."

"Which is why we're still all alive," Brutus said.

Devil's expression did not change, even though it made him want to squirm like a young lad with his first compliment, while also taking the city to the sword, when his men looked at him like that. He would not let them down. They had been through too much together. Mud, blood, freezing their arses off at night, sweating sickness between being shot at. Inept officers in charge who did not care for much beyond their luxuries and renown.

"What do you want me to do?" Brutus asked.

"Nothing," Devil said. "I'll go to the clubs, let myself be seen. And heard."

Brutus snorted. "Aye, that ought to do it."

KITTY RUMINATED ON the book and the inked note for the rest of the day and did not come to any brilliant conclusions. It was a coincidence—it had to be.

An odd one.

And by the time the sun set, Kitty was no longer certain she believed in coincidences. Still, it left her no further ahead. It was hardly a map to Lady Caroline's location. For one thing, there had to be thousands of oak trees in England.

She needed to know who the note had been meant for. The thieves had not found it. Or had they left it behind? That made no sense at all. None of it did. All Kitty knew was that she needed to know more about Lady Caroline and Lord Portsmouth.

And then the invitation arrived. Presumably it had been sent to the house, but Aunt Priscilla had also sent a note to the shop. Lord Portsmouth was hosting a dinner—no doubt originally meant to be a celebration of his recent nuptials to Evie.

Over Kitty's dead body.

The Caldecott family's presence was not a suggestion. It would quell some of the rumors if they were in attendance. Evie had not run from the earl and everything was proceeding at pace. Look, her older sister was right there drinking pink champagne and eating mushroom caps filled with soft cheese. Or whatever it was that was served at such dinners.

Aunt Priscilla's note was not subtle: *Do not embarrass us and do not forget that Evie is in Paris.*

Kitty might have preferred a night joining the mudlarks sifting through the stinking mud of the Thames for teeth and treasure, but they needed everyone to assume Evie was in Paris. Or at the very least, not hiding from Lord Portsmouth. He especially needed to believe it for as long as possible. Or, at least, be willing to *pretend* he believed it.

Not to mention that it would be so much easier to sneak through his house and rifle through his belongings with an invitation.

Chapter Eleven

THE PARTY WAS as awful as Kitty assumed it would be.

As a harbinger of doom, the carriage ride over was suitably ominous. The hired hackney smelled like fish pies and cheroot smoke. Her father was already thoroughly soused and stumbled climbing up the steps, ripping the knee of his breeches. Aunt Priscilla vibrated with barely concealed nerves and outrage that Kitty still refused to divulge Evie's whereabouts.

Kitty just wanted to get there so she could get home again and crawl under the coverlet with her newest romantic novel. The monster hero was a Minotaur and oddly kind.

She would have preferred a Minotaur to anything this night had to offer.

She wore her best gown, which she knew perfectly well was nowhere near good enough for a dinner party at an earl's townhouse. It was a cheerful yellow, paired with her only pair of elbow-length gloves. It was the same one she had worn to the Devil's Night.

"I wish you'd have let me scrub away some of those freckles," Aunt Priscilla muttered. The closer they got to Grosvenor Square, the sharper her edges.

"That's not how freckles work, Aunt P."

"Well, they make you look dirty. And don't call me Aunt P among the *beau monde*."

"Yes, Aunt P." Kitty softened the response with a small smile. She was nervous too. Regrettably. She would never let them know it, the way no one would see her exhaustion or anger when washing splatters off her shop windows.

"I don't have to remind you how important tonight is," her aunt charged on.

But she would.

"It's your fault, you know. If you would just tell us where Evie—"

"I don't know," Kitty replied.

"And *I* don't know how my brother raised such an ungrateful liar."

Aunt Priscilla elbowed the baron so hard that he woke with a shout of "One more round, I'm good for it, I swear." He blinked at his family. "Eh?"

It might have been funny if it weren't so aggravating. At least that was one thing Kitty and her aunt agreed on, if their exchanged glance was anything to go by.

"Oh, get yourself together, Francis," Aunt Priscilla snapped. "Honestly, you've become worse than even our grandfather was. And they wrote a song about him at the village pub."

"Every gentleman has a tipple or two."

"You stink of the alehouse. Gentlemen drink *wine*."

It went without saying that they could not afford wine.

"Kitty's little shop is doing well enough—she could buy me some wine." His eyes were mournful. "Eh, tabby-cat?"

Kitty looked outside, focusing on the lights of Grosvenor Square. They poured from the windows, swung from the dozens and dozens of carriages clogging the street, flickered from artfully placed torches. It was something out of a fairy tale: grand houses of pale stone, warm honey light, glittering glass windows. People poured out of the painted carriages in silk gowns, snowy cravats, diamonds flashing, gold buttons gleaming. It did not even smell like London; here it was beeswax and perfume and gardens thick with lilies and roses.

She had never wanted to be anywhere less.

Oh well. Frying pan into the fire, as they said.

The townhouse was a perfect gilded treasure. Elegant, sophisticated.

With a heart of rot.

By the time Kitty had given her cloak to a footman, her father had already vanished into the back parlor where the card games were underway. Her aunt shot her one steely warning glare and went to greet Lord Portsmouth with effusive deference. It was hard to watch. He turned in Kitty's direction, and she curtsied, bile rising in her throat. There was something deeply cruel to the way he smiled. Something not right.

Music spilled through the shining rooms, played by an orchestra hidden behind a screen of ivy in the ballroom. The air was hot and sweet. Kitty knew not a single soul.

Not a single soul who would admit to knowing her, that was.

She spotted several customers who recognized her with mild panic, as if she were going to start shouting over the violins that she had just received a new romance centering on a many-tentacled kraken prince that might interest them. She nearly chuckled at the thought and tucked herself quietly among the chairs set out for dowagers and wallflowers. In a few minutes, no one would remember she was here at all.

Perfect.

It was lovely to drink champagne and eat leek tarts and parmesan biscuits. To hear music again, so beautifully played.

It was even lovelier to slip away to the library.

IT ONLY TOOK a single glance to know that Lord Portsmouth did not deserve his library.

It was, quite simply, magnificent.

Polished oak shelves, lamps in every corner, and hundreds of books from wall to ceiling, immaculately bound and sorted. She let out a little sigh, as if she had just wandered into a thousand-year-old church full of the bones of saints and holy men.

She did not want to admire a single thing that belonged to the earl. But all organized alphabetically, dusted, with painted titles in gilt catching the lamplight, it was a remarkable sight.

And it would take her hours to inspect. Glorious hours, but hours she did not have to spare.

Her first turn about the room presented a shocking lack of novels and poetry. A crime, in her opinion. And a little unusual in a house that had seen three wives to date. She plucked books off the shelves, flipping as quickly as she could, searching for little notes.

She did not find any. And, regrettably, she was found.

"Oh ho, what have we here, gents?"

Three young men, drunk, bored, and indulged, stumbled into the library. One of them winked at her. He was tall and golden and clearly considered himself as charming as a prince from a fairy story.

Kitty never did like the princes. She preferred the dragon. Every. Single. Time.

And she was fairly certain tonight was not going to change her opinion on the matter.

She knew how to recognize men like Lady Susanna's husband, who escorted his wife to discuss shocking novels in a small shop outside of Mayfair. Men like Clara's new sea captain husband.

These were not such men. These were the worst Mayfair had to offer. They oozed entitlement and privilege and arrogance. Not to mention wine. Her aunt was perfectly correct on that score: gentlemen did drink wine. By the barrelful, apparently.

And they were between her and the door. She curtsied and tried for a quick exit regardless. She already knew it was not going to work.

"Where are you going?" the dark-haired one drawled. "You'll hurt our feelings."

Kitty had several things to say about their feelings. None of them were complimentary. Nor would they be remotely helpful in this particular predicament.

Not only did she prefer the dragon, but she also vastly preferred scrubbing day-old egg off the shop pavement on the hottest day of the year to *this*.

"Pardon me, I am expected," she murmured. Her pulse was a distracting, fretful sound in her ears. She was a mouse trapped in the larder and did not care for it.

"No one's missing you." The third gentleman snorted derisively, but she still liked him best, as he was far more concerned with the brandy decanter on one of the tables than her.

"Anyway, this is supposed to be a celebration." The golden prince sauntered nearer. "And it's deadly dull."

Kitty had no intention of being the entertainment. "I really must go."

"I don't think so." He closed in, grinning.

When Devil stalked her into a corner, there was something thrilling about it. A recognition that though he was perfectly dangerous, he meant her no actual harm.

Not so here. She considered throwing a book at the prince's head. It might buy her just enough time to dart toward one of the doors. It might not. At least it would be satisfying.

"St. John, what are you—" A young woman glided into the library, her sudden smile just as sharp and poisonous.

Kitty swore under her breath. This would not help matters. She knew it instantly.

The lady clicked her tongue like a disapproving governess. "Shocking lack of chaperone," she said. "What *will* the dowagers say?"

The dark-haired one snorted into his brandy. "Nothing that would entice any of us to marry a bookseller, I can assure you."

"Wait, I've heard about you. And the books you sell." The blond prince was not the type to lecture Kitty on wickedness—he was the type to expect her to offer herself along with her books. "Bit of a wild one, aren't you? I can tell, the hair and all."

"Yes," Kitty said drily. "Accounting ledgers and calculating price margins are terribly exciting."

"Eh?" He shook his head. "Come and have a drink with us."

She did not like the look in his eye. "No, thank you."

She edged toward the other door and contemplated hurling herself right out the window if it became necessary.

"Oh, come now, no one sells books like that and still acts the demure wallflower."

"No." She wondered if gagging might be clear enough for him to understand. She did not count on it.

Their lady friend would not offer assistance. She watched the proceedings with a nasty smile. They clustered together like poisonous berries on the vine. And Kitty did not have any gold paint to toss at them.

She did have a decanter of brandy. She took a step to the side and knocked it over the table toward them. They jumped back out of instinct born of generations of clean lace or tidy ruffles and shiny shoes.

Kitty took the opportunity to dash out of the other door while the dark-haired one stared mournfully at the broken decanter pouring liquor at his feet. "Deuced waste."

KITTY DUCKED INTO the servant stairwell, where no one would even think to look for her. The servants were too busy running back and forth with sewing supplies and tea for the ladies' retiring room, more wine and champagne, platters of soft bread, cheeses rolled in peppercorns, ribbons of cucumbers in salt. There were a thousand tasks that went into a grand affair such as this one, too many for them to pay her much mind.

She darted up to the second floor, toward the family chambers.

It was a monumentally stupid plan. But it was also the last time she was likely to be able to roam unsupervised through the Portsmouth townhouse. Surely the missing countess had left something behind in her bedroom. A clue. Another letter. *Something.*

It wasn't safe, but then, neither was Evie.

Lamps burned low between tables set with towering displays of flowers that stabbed at the painted ceiling. It smelled of lilies and furniture polish. Oil paintings marched along, scrupulously hung at just the right intervals. As Kitty did not exactly know what she was looking for, she poked her head into each bedroom she came across.

The master suite was obvious, stately and luxurious, and Kitty ducked back out immediately lest Portsmouth's valet be waiting inside. Her father had had a valet for a few months: a small Frenchman who terrified her father into being fashionable. Aunt Priscilla had adored him.

The lady of the house usually had a bedroom adjoining the main suite. Portsmouth was too traditional to have it any other way, which was obliging. The bedroom was quiet, with the feeling that rooms had when they were not lived in. The coverlet was a pearly gray, as was the silk wallpaper. It was elegant and pretty. Perfectly Mayfair.

Like hell would Evie be trapped here.

Kitty opened the drawers to the writing desk and searched the armoires and the scrollwork chest at the foot of the bed and found...nothing. No helpful diary, no map with a big "X" marking where Lady Caroline had run off to. Nothing under the cushions embroidered with silver swans; nothing under the mattress.

Nothing until she sat back in frustration and her finger caught something. The loop of a black ribbon tied to a torn bit of paper, rolled up tight. She recognized the handwriting from the *Desires of the Duchess.*

Do not trust Portsmouth. Run.

A warning from his previous wife to his next wife?

She had finally found something.

And then *she* was found. Again.

Bollocks.

CHAPTER TWELVE

I T OCCURRED TO Kitty, too late, that she was not particularly good at this subterfuge business.

She ought to have stayed and taken lessons from the Spinster Society. Lessons in hiding, running. Stabbing. Definitely stabbing.

But here she was, prowling through the private personal rooms of the Portsmouth house with nowhere to hide. There was no time to wedge herself under the bed. She had already been spotted. There was only time to shove the scrolled paper down the front of her stays and then turn around with a startled, innocent expression.

Which froze on her face the moment she realized it was Lord Portsmouth himself who had found her.

Her heart stuttered sickly in her chest before leaping into her mouth, presumably trying to abandon ship altogether. Not that she could blame it. The earl filled the doorway connecting to his rooms. He may as well have been carved from marble: cold, cruel.

This was no way to convince him Evie was merely a young girl suffering from nerves on a trip for her wedding trousseau. Kitty had made a monumental mistake.

She already knew that, but it was quite something else entirely to be presented with it so plainly. Her mind raced and tripped over excuses, apologies. Should she try to laugh it off? Act as though she were lost? What earthly reason could she have to be here?

She tried to smile even though it felt too tight on her face. "I do apologize for intruding," she said, hoping her voice did not sound as squeaky as it felt forced through a dry throat. "I could not help but want to see where my little sister will be living."

Lord Portsmouth did not look convinced. But he also did not look like he wanted to toss her headfirst from the window. Much.

She shifted awkwardly. "I should get back."

"About your sister," he said coldly.

She halted. "Yes?"

He had not moved, but he made her skin crawl. "We both know she is not in Paris."

"She…" Kitty trailed off. She did not know how to maneuver through this.

"You are smarter than your father by not insulting my intelligence."

She had every intention of insulting his intelligence, just as soon as she had a viable escape route. As well as his honor, his face, the scent of his hair pomade…

"She will marry me," he continued. "In two weeks' time. I don't care where she is or how you bring her to me, but she is mine."

Kitty straightened, cheeks flushing hotly with anger. "She belongs to herself."

"I think you'll find that's not true," Lord Portsmouth said with careless arrogance. "Don't antagonize me, Miss Caldecott. I have no patience for spinsters. Or girls who run from their duties."

The threat sliced between them. Primal instinct made Kitty's leg muscles twitch with the need to run, as if this were a dark cave with the tide inexorably rising, cold and deadly, instead of a stylish townhouse bedroom with silver candlesticks and boxes filigreed with gilded paper.

"You are nothing," he added. "Your little shop is vulgar. Your house is rented. And all of it you retain because of my noblesse. Remember that. One match is all it would take."

Kitty refused to flinch even though her palms went damp.

"In fact, you may just be the incentive I require. Obliging of you to present yourself."

Run, run, run.

"There you are," Devil said from the doorway, the light haloing behind him like he were an avenging angel. Or a devil, as the case may be.

He did not belong here any more than she did, but he also belonged anywhere he damn well pleased. It shone from the line of his shoulders, his etched jaw, the glitter in his eyes when he looked at Kitty, head to toe, as if searching for injuries.

When he looked at Lord Portsmouth, there was nothing of the drawing room in his face. He brought the battlefield with him. Invisible swords and daggers whistled free from scabbards between them.

"I've come to claim my betrothed," he said, warning in every syllable.

Lord Portsmouth scoffed. "Her?" Disdain dripped from the word.

Devil smiled, though his eyes stayed hard. "Careful."

Lord Portsmouth was an earl. But so was Devil. And his reach extended far beyond the usual social power given to the title. Lord Portsmouth knew it. And he didn't like it.

He bowed mockingly, and Kitty knew full well it was a temporary truce. Not even a truce—a line drawn in the field to be examined and fully tested later.

"Felicitations," he said.

Devil nodded and offered his arm to Kitty, not taking his eyes off Lord Portsmouth.

Kitty's pulse was a boat tossed by the waves. She didn't know what was happening, only that something lurked dark and deep beneath them. She took Devil's arm, like any fine lady would, because she might be out of her depths, but she was not a fool.

Devil was a different kind of danger. One she welcomed. She did not tuck herself into his body on point of pride, but it was deeply tempting. He had brought air back into a room rapidly shrinking around her.

"Thank you," she murmured as they made their way down the hall to the main staircase. Guests milled below. "They'll see us. I should take the back stairs."

"Too late now," he said calmly.

He was right. Lord Portsmouth had found her in a bedroom unchaperoned, later located by Devil, who had announced their betrothal. There was no sweeping this particular rumor under the rug. She stifled a sigh.

"What is it?" he asked.

"I'm just thinking of the mess I'm going to have to clean off the front of the shop."

"You think the Ladies' Association for Moral Standards will disapprove of me?"

"Without a doubt."

"And do *you* disapprove of me?"

"I am currently more concerned about every single unmarried woman here who wants to marry you. And half the married ones as well." The glances were starting to find them. Whispers flew back and forth like songbirds finally free of the cage.

"And I chose the only lady who is not interested," Devil remarked, faintly amused.

She did not correct him. Of course she did not want to *marry* him.

Other things, absolutely. Most definitely.

A matron raised her quizzing glass. Heads turned.

"Don't you dare wilt," Devil said, as though he were suggesting she try the lobster canape.

Kitty glared at him out of the corner of her eye. "I do not wilt."

The guests parted slowly to give themselves time to stare at Kitty's hand on Devil's arm, her thin glove against the rich superfine of his sleeve. The gold button on his cuff cost more than Kitty's gown. The trio who had insulted her earlier stared, half smirking, half in shock. Devil paused. "I'm sure you wish to congratulate Miss Caldecott," he said, icily polite. "On our betrothal."

They blinked. Their entertainment had changed and they did not know the rules. Kitty was supposed to be fair game, too lowborn to be a threat. Beneath them. A woman who sold filth. It occurred to Kitty that Devil had made her feel rage and desire and confusion. He had even made her feel seen and cared for, with a single cup of tea. All of those things and more, but never looked down upon. Not once.

"Well, Lady Ingrid?" Devil pressed lazily. "St John? That is the name you signed that vowel with, is it not? Your father's courtesy title? It does not suit. You do not strike me as the courteous sort."

It was a simple question with all the power of a cannonball. No one crossed the Devil. That was one fact embedded into Mayfair society.

And they had offered insult to his fiancée.

The golden prince paled to the unflattering color of soured milk. Kitty nearly chuckled. He bowed to her jerkily, like a puppet with too-tight strings. "Congratulations, Lord Birmingham."

"Pardon?"

He realized his mistake, he immediately and nearly danced a jig in his haste to bow at Kitty. He looked queasy. "Congratulations, Miss Caldecott."

His friends echoed the sentiment, wide eyed and nervous. Kitty knew they would babble the story for days to come just as soon as they were out of earshot. Devil had taken on Portsmouth in his own house, and now he was using the gossips to spread the word that Kitty Caldecott was untouchable.

He leaned forward, just slightly. "I heard what you said to my betrothed."

St. John gulped. He looked queasy enough that Kitty stepped

back out of prudence. She did not wish to ruin her best dress. "I… That is…"

Devil simply *looked* at him, without another word, until he bowed again and stumbled away, sweating.

"You need to teach me how to do that," Kitty murmured. "Did you really hear what he said to me?"

"No. I guessed. He is not clever enough or creative enough to surprise me." His forearm tightened under her fingers. "Shall I kill him for you?"

Kitty choked on a laugh.

Devil did not laugh.

They continued through the crowd that parted hastily to let them through. A footman waited with her cloak as if summoned through the sheer magic of Devil's will. Devil drew her toward his own well-appointed carriage rather than letting her walk toward St. James to hire a hackney. It was simple, clean, and smelled of the oil from the lamps, scented with lemons. The seat cushions were black damask, the walls polished mahogany. The curtains were a deep, full red, like spilled wine. It was a fitting conveyance for someone nicknamed for the Devil. Sin and sensuality.

Kitty took a proper deep breath, the first of the night since she had stepped through the doors of the Portsmouth townhouse. "I think I would have remembered getting engaged."

"You asked for my help."

"Not like that!" The gossip would be thick as honey off the comb. Still, it was no doubt preferable to whatever Portsmouth had in mind for her.

"You should have been specific, Miss Caldecott. The first rule of wagering. Always specify terms."

"I shall have to cry off, I suppose," she said. "Or you will and ruin my reputation. Well, what's left of it. Still," she added. "Thank you."

"I think you know Portsmouth is not to be trusted."

"Believe me, I know."

"And yet you flitted about his bedroom."

She rolled her eyes. "I was not flitting. Honestly, who flits? And I was in his wife's bedroom, if you must know."

"Why?"

"I'm not sure that's any of your business, actually."

"Well, you are going to be my wife."

She grimaced at him. "Ha."

"You wound me."

"You look fine to me."

"Cut to my very soul."

She tilted her head. "Do you have one? Being the Devil and all?"

His jaw hardened. "No."

She narrowed her eyes. She did not like the altered gleam in his gaze. "Don't be silly—of course you do."

"You've heard the stories."

"I think I, of all people, know not to believe gossip. Last I heard, I was leading virginal young debutantes into the cellar of my shop for distinctly nefarious purposes. There was also talk of a debutante revolution."

"Virginal sacrifices should be my lot, don't you think?"

"I suppose you were taking too long."

He smiled. It was quick and crooked, and a true smile. It made her feel warm. Strangely vulnerable.

"Now what?" she asked.

His smile lingered like a hot coal on a winter morning. She wanted to keep it safe. She had slid closer to him without conscious thought. He had leaned forward.

"You tell me," he said, voice rough.

"This is madness." And not just because she was technically blackmailing him. A gentleman and an earl like Lord Birmingham, a *man* like Devil, would not think twice about someone like her.

And yet...

There was no denying something heated the air between

them, charged until it practically crackled. The memory of their one kiss blazed and burned.

"Perhaps we just need to get it out of our blood," she suggested. Out loud. Like a cabbagehead. He was no doubt used to considerably sultrier.

"Sounds very reasonable," he murmured, not looking the least bit put off. She liked him in that moment. Not just wanted him but *liked* him. "Downright scientific."

She had read too many novels like this. She knew exactly what she was doing and all the ways it could go wrong. *Would* go wrong.

But for right now, in this private, dark corner of the world, she did not care.

She leaned closer, hands resting lightly on his thighs, and tilted her head up expectantly. She had initiated their first kiss. Would he initiate this one? Was he only doing this to pass the time? Was she a complete idiot?

Did it matter?

Devil pushed his fingers into the hair coiled at the nape of her neck, tightening until she made a small sound, very much like a moan. His eyes were stern, searching. "This has nothing to do with our trade."

"Of course not." Kitty snorted, which was the least alluring sound she could have chosen, but his posture softened slightly in response. "This has everything to do with your pretty face."

"Pretty?"

He did not smile, but she could still tell he was amused. Why was that, she wondered? And then his thumb stroked the bare skin of her neck and she stopped thinking altogether. She nearly purred. "Unfairly so," she managed instead. "It's quite annoying, actually."

"I'll keep that in mind." His mouth was so close to hers that her lips actually tingled in anticipation.

"Do try not to smolder." She might go up in flames.

He smoldered. Of course he did. The heroes in books always

smoldered.

But the devils?

Kitty might not survive, and she was still wearing every stitch of her clothing. He dragged his mouth across her jawline, across her collarbone, down her arm to loosen the ribbon securing her plain glove above her elbow.

With his teeth.

The scrape of them against her skin, following the glove and nipping gently at her wrist made her head swim. The other glove landed on the seat beside her, and she wasn't entirely sure how he had managed it. Her breasts pushed against her neckline. He had barely touched her, and was already building and building the tension until she trembled.

She wasn't strong enough for this.

To hell with it.

She grabbed his cravat and tugged. He chuckled like an ordinary man and not at all like a devil, before scooping her forward in one swift movement so that she straddled him. The devil was never far away. The softness between her legs heated, dampened at the sudden pressure of him against her where she ached the most. His breathing was rough when he finally kissed her, and it made her feel like a queen.

He licked into her mouth slowly, as if she were a delicacy, as if he could kiss her for the next hundred years and not be sated. She rocked against him—or the sway of the carriage did it for her; it hardly mattered. She was made entirely of need and desire and desperation. For him.

That might be a problem.

Later.

This moment was for mouths and hands grasping and heat shooting into her core when his thumbs dug into her inner thighs. She hoped there would be bruises, a mark to remind her that this was not a dream. She kissed him back, wanting, taking. He growled something deliciously filthy into her neck that she did not quite make out. She nearly asked him to repeat it, but his mouth was already at the top of her breasts, sucking at the tender flesh. She squirmed, panting, as sensations bolted into her quim like loosed arrows.

His touch roamed higher, thumbs dragging toward her folds. A gentle stroke, a tease of a promise. "Devil," she gasped.

"My name is Rhys," he murmured, stroking deeper into her slickness. "When you scream my name, make it the right one."

His fingers drew her slipperiness up and around her bud, before delving deep again and robbing her of coherent thought. Of anything but Devil. *Rhys.*

"Go on," he said, nipping at her earlobe as he kept stroking, kept rubbing and teasing. Hot tension built inside her, tingling up her thighs, trembling deep in her belly. In and out and around, around and in and out, soft then deep, he built a rhythm that threatened to consume her.

She wanted to let it.

"Go on," he demanded, rough and soft at the same time. The combination did something to her, snapped whatever last thread kept her tethered to reality and rules and reason.

There was only Rhys and the pleasure he summoned to destroy her.

She knew intimately why one might choose a devil. No one else knew how to make you burn from the inside out. Her climax rocked through her, all trembles and quivers and long spasms that made her whimper. *"Rhys."*

"That's it." He sounded so pleased, so hungry for her pleasure, that she clenched around his fingers again, just a little. She wanted him in her hands, inside her body. *Now.*

But he was a devil through and through.

"Ah ah," he drawled when she reached for him. "Not until you're begging for it."

She was fairly certain she had already begged. She had no recollection of anything she might have said between moans. She rubbed against him wantonly, and he groaned.

It sparked through her, that sound. Made her feel like more

than a queen. Made her feel invincible. Frantic.

He eased one breast free, sucking hard. She bucked, sensitive and painfully aroused. She might have moaned. Definitely moaned.

"What was that?" He tormented her with a smug, crooked smile against her skin.

"*Rhys.* Please."

"Better."

She was beyond embarrassment. Begging was not a wrench of her dignity. It was merely another kind of release, one she had not realized she wanted. Besides, a strange sort of joy bubbled underneath the desperation and the desire. A game she was more than willing to play.

Challenge accepted.

She rubbed against his erection again, harder, driven by primal instinct, wanting to make him gasp the way she was gasping. The friction made her even wilder, the way he canted his hips to meet her. Demanding. Hard.

And then he stopped.

He just…*stopped.*

Kitty blinked at him, disoriented, wanting to howl at the interruption. Was the carriage being besieged? Was there fire? The king's army? There had better be considerable threat to life and limb. Why on earth would one stop otherwise?

And then she knew exactly why one would stop.

Devil's fingers brushed over her nipples as he pulled the little scroll from between her breasts. That would not be enough to stop him, surely. A mere curiosity. Surely women slipped all manner of things into their stays—ribbons, hairpins, a coin for emergencies. He unrolled it, skimming the words. *Do not trust Portsmouth. Run.*

"Kitty." The way Devil said her name had her straightening. It was the command of an earl, and of a man who routinely held other men's fortunes in the palm of his hand and flicked them away like they were dust. Unyielding. No longer the command of simply a lover.

"Devil," she returned tartly, mostly because it still activated some kind of shivering over her skin. He made her feel coddled and then hunted.

Yes, please.

No. *No.*

Damn it, Kitty.

His eyes darkened. The lazy snap of his voice—the underestimate-me-if-you-dare languidness of it:

"I think you had better tell me everything, Miss Caldecott. *Now.*"

CHAPTER THIRTEEN

D EVIL STILLED, SUDDENLY a warrior alert on the battlefield. Searching for any hint of attack. For the enemy.

While she was still straddling him.

She did not want to regret this delicious moment outside of time and place. There were too many regrets already. She shifted to slide free, but his hands tightened on her hips, keeping her still. "Explain," he said softly, darkly.

"It's nothing to do with you."

"What were you doing in the countess's bedroom?"

"Why?"

"Because it's not safe."

Her head whipped up. "Don't you dare suggest that I do not know the seriousness of...whatever this is. My sister's life hangs in the balance." Because she craved the feel of him between her thighs, she pushed back, away. "Let me go."

"I don't want to," he grumbled, even as he released her.

She scooted back on to her seat, yanking her skirts down where they belonged. Her body was deeply, deeply confused. And rather irate that she had moved away instead of closer. He lounged like a king on his throne, not at all discomfited by the fact she had just come on his fingers. It made her want to kick him.

"I know that look." He trapped her leg between his knees. "Last time you followed it with a facer. I don't fancy being kicked either. Tell me about the message instead. Who wrote it? Where did you get it?"

She crossed her arms even though she knew it made her look petulant. She was starting to *feel* petulant, truth be told.

"Did you find it the countess's bedchamber? Is that why you were there?"

"Yes."

He cursed, low and vicious.

"Don't you think it odd that Lady Portsmouth's bedroom was so…empty? Nothing left of her at all. Not even a single portrait of her in the house." She paused. "Of any of his previous wives, actually."

"The earl is not exactly what you would call sentimental."

"Not to mention the fact that he's a murderer."

"That too. He has always wiped away any trace of his wives. Claims it's so as not to make his new bride uncomfortable."

"Untimely death is uncomfortable," Kitty muttered.

"Where did you find it, exactly?"

"Hidden behind her bed." She rubbed at her breastbone. Portsmouth meant to make her sister just another woman he erased from the world.

Devil watched her steadily, every inch the man who held a hundred fortunes in the palm of his hand on a regular basis. "What else?"

She blinked. "Pardon?"

"There's something else you're not telling me."

She tried not to wriggle in her seat. Willed herself not to flush nervously.

"Kitty," he said, "this is serious."

"There's a chance Lady Caroline is not dead, only missing. Or on the run. If I find her, I can… I don't know," she acknowledged. Do *something*."

"I thought the whole point of your blackmailing me was so *I* would do something."

"And have you?"

He narrowed his eyes. "Yes."

"Truly?"

"Yes."

"And are you going to help me find Lady Caroline?" she asked.

"Are you going to let me do it alone?"

"Absolutely not. I'm perfectly happy to take Portsmouth down. But I won't put you in danger to do it."

She shrugged one shoulder, let it fall. "That doesn't matter."

"The hell it doesn't."

THE WOMAN WAS a menace.

This was not a new revelation—he already knew she was a menace—but she insisted on proving it at every opportunity. Climbing up buildings, sneaking into Portsmouth's house. Already finding out more about his last wife than the magistrates or constables had managed.

Coming on Devil's fingers, gasping and clenching around him. It had taken every ounce of resolve to stop when he found the note. And that was only because fear for her was like a dousing of icy water down the back of his neck.

Who knew what Lord Portsmouth would have done to her?

Nothing good, not with his infatuation with her sister. Not with his character. Devil had seen rats among the corpses on the battlefield at Waterloo whom he would trust more than fucking *Portsmouth*.

It was not a secret that his wives had all perished under convenient circumstances. Kitty was right to be scared for her sister. She ought to be terrified.

If only fear proved a deterrent for Miss Kitty Caldecott. He already knew it would not.

And now he had claimed her for his own.

It had felt too right, thrumming through him like fate, which he did not believe in. But she was his now. *That*, he believed in.

And he would protect her. He had done things on the Continent that Portsmouth could not dream of. He might be a threat, a murderer.

Devil was worse. London knew it.

But perhaps it was time for a reminder. He did not have time for missing shipments or broken doors.

And he definitely did not have the patience for threats against Kitty.

It hardly mattered why, or that he had known her for less than a month all told. He knew it in his gut, and he had learned long ago to listen to primal instinct. He had met her once before but she did not remember it. He did. He recalled it quite clearly: she had marched up to Brutus, who was collecting vowels and payments for wagers and listening to her father's pitiful excuses. Devil had not bothered to listen; he had heard them all before. The baron was pleading and sweating. Nothing new.

Until Kitty had marched into the club, which very specifically did not allow women, glared at her father, and then handed a pouch of coins to Brutus. "It's all there," she said, lifting her voice so Devil could hear her, as if he had not leaned forward to get a better look at the woman with the red curls and the gray eyes that threatened to burn the building down around them. He remembered there were ink stains on her fingers. A mended tear in the hem of her dress.

"That's the last of it," she snapped at the baron. "Tell Aunt P to leave Evie out of it."

And then she marched away without a single backward glance at the men staring at her, at her father, even at Devil. He did not think she had even noticed him.

Magnificent.

And then she had picked his bloody pocket. Let him kiss her in her bookshop, let him touch her in his carriage until he was so hard he had genuine concern over injuring himself.

And now he was back at that same club, not the Sins, just one of the many that catered to gentlemen's entertainment. It had become his favorite haunt since that day, all because of her.

Worrying.

But fine as long as no one else noticed.

Such as MacLeod, that gossip. Or Granny Brutus, who kept sending him bits of the most awful poetry in case "his girl liked poetry."

His girl, as she put it, preferred scandalous novels that would make the most hardened rake choke on his own ill repute.

Devil tried to put her from his mind, or at the very least not appear as though he were contemplating things like poetry and the hot, silky feel of her around his fingers. In this place, he needed to be Devil: aloof, terrifying, ruthless.

Simple enough.

Especially if he let his mind wander to the fact that someone had broken into her shop. That people regularly tossed rotten vegetables in her direction. Made unseemly remarks. *Insulted* her.

Never again.

"Devil?" The man's voice shook as his throat bobbed. "Never mind, you're busy."

Devil looked up at the sweating viscount and set his glass of port down. "Speak."

"About that wager…"

Devil did not blink, did not say a word.

"I just need a little more time." The viscount gulped as Mac-Leod made his way through the members playing cards, smoking cheroots. He shouted for more wine as he sat next to Devil. The candlelight shone off the scar that sliced halfway across his throat. He gulped again. "I'll have it for you tomorrow. One thousand pounds. Tomorrow."

"Good choice," MacLeod said mildly.

"What are you doing here?" Devil asked him as a footman brought another glass of port. MacLeod shook his head and asked for coffee instead.

"What are you doing *here* without anyone to watch your back?"

"No one has tried to kill me in weeks." It was an occupational hazard when collecting debt vowels was your occupation. Devil wouldn't miss it. But he did not regret a single bit of it either. It had served its purpose.

"That you know of." Macleod snorted. "Because I'm that good."

"How do you get through doorways with that fat head of yours?"

"I manage."

The hum of the crowd intensified around them as the night progressed, members falling more heavily into their cups. It made them at once bolder and more desperate when they inevitably approached Devil to beg for an invitation to the opening of the Sins, or for mercy.

Devil was not handing out either that night. He was only offering the threat of his presence.

When Portsmouth arrived, Devil's eyes narrowed.

Macleod whistled softly. "I haven't seen that look on your face since the war ended."

Portsmouth greeted the other members, motioning imperiously to a footman for a drink. He snarled with scorn when it was not delivered quickly enough.

"Portsmouth, I thought you were supposed to be celebrating your impending nuptials," someone shouted from a nearby table. "What happened, old man? Not up to it?"

His companions laughed. Portsmouth stiffened. "I'm not a butcher's son after the nearest barmaid. I can afford to wait for the right lady," he said.

"I've got a wager in the books that says you can't."

The tension in the air was palpable, sharp, but still not sharp enough to cut through the haze of drunkenness at three o'clock in the morning. Half the men made commiserating, sympathetic murmurs; the others mocked louder. The club betting book was passed around.

"The chit is the daughter of a minor baron. Couldn't find another duke's daughter, eh?"

"The chit is beautiful, at least."

"Her sister is a disgrace. Runs that bookshop. That the family you're keen on marrying into, old man?"

"My wife loves that shop—shut your gob."

On and on it went, with Portsmouth ordering another drink and then another, silently seething.

"Is he going to be a problem?" Macleod asked.

"Not for long," Devil replied.

CHAPTER FOURTEEN

WHEN KITTY SNUCK out of the house far too early the next morning once again in order to avoid her aunt, Devil was waiting on the front step.

For her.

She nearly collided with him, jerked back to stop her nose from smashing into his chest, pulled something in her neck, and then nearly toppled over.

For a woman accused of all sorts of wanton wickedness and immoral deeds, she was proving to be spectacularly unseductive.

She had read enough books to be intimately familiar with the desires of men and monsters, from Minotaurs to winged fairy kings. It seemed unfair that absolutely none of the seductive wiles had rubbed off on her.

She was still just Kitty: red haired, freckled. Short. Not to mention physically catapulting herself off the most sought-after man in London.

He caught her by the shoulders, steadying her. "Are you on fire?"

"No. Of course not." It was possible her pride was going up in flames.

"I just wondered. I've seen racehorses run slower."

She frowned at his pretty face. Why did he have to be so pretty? Sculpted, delicate, rugged. None of those things should work so well together. And wasn't their very brief interlude in the carriage meant to erase this kind of distraction? His face meant nothing to her. Nor did the warmth of his hands through the thin material of her dress. The smell of incense that clung to him, amber and sandalwood.

"What are you doing here?" she blurted out. It was too early for anyone to expect sonnets and soliloquies from her. She might be able to manage a naughty limerick.

Devil's mouth quirked. "A naughty limerick?"

Kitty closed her eyes briefly. "Did I say that out loud?" She really needed several more hours of sleep and a trough full of tea.

"I find your forthrightness refreshing."

"Mm-hmm," she murmured, doubtingly.

Very doubtingly.

In her experience, men like Devil—of which, to be fair, there were likely very few—still preferred powdered bosoms and red lips and sultry, agreeable smiles. A modicum of grace.

"You'd think so," he said, still amused. "But you'd be wrong."

"I said that out loud too?" She groaned. "I really can't be around people this early in the morning."

"I'll keep that in mind," he drawled. Like a man who planned to see her early in the morning.

Every nerve ending flared spectacularly awake. It was too early for *that*, too.

Someone should tell it to her thighs and her belly and that ticklish spot behind her ear.

She took a deep breath, another. *Get a hold of yourself.* "You are between me and my breakfast."

He frowned. "You haven't eaten yet? What about your cook? What does she do in the mornings?"

She did not tell him *she* was the cook and that some mornings it was just too much hassle to even contemplate. She managed for Evie. For herself, Kitty was fine with tea and a muffin from a cart. Especially at the moment. Poisoning her father and her aunt's morning tea was likely bad form. And entirely too tempting.

"Why are you here, Lord Birmingham?" she finally asked, gathering the scraps of her dignity around her, such as they were.

His frown deepened; his voice roughened. "I thought I told you to call me Rhys."

She forbore reminding him that he had said so with his tongue tracing along various parts of her anatomy.

But since he was not giving in and he was still blocking her way, she repeated, "Why are you here, *Rhys*?" She'd meant it to be faintly mocking. Wry. But as it immediately conjured up the memory of his hands moving skillfully under her skirts, she'd somewhat missed the mark.

"I'm here for you."

That conjured up all sorts of new ideas.

Not helping.

He had steered her to his waiting carriage before she quite knew what he was about. Sir Reginald hung nearly halfway out of his window to watch them. He was going to land right on his head if he leaned out any further. A curtain twitched upstairs, over their heads. Her aunt's room.

Kitty all but leapt into the carriage. "If you want to talk to me, you can drop me at the bookshop," she said. Devil's carriage was just as luxurious in the light of day.

"Certainly."

But when the carriage pulled to a stop, she peered out of the window. "Bollocks." She turned to glare at him. "*You* are not in your right mind."

ESCORTING KITTY WAS like escorting a firecracker. A particularly stubborn, quarrelsome firecracker.

He liked that about her.

These days the people who were brave enough to deny him were generally desperate. Even then, they were just as willing to fall over themselves to gain his favor, to do exactly as he asked in the exact manner in which he asked them. He knew several ladies who would have hurled themselves bodily into this particular shop had he suggested even a hint of interest.

Not Kitty.

She dug in her heels, expression blazingly and adorably mutinous. Her freckles smoldered like sparks. "Are you insane?" she asked again.

Pedestrians glanced at them curiously, as did one of the shop clerks. When he recognized Devil through the glass, he bowed his head in greeting. Carriages continued to trundle along behind them, horses snorting, wheels creaking. A dog barked at them from the end of a braided leash. Still, Kitty did not move. Not one inch.

He'd wanted her before—that was no secret. He wanted her even more now.

She glared up at him. "No."

He leaned one shoulder against the doorjamb, perfectly willing to wait her out. If he knew anything, it was patience. The clerk stilled at his subtle gesture. "What's the problem, little firecracker?"

Her glare narrowed further. "Little firecracker?"

"You are practically breathing fire."

She rolled her eyes. "I have red hair, yes, very clever. And I'm short, well spotted."

"You have fire in your veins, Kitty. Your hair has nothing to do with it."

He had confused her, just a little. Good. She bewildered him daily, and it was high time he returned the favor. She was distracting. It was unacceptable.

And yet here he was.

"De—Rhys, you can't be serious. I'm not setting foot in there with *you*."

"You make it sound positively sordid," he drawled, mostly because he knew the drawl would needle her. And he liked her needled. It made her even more honest. Distracting *and* refreshing. "It's just Rundell and Bridge."

"'Jewelers to Their Majesties,'" Kitty read from the sign as though Devil had taken a wrong turn somewhere, "'His Royal Highness the prince regent and the royal family.'"

"Yes, I can see that."

"Why?" she asked bluntly. Suspiciously. It made him want to kiss her until she was soft and warm against him. Breathless.

"I am shattered that you do not remember our betrothal," he said.

He saw the exact moment she wrestled her expression into something suitable, because before that he had seen more than she wanted: curiosity, temptation. Horror.

Horror.

Why? Because he was the Devil? She had not let that intimidate her one bit yet.

She straightened, still on fire, only this time she was a flaming arrow pulled back in the bowstring. "We had a…moment in your carriage," she said plainly. "No need to get hysterical."

Hysterical? *Hysterical?*

Devil was known for his unruffled calm when assaulted with panic and pleading and outright violence to his person. Even the odd assassination attempt did not faze him overtly.

And here she was accusing him of being overwrought. Like an elderly aunt being sent to the seaside for her nerves.

Someone snorted nearby. Devil did not look away from Kitty. He knew exactly who was hovering like a fretful nursemaid. "Go away, MacLeod." *MacLeod* was the one who ought to go to the seaside for his nerves.

MacLeod did not, in fact, go away. Even though he was one of the few men in Mayfair not in debt to Devil, he insisted on acting as though he were, determined to protect him. Even though Devil paid men for that very purpose. MacLeod refused to take payment and refused to accept anyone else would do as good a job as he did.

And the bastard was right.

What was more, if Kitty kept looking at Devil as though he were fretful, he really would pull her into that alley and kiss her senseless. He might anyway.

"I am not hysterical," he said instead.

"It's perfectly normal," she offered. "And I'm sure it's very gentlemanly of you. But I'm hardly worried about my reputation."

A muscle twitched in his jaw, even as he fought a smile and the very inappropriate urge to slide his fingers under her thin dress until she moaned. "According to all of Mayfair, we are betrothed," he reminded her. "And a betrothal means a betrothal ring. I don't make the rules."

"You're not exactly known for following them either," Kitty pointed out drily.

She was not wrong. Earls did not run gaming hells or bacchanals twice yearly. They did not enforce debts. They did not run away to join the army after a fight with their father at the age of twenty-three because war on the battlefield was preferable to war everywhere else all of the time. They didn't leave their thirteen-year-old brother behind.

"That's all this is?" she pressed.

"Of course." *Like hell.*

"Oh."

Was that a hint of disappointment? He decided it was, because he wanted it to be.

"Portsmouth is dangerous," he reminded her. "This way you will be under my protection. You wanted my help, remember? Demanded it, in fact."

"I don't need—" Kitty snapped her mouth shut. She might not want his protection, but she needed it. For her sister. She was too clever to deny that.

And he would not have her traipsing about London, kicking over Portsmouth hornet's nests without him.

Not happening. Ever.

"I supposed it's just a ring," she said softly. "But I might have one left at home I can use."

Something recoiled in him at the thought. That she had sold

too many of her belongings to pay her father's debts. The baron had a lot to answer for.

"No."

"No?"

"No." He opened the door and nudged her inside. If she was going to wear a betrothal ring, it was going to be *his*. And that, as far as he was concerned, was that.

The shop was impeccably presented, with glass cases waiting for perusal, catalogues stacked just so, sketches framed on the wall. Most of their work was made to the buyer's custom specifications, but there were always pieces available. Some were returned because the colors were wrong, the setting not to taste. The buyer suddenly in debt and unable to pay. Devil had been offered so much jewelry he could have opened his own shop. In every city in England. But he wanted something particular for Kitty, something just for her.

Diamonds and pearls were the fashion, available in all shapes and sizes. There were lockets, rings, necklaces, ear bobs. Buckles for shoes. Brooches. All described and detailed in catalogue books, the rest pinned to rich, dark velvet. Even on a bright day, candles burned, glinting and glimmering off a multitude of gems.

"Lord Birmingham." The clerk bowed. A crystal pin shaped like a sword gleamed from the intricate folds of his cravat. His buttons were inlaid with opals.

"Evans," Devil returned, more concerned with the way Kitty had stilled, her smile tremulous. She rubbed at her breastbone. She was uncomfortable. Waiting for some kind of insult.

He very much wanted to see London kneeling at her feet. Bloodied, if at all possible.

"Miss Caldecott this is Evans," he said. "Miss Caldecott is my fiancée."

Evans did not blink. He was too well trained and too professional for that. "May I offer my congratulations?"

"Thank you," Kitty said softly.

Devil found he did not like it when she was nervous, quiet. It did not sit right. Not when he had once seen her throw a rancid potato back at a vicar, spewing the kind of profanity that would have shocked several members of the criminal underworld.

She was a veritable force of nature. And he would not have her shrink down for any reason.

"We're here for a ring," he said, flattening his hand on her lower back when she shifted to bolt. She stepped on his toe. Hard. He tried not to smile. He did not even try to *not* feel smug satisfaction. There she was: a flame finding its wick.

"Something simple," she added, looking utterly horrified when Evans led her immediately to a display box of diamond and pearl rings large enough to give her hand cramps.

"Something beautiful," Devil corrected her. "Sapphires, I think."

Her eyes glowed, just a bit, when the new rings were procured. They were as blue as a Scottish loch, ringed with a stormy gray.

"Why sapphire?" she asked him, reaching out to touch one, then jerking back as if she were going to be scolded.

"It's the color of your bookshop," he replied with a shrug. "I assumed it was your favorite."

She stilled, stared at him for one long moment, and then pointed to a ring with barely a chip of blue. "This one, please."

He raised an eyebrow. "Try again."

She crossed her arms. "What if that's the one I like best?"

"Then that's the one you'll have, but since it's *not* the one you like best, try again."

"You're very sure of yourself."

"You're not the first to say so."

"It's very annoying."

"That has also been said."

She huffed out a sigh, muttering something under her breath he chose not to hear. Evans folded his lips inward as if trying not to laugh or gasp in shock. Kitty had that effect.

"We also have some lovely lapis lazuli," the clerk offered

tentatively.

"Not nearly good enough," Devil said.

Kitty snorted. "Now you're just being ridiculous."

"If she won't choose a ring, we'll take that one." He pointed to the most ostentatious sapphire, best suited for a dowager duchess who liked to show off. Kitty winced. She *physically* winced.

"You're impossible," she said. When she finally glanced at him, the hunger he felt must have shown in his face, because she stilled. The soft, delectable pink flush deepened, dipped under her neckline and made him think of all the places on her body that same shade.

He hardened instantly and very nearly groaned out loud. He wanted to trap her against the table and chase the pink flush traveling down her neck with his mouth. His tongue.

He was being undone by a modest neckline, a pink blush, and a smattering of freckles. Utterly undone.

He cleared his throat so his voice would not frighten her. Or encourage her. Even Devil ought not parade through London with a cockstand so painful it reminded him of his days as a young man. Where was his infamous indifference now? His cool, calm stoicism?

Crushed under the dainty foot belonging to a dainty woman with the vocabulary of a sailor and the arm of a cricket player.

When Kitty hesitated over a ring featuring a flower with sapphire petals and a pearl center, he pounced. "This is the one."

She blinked.

"Isn't it?" he asked.

"Yes," she admitted. "Thank you."

"We'll take a pair of sapphire earrings to match as well," he said to the clerk. "Have those sent to me when they're ready."

"Of course, your lordship."

Kitty widened her eyes at him. He pretended not to know what she meant.

He did not pretend to not be enjoying himself immensely.

Funny that he was known for orchestrating the kind of entertainments that thrilled even bored, jaded aristocrats, from gaming hells to soirees at Vauxhall Garden to week-long house parties. Debutantes, *demimonde*, dukes to dairy maids. He had seen it all. None of it caught his attention. Not the way Kitty Caldecott did.

"I really don't need earrings," she said.

"And a necklace as well," he decided. "Something striking. Diamonds with sapphires. Impress me."

Kitty swallowed back a comment. She had clearly realized that every time she protested, he would add something more extravagant. More expensive. She deserved the very best. Sapphires, diamonds. Books would be better, of that he had no doubt, but they would not help protect her. They would not make the statement that needed to be made. "What about a tiara?"

"Absolutely not," she snorted, forgetting her awkwardness. "Exactly which invitations do you think I am extended that require me to have a diamond tiara?"

Anger tightened in his chest. Anger at the people who dared throw rotten fruit at her door and insults at her person. Never again. She would be invited to the damn palace if she wanted to be.

He knew without asking that she did not want to be.

"A tiara too," he told the clerk as he ushered her outside before she could protest. "And a gold inkwell, also with sapphires. Etched with a griffin."

She paused, tempted.

"We do not make inkwells, your lordship," the clerk said apologetically.

"You do now." Devil let the door shut behind him, confident in his ability to get what he wanted.

"It's too much," Kitty insisted as they stepped onto the pavement, crowded with shoppers and footmen and maids running back from market. The sun picked out the amber threads in her hair and turned them molten. He wanted to toss all of her hairpins into the street.

"You can sell the lot, if you wish," he told her. "And buy your sister a hundred more hedgehogs. Or settle a dowry on her. Buy her a house."

"I could? I mean, I couldn't."

He had her. She might be uncomfortable accepting luxury for herself, but she would do anything for her sister. She took care of Evie, obviously. Enough to blackmail Devil and go up against Portsmouth. She took care of her useless father. Her acidic aunt.

But who took care of her?

And why did that bother him so much? As did the thought that she still had not had her breakfast. They would stop at a bakery on their way to the Golden Griffin. Ten bakeries.

He was too busy deciding how many loaves of sugared bread she would let him buy her that it was only long experience that registered a shout from nearby and MacLeod suddenly running toward them from the opposite direction. Devil reacted without conscious thought, purely on habit and instinct.

Danger.

It took on a sharper edge when Kitty was in the vicinity.

Unacceptable.

CHAPTER FIFTEEN

T HERE WAS A dagger in his hand even as he pushed her against
the brick wall, covering her entirely with his body. She
squeaked in surprise. There was a second dagger—he knew
because he felt it slice into his upper arm before clattering against
the wall. A searing bite of pain, inconsequential until he was
satisfied Kitty was safe.

He turned, his back still shielding her. Only a couple of pedestrians had noticed, one of them pale as boiled parsnips. The
others walked on, unconcerned. London—love it or hate it, it
would not change, not for anyone.

Macleod glared between the passersby, between the carriage,
the froth of London obscuring his view. "I sent Michael after
him."

Kitty tried to peer around Devil, but he would not let her. He
was not convinced it was safe yet.

She poked him in the kidney. He ignored that too, glancing at
MacLeod. The other man nodded. "Safe enough now, I reckon."

"Excuse me." Kitty pinched him. Hard. "You're crushing me,
Lord Birmingham." He eased away reluctantly. She popped away
from the wall. "What on earth just—You are bleeding!" Outrage
darkened her eyes from gray to nearly black. Outrage for him.

He looked down at his sleeve. "I liked this coat."

"Rhys!" She looked around frantically, finally plucking a

handkerchief from a passing gentleman who protested until he saw the look on Devil's face. And the blood spattered on the pavement at his feet. He hurried away as Kitty folded the thick material and pressed it to Devil's wound. "You need a doctor."

He smiled at her.

She glowered. "Do *not* smile at me like that."

"Like what?"

"Like I'm a silly woman. You've been *stabbed*."

"Barely."

"Choke on your pride, *Lord* Birmingham. You're having it looked at."

Devil grinned. He couldn't help it. Despite the simmering fury he planned to take out on the attacker when Michael dragged him back.

MacLeod blinked at Devil, who could not remember the last time his friend had looked so shocked. "You're smiling."

"Shut it."

Macleod nodded solemnly to Kitty. "You're right. He does need a doctor."

DEVIL, BEING AS stubborn as a boatful of cats, would not let Kitty summon a doctor. He even insisted on stopping at a bakery to procure bread and marmalade for her breakfast.

He really was a madman.

She tried not to like it so much. Especially as he was still bleeding. For her? Possibly. Had the knife been aimed at him or at herself? Either way, he had shielded her.

He let her bully him into her shop, which sported gleamingly clean windows, thanks to Wulf's standing guard overnight. Devil nodded his approval. "Continuous guard."

Wulf noticed the tear in his sleeve, the bloody handkerchief, and nodded back. "Aye."

Kitty brought Devil to her chair in the back room and was gratified to find there was still clean water in the kettle over the cold ashes of the grate. She made quick work of gathering a cleaning bowl, more rags, soap. She had thread somewhere, but she had never stitched up a person. She did not think he would appreciate a griffin embroidered in gold thread on his arm.

He shrugged out of his coat. She could hear the sounds of his cravat being pulled loose. She turned just in time to see him pull his lawn shirt over his head, baring his torso. He was solidly muscular, more sun-kissed than she would have imagined for an earl, and dusted with hair. She tried not to stare. To salivate.

And then he shifted so that his wound was visible, and all of her prurient interest slid away. It was not a deep wound, but it was ragged. It looked painful. She sucked in a breath. "Sit down."

He lowered himself into a ladder-backed wooden chair with a careless groan, as if he had gone for a long, exerting walk instead of being attacked in broad daylight on Ludgate Hill.

"Oh, Rhys," she murmured, dabbing at the blood with a clean, wet cloth. It had once belonged to an old nightshift she had pulled apart for rags.

"This is not the first time someone has tried to stab me," Devil said, unconcerned. "It's not even the fifth time."

She sniffed. "That does speak well to your character. If people keep trying to poke you with sharp weapons, you might consider improving your personal manner."

He shrugged. Blood pooled and dripped on the floor.

"Stop that—I just had it stanched." She pressed harder. "You really should see a proper doctor. I mostly have salve for bruises."

He nudged the cloth aside for a moment. "It won't need stitching. It didn't cut me deep."

She lathered up her soap, plain and not at all scented with roses or sandalwood or whatever he was used to. He winced when it came into contact with his wound. "Does it sting?" she asked.

"A bit."

"You probably should try harder not to get stabbed, then."

"Probably."

The water rinsed away, pink and soapy. She swallowed.

"Why aren't we sitting over there?" Devil asked, gesturing to the reading room with the embroidered cushions and the oil lamps. It was marginally more spacious, but she imagined he'd pointed it out only to distract her. As she had no wish to become any queasier, she let him.

She did not see a long career as a nursemaid in her future.

"That is the ladies' reading room," Kitty explained.

"And the men?"

"The men have access to every other reading room in London. Every other physical corner of every other building from here to Inverness. They don't need my sliver of a reading room."

Devil nodded. "I suppose that's true enough."

The fact that he considered the matter without being defensive, and then actually agreed, made her fall a little bit in love with him.

Just a little. Not enough to worry about. Like a small cold, easily remedied with rest and lemon tea.

"When *I'm* allowed in Parliament, then they may attend my reading room," she said, scrubbing his wound harder. The blood barely bothered her now—hers was boiling too hot.

"A radical," he said.

"Merely rational," she corrected him.

He did not look offended or insulted or condescending. Only interested.

It made her too aware of his nearness, the ridges of his chest, the hair tapering under the waistband of his breeches. Too drawn to the curious, understanding man under the shiveringly cold indifference of Devil.

She wrapped a clean, dry cloth around his wound, tying it tightly. "You'll need to make a honey dressing." She did not tell him she did not have honey. It was an exorbitant luxury at the moment.

Her fingertips brushed his arm. The muscles and tendons rippled under her touch. If he turned his head even a little, his mouth would brush against hers.

She stepped back. Mostly because devouring an injured man in her back room was probably not the right thing to do.

But he was not having it. He snaked his arm around her waist and tugged her forward—not just between his knees, but turning her so he could perch her on his lap. "What are you doing? Your arm!"

"My arm is fine," he murmured against her throat. "Thanks to you. You took care of me." His teeth scraped lightly over her skin, and she shivered. "Let me take care of *you*."

"This isn't a wager. There are no reciprocal terms."

He bit gently on the spot where her neck met her shoulder. Heat tingled through her core. He was entirely too good at that. "We already agreed one has nothing to do with the other," he said, firmly, with more than a hint of command. "This pull between us exists on its own."

It was a lovely fantasy. She was willing to let it be true for a little while longer. Reality would always find them. She didn't have to draw a map. She squirmed, feeling him harden against her hip.

"Sit still, firecracker." His voice was rough now, threaded through with want and need. She was already gasping a little by the time she turned her head so she could claim his mouth, or him hers. It didn't matter. It was enough that their tongues tangled, their breaths mingled. He made her feel as if she were floating, but also anchored so thoroughly and deeply to him that she could do anything. Ask for anything. Feel everything.

He drew her skirt up, fingers moving up her inner thigh until he cupped her quim in one big hand. "You're wet for me," he groaned as if she had offered him everything he had ever wanted. He lounged like a king, pinning her in place. Taking in order to give. Commanding her body better than she ever had.

It made her wild.

She rubbed against him, mindlessly seeking friction. He was stealing her breath with his breath, with his touch, stroking her bud, before the invasion of two fingers rubbing against her inner walls, stretching her just so. She gasped and he retreated, returned, sliding through her wet heat. She clutched his arm, frantic to get closer.

He winced. Barely, but it was enough to stop her. She froze. "Your arm."

"To the devil with my arm."

"Was that a pun?"

"No, a desperate attempt to keep you focused."

"I *am* focused," she said, reluctantly slipping off his lap. Her heart was still tumbling, pulse flinging through her from her throat to her quim. Her body tingled with the abrupt distance from him, her arousal disoriented, still seeking, searching. "You're injured."

"I'm fine." He met her gaze, eyes glittering, mouth quirking. "Come here, firecracker."

She took a step back, and even though she felt quite desperate, she was smiling. There was something new between them, something that was not all teeth. "You really are the Devil."

"Let me prove it to you."

"Even the Devil needs a rest," she returned crisply, easing behind the table. It felt prudent to put something between them. The fanged desire still sparking though her was deeply unimpressed with her choice.

She didn't much like it either.

"Kitty," he murmured in a way that nearly had her moaning aloud. She swayed toward him.

"You'll bleed on my floor," she said, gripping the edge of the table hard enough to bite into her flesh. To clear her head. To stop her from reaching for him.

"I'll clean it up."

"I can't exactly picture you holding a mop."

"I'll have Wulf clean it up," he amended instantly.

She grinned. She couldn't help it. Under the persona of hard, vengeful earl, there was a likeable man who did not take himself as seriously as the world thought he did. It was deeply appealing. She nearly told him she thought he was amiable just to see the expression on his face.

Instead, she forced herself back into the moment. An earl and a shopkeeper, a pretend betrothal to help her save her sister from a real one. Missing wives. Attacks on the street.

"Do we think it was Lord Portsmouth who sent the man with the knife?" she asked. "And was he sent for you? Or me? But why would he bother wanting to kill me?"

"If he was trying to kill you, he won't see the dawn." The glint in Devil's eyes was glacial. The kind of fury that was so cold it nevertheless burned down entire cities.

Kitty blinked. "Oh my."

So much for amiable. Unfortunately, this was equally attractive.

Misreading her, Devil reached for his shirt. Travesty. He should never wear a shirt. "If you wanted a different kind of help, you should have stolen from a milksop."

"I am not very keen on being murdered, actually," she said crisply. "So I am fairly certain I stole from exactly the right person."

He blinked back at her. "You're really not afraid of me, are you?"

She tilted her head. What a contradiction this man was: powerful yet oddly vulnerable, as though he was not used to being seen. Stoic and curious, cold and hot. Oh, she was in trouble. "Do you want me to be?"

"No," he replied quietly. "Not you."

"But everyone else?"

"I don't care about them. They can go to hell. I'm not a kind man, Kitty."

Ha. She was beginning to see right through him.

"You saved my life," she said. "And I've been called a violent termagant too many times to get swoony over a tiny threat of murder."

Although she was quite sure it had been a promise and not a threat. Never mind. She was also quite sure she should not find it so comforting. She'd told him he ought to work on his character, but obviously she should do the same.

"Who has called you that?" he demanded.

She snorted. "Who hasn't?"

He did not look amused. Being stabbed and bleeding all over himself amused him, apparently. Her being insulted did not.

She was in so very much trouble.

WHEN DEVIL RETURNED to the Sins, Michael had already found his attacker, as suspected. Macleod had tied him to a chair in a small back room mostly used for storing supplies for the housemaids. The man was shaking and Devil hadn't even opened his mouth yet. He shut the door behind him, disgusted.

The man whimpered. His jaw was bruised, blood on his teeth.

Macleod snorted. "This one's not exactly brave."

"Stupid, though," Devil said. "For putting a lady in danger. *My* lady."

The man visibly gulped. Devil recognized him—an earl's third son with an addiction to horse racing. Cock fighting. Bear baiting. Devil couldn't abide that kind of gambling. He'd seen too much death. Too much violence to be impressed by violence for violence's sake. He made a point to wager on the bear.

"Emmett," he said.

Emmett jerked at this name.

Macleod handed Devil a debt vowel, even though he did not need it. "You owe me three thousand pounds," he continued coldly. "Killing me won't wipe out your debt." And yet someone always insisted on testing the theory. "More importantly, you came at me in the vicinity of Miss Caldecott. I could happily toss you in the Thames with a stone around your neck for that."

He had never done any such thing. But Emmett didn't know that, judging by the state of him.

"Christ, man. If you piss yourself in here, you're only going to make me angrier." Devil leaned over, barely restrained violence in a superfine wool coat. "Tell me about Portsmouth."

"Wh-what?"

"The Earl of Portsmouth. Have you been talking to him?"

"N-no," Emmett stammered. "Why would the earl talk to me?"

As Devil presumed, but he would not leave it to chance. "You attacked me of your own volition?"

When Emmett did not immediately answer, Devil arched a brow.

"Yes!" the man finally replied. "I... Three *thousand* pounds. I can't..."

"I didn't make the wagers," Devil reminded him. "*You* made them. You're obviously banned from any future Devil's Nights and from this club. In fact, you are banned from London altogether."

"From *London*?"

"It's time you disappeared."

London assumed Devil went around murdering people for fun. It was hardly necessary. He only needed the illusion of it with the certainty of retribution and consequences for crossing him.

"Let's make it from England entirely."

"But where would I go?"

"Not my problem." He could call a magistrate or a constable, but Emmett's father was an earl and it would not make the kind of statement that needed to be made. Miss Caldecott was off-limits.

Emmett was choking on fear and a bit slow to realize his good fortune. "But..."

And Devil's patience had run out. "If I see you again, it will be the last thing you see."

Macleod shook his head. "Mate, the other way to disappear is facedown in the river. Say thank you and run, idiot."

Emmett visibly gulped. "Thank you."

"Go on," Devil said, slicing through his ropes. He was not careful about it. "You have until sundown. Run."

CHAPTER SIXTEEN

THE FIRST STEP to taking down a powerful and corrupt earl was surprisingly akin to a regular day for Kitty.

It had to do with books.

If the note she had found was written by Lady Caroline and sold off as part of her belongings, Kitty was going to have to trace those belongings to various estate sales and buyers. She had already gone through the rest of the items in the box purchased for the shop and found nothing unusual. No more notes, no letters.

Lord Portsmouth had his wife's life packed into boxes and handed the lot over to an auction house. Tracking the various sales had taken some doing, mostly bribes Kitty could not afford, and then a single suggestion of a visit from Devil and a list had miraculously appeared.

Effective, if vexing. Clearly, there were benefits to people thinking she was the future bride of the Devil.

She herself tried not to think about it too hard. It made her feel odd. Hopeful, hopeless. Unmoored. Too aware of her body and worse, of all of the things she could not let herself want. That part was nothing new but it was sharper, more raw. Devil would never marry *her*.

Not that it mattered. Because it most certainly did not. Today was for following another lead. Another private library.

And dealing with her father, apparently.

She could count on one hand the number of times he had visited her at the shop. He disdained its very existence, the proof that her mother's family was in trade when he had only been given a barony as a life peerage because had helped the War Office with some kind of secret invention. Something about a new rifle? Cannonballs? She had never been able to figure it out. But it had made him scads of money. For a very little while. Doing something very much like trade, she felt the need to point out.

Also, it was the only thing keeping him in bread and mutton stew and other necessities.

Her grandmother, his mother-in-law, refused to sell him the store, refused to even talk to him. The day he had lost the majority of his fortune on a single roll of dice, she had sent him raw chicken hearts. Which had sat in the sun for some time before postage.

And now here he was, nose faintly wrinkled as he came through the door in a gray coat with enameled buttons he ought to have sold already. She made a mental note to sneak into his room and remove them. They would buy Galahad enough food for the rest of the year.

"Why does it smell like soup?" he asked, confused.

"Someone hid rotten onions in the back alley two weeks ago." She shrugged. "We haven't found the last few yet." Miss Peridot had been outraged at the waste of it.

"Why would someone do that?"

"I couldn't say," she replied, even she could say, and at great length.

"And did you know there is a giant on your doorstep?" her father added. "He's somewhat off-putting."

"Yes. He works for Lord Birmingham."

"Good, good. That's good." Her father smiled, and it made her stomach hurt. She knew that smile. It was wheedling, hopeful. "He takes care of you already. He'll make a fine husband. And a fine son-in-law."

She rubbed at her breastbone, which had also started to ache. She did not want to hear the rest of what he had to say.

"I need funds, Kitty. Just to get me through the rest of the month. There are several games that I just know would solve my problems."

She sighed.

He continued, undeterred. "That hell in Covent Garden is going to send that bruiser of theirs after me. You could have Birmingham talk to them."

By talk to them, he meant have her pretend fiancé pay off his astronomical debts. Devil, who had crafted his reputation on the fact that everyone paid their debts. It was beyond absurd to even contemplate that he would intervene to forgive a wager he was not involved in when he would not forgive those he *was* involved in.

"Father, no." She knew he wouldn't stop. He would hound Devil in the very streets, begging. It made her itchy just to think about it. She rubbed her breastbone again. He wouldn't listen to her. He never had before. "If you bother him, he'll ban you from the Sins," she pointed out.

That, at least, had an effect. His daughter's pride meant nothing, but being turned away from the most infamous gaming hell when it finally opened? That would drive him mad.

He frowned. "That seems unjust." He glanced around, more frantically than she liked, then wiped his face, shoulders slumping alarmingly. "I did not have breakfast. You left early again this morning. Do you have any rolls? A muffin?"

He did look pale. Perspiration beaded his upper lip. "Are you ill?" she asked, concerned despite knowing that there was always something behind the simplest of his questions.

"I feel a bit weak, is all. A bit of breakfast will fix me right up."

She nodded. "I have currant rolls in the back. I'll get you one."

"Thank you, Kitty. You've always been a good daughter."

A good daughter who should have known better.

When she returned with the last roll, her father was gone.

So was her lockbox with her money.

KITTY WANTED TO throw things.

She wanted to rail and rant.

She wanted to cry.

She did none of those things. For one, it would have alerted Wulf, who would have wanted to know what was wrong. And he would tell Devil.

And there was nothing anyone could do that would make a lick of difference to the fact that her father had stolen from her.

Again.

He was obviously panicking—that was the only time he rifled through her trunks at home or came to the shop with teary, hopeful eyes. It was her fault for being distracted. She knew better than to leave him alone with the shop's money. She *knew* better.

It made her feel a hundred years old and with iron for bones. Like the entire bookshop was suddenly perched on her shoulders, pressing down, down, down.

At the least old man with the placard hadn't even tried to spit on her when she arrived. Last month he had thrown soup at Kitty. He was very old, and so she could not even throw the clay bowl back at his head. Once Devil broke their betrothal, she would have to find a better way to keep the rabble from her door. Sharp sticks. A spear. A trebuchet, maybe. A friendly pig who would eat the slop with glee.

Meanwhile, she would salvage the day. She could sit here worrying about Evie, staring out the window for Portsmouth's men, mad at her father—worse, disappointed—or any of the thousand tasks that needed doing, or she could forge on with her investigation. Her plans and plots and conspiracies. Her one tiny, hard-won lead.

Lord Tadworth was a collector and a recluse who had turned

down every letter, every invitation, every request and offer Kitty had ever sent over the years. She tried to form some sort of connection to most avid book lovers as a matter of course, but he did not like to leave his mansion and he liked visitors even less.

Devil, of course, was not in the habit of taking no as an answer. Mostly because so few people offered it.

Not only did he receive an invitation for tea, but it included a tour of Lord Tadworth's extensive and famous library.

It was irritating.

Devil was likely to agree as she marched to his club to inform him of his new plans for the afternoon.

THE SEVEN DEADLY Sins pleasure hall was exactly as extravagant as it should be.

The building itself took up almost as much space as the palace the prince was building for himself. It gleamed white, with fluted columns on either side of the red door and above the portico. There were roses, marble urns, ivy growing up the walls.

Kitty stepped through the iron archway, past the steps leading down to the coal bins and the delivery entrance. The front door was painted red, because a house associated with the devil must surely have a red door. Everything else was expected: soaring columns and carved pediments and freshly washed glass gleaming. No brimstone or writhing souls to be found.

Not even a sign declaring members had found the right place. Only a door knocker in the shape of a flame. And the sounds of construction within, the smell of sawdust and paint.

She had never been here, of course. Ladies did not visit men unchaperoned. Or at all. And certainly not at an already-infamous pleasure hall. And while she was not technically a lady of the *Ton*, their rules still dogged her steps. Still, she was not an aristocrat, and she had never had a chaperone, even as a young woman. And now she was twenty-nine years old and firmly on the shelf.

But also betrothed.

Her already complicated life had certainly gotten even more

complicated of late. A sinfully handsome earl tended to do that.

The door swung open before she could dwell on it further or give in to the nerves that were inconveniently swirling in her belly. She was Kitty Caldecott, Purveyor of Filth and Moral Threat to the Decency of Good Society Everywhere. She could greet a butler of a place named after the Deadly Sins and bully the Devil.

"Hello," she said cheerfully to said butler. He was made entirely of muscle. And teeth.

"I'm afraid the earl is not accepting callers, Miss…?" She could not place his accent. It was soft and lovely.

"Miss Caldecott," she supplied. "And of course he is." The place was too busy and opening night loomed too near for him to be anywhere else, doing anything else.

The butler blinked at her before smiling. He still looked capable of breaking a man's spine with his bare hands, but now he was at least cheerful about it. "Miss Caldecott, of course. What a pleasure—do come in." He frowned over her shoulder. "You did not come alone, surely?"

"Wulf followed me very discreetly the entire way here," she said drily. Godric remained at the shop, fending off vicars and cross ladies and soft fruit hurled from carriages. She must remember to bring him a piece of cake. She knew exactly how tiresome that particular work was.

The foyer was easily the size of a house built for a family of ten. It was a spectacle of epic proportions. Kitty had never seen anything like it. Every inch of every wall had been painted with murals in rich jewel-tone colors. Angels soared overheard; dark forests stood sentinel on either side of the hall. Lucifer fell, his wings glowing and scattering embers. Nymphs peeked from behind stones dotting a pastoral hillside.

And mirrors hung from floor to ceiling, amplifying the light of chandeliers and the oil lamps. It was dazzling.

Beyond, doorways over which hung gilded signs painted "Envy" and "Gluttony" opened to even larger spaces. Envy was a ballroom appropriately painted in green, with a dais for an orchestra and a balcony for an opera singer. Gluttony was on its way to becoming a banquet hall, with red tapestries and carpenters putting the final touches on a long table with lion heads. As Kitty stared wide eyed, a young lad who could only be a boot boy, judging by his age, stared at her. "Ladies aren't supposed to call on the Devil. They wait for *him* to call."

"Pierre," the butler snapped. "Hush."

Kitty smiled. "The fine ladies of Mayfair may have the time to sit about waiting for the Devil, but I do not."

"Oh, I like her."

A young man approached from the main ballroom, his hair pomaded just so, the gold buttons on his waistcoat gleaming. He was the very picture of a fashionable man about town, if not for the purpling bruise around his eye. "You!" Kitty cried, recognizing him instantly.

She was not concerned about being overly familiar. Once you had been at war with the enemy on the steps of the Golden Griffin, you were family. Those bonds were forged in blood and rotten eggs. And, in this case, gold paint.

"And *you!*" he returned, a wide smile splitting his handsome face.

"You know each other?" The boot boy was agog. He was clearly the first to get the gossip to bring down to the servant hall. It would give him currency for the rest of the day. Possibly the week.

"We're old friends, Miss Caldecott and I."

"We are." Kitty grinned. "Although I don't actually know your name."

"Good point." He bowed. "Thomas Rochester. You can call me Tom."

She stared at him. "You're related to Lord Birmingham?"

"He's my brother. Try not to hold it against me." He glanced at the boot boy, who was twitching with excitement. "Go on, little man, what are you even doing up here?"

"The earl's valet wants me to add champagne to the boot-black for the members." His eyes were wide as plates. "Frightfully posh, don't you think?"

"Very elegant," Kitty agreed solemnly. "Not to mention a little bit ridiculous," she added in an exaggerated whisper.

"You think so too?"

"I do," Kitty confessed, just before the butler shooed him away.

"I apologize for everyone here," the butler muttered.

"Shelby despairs of us." Tom's eyes twinkled. "He's usually at the house, but I confess we are not any better behaved over there. I hear you're going to be my sister."

"Oh. Um."

He winked. "Don't fret. I don't expect you to reform him."

"That's a relief." Kitty did not know what else to say. She smiled weakly. Did he know it was a sham betrothal? What exactly had Devil told him? "He must have a study here?"

"Just down that way."

She peered down the hall. "I don't want to give him fair warning. He might climb out the window."

"That, I highly doubt. Third door on the right. Past the atrocious statue of Pan I gave him last Christmas. It was meant to go in his bedroom."

Tom was quite correct, as it turned out. The statue was vaguely terrifying, but mostly because it stood out so starkly. Pan was all goat legs and horns and a happy, mischievous grin. The sheep at his feet…was not.

Statues of lambs should not be life-sized in the hallway. Nor should their eyes follow you around.

"His name is Oatcake," Tom called out helpfully.

"No, thank you," she called back. If she said his name, he might wake up. It seemed entirely possible.

She knocked on Devil's door, because though she was uncouth enough to barrel ahead before the butler could introduce her, she was not *entirely* without manners. Aunt Priscilla's opinion not withstanding. It was only that they were going to be late. And it was the first lead she had found in days. And she'd felt dreadful all day, and suddenly she did not feel dreadful.

"Come," Devil ordered.

She tucked her tongue firmly into her cheek and decided not to answer with the first, most shocking thing that leapt to her mind at such a command. She entered the study, expecting bookshelves and leather chairs and brandy decanters.

She was not expecting a stunningly beautiful woman in her early forties with lustrous silver-shot black hair and the sultry elegance of Aphrodite come to life.

Kitty did not expect it because Kitty was an idiot.

CHAPTER SEVENTEEN

KITTY'S STOMACH DROPPED so fast it might have bounced off the parquet floor. She couldn't be sure, as a hot flush of embarrassment was currently turning her bright red and making her eyes burn.

He was Devil.

He was the Earl of Birmingham.

And she was Kitty Caldecott, shopkeeper with a father in debt up to his nostrils.

Devil rose from his chair, unjustly handsome and at his ease. "Kitty. I—"

"I'm so sorry," she interrupted hastily. This served her right. For pushing through without thinking. For letting her head be turned.

Idiot. *Idiot.*

She tried very hard to smile at the woman but wasn't sure her face was working properly. "Entirely my fault."

She whirled on her heel and darted for the safety of the hall and Pan's judgmental sheep.

"*Kitty.*" Devil caught up to her almost immediately because he was twice her height and life was just that unfair. His hand curled firmly but gently around her elbow. "Wait."

"I'm so sorry," she said again, physically unable to meet his eyes. They were too green. Too clear. And she just wanted to disappear. "I didn't mean to intrude."

"Just come back inside."

She finally looked at him, mostly so he could see the depths of her horror at the suggestion. She had already humiliated herself. Why on earth would she tarry? He was sadistic, clearly. Or his sense of humor needed immediate work.

He just shook his head, amused, fond. He had the audacity to look *fond*. Because he was sophisticated and debonair. Being caught by the woman he had fondled in a carriage with another woman far more suited to his rank and privilege was nothing new to him.

It was bloody well new to Kitty.

He hadn't done anything wrong, not really. She had no claims on him. And she did not believe in jealousy.

Technically.

But she also did not believe in stewing in her own misery. Or worse, awkwardness. She was too used to bearing insults with a smile. Not this time. Not like this. Not here.

"Listen to me, firecracker."

Not pet names. She could *not* handle pet names. Not right now.

Someone was hammering nails again. Or was that just the headache suddenly invading her skull? Devil tugged her back over the threshold. She ought to have kicked him in the kneecap and bolted. She couldn't think why she didn't.

"Mrs. Dimitriou, may I introduce Miss Caldecott?"

The woman put down her cup of coffee with a smile. "A pleasure, Miss Caldecott. Please call me Yelena. I've heard so much about you."

"I am sure you have." Kitty finally smiled, and it was so self-deprecating she actually *felt* Devil scowl down at her.

"I just adore your bookshop."

"Oh. Thank you." She did not know what to do with her hands. She rubbed her breastbone.

Devil took her wrist gently, folding his fingers around hers. "I asked Yelena here to meet *you*, actually. So you have excellent timing."

Why was he prolonging her torture? Why would Mrs. Dimitriou want to meet *her*?

Oh.

Idiot, once more.

Yelena must want to reassure herself that their betrothal was a sham. That she had nothing to worry about. Had Devil not talked to her about it at all?

This time Kitty scowled at *him*. He blinked, taken aback. "What?"

"Did you not tell her we aren't really engaged? Did she have to find out through the gossips? Devil, really."

"Are you scolding me?"

"Poorly, if you need to ask. *Very* poorly, in fact, since you won't stop smiling at me." Her eyebrows drew together. "What's wrong with you?"

"He's a man," Yelena remarked drily.

"Hey," he said mildly. "But a fair point."

"We are not lovers," Yelena continued, "if that's what worries you. He has not wronged me."

Kitty was still tense as a bowstring but felt a little bit less like the arrow that might ricochet around the room smashing very expensive things she could not afford to replace. She took what might have been the first breath since barging in. "Oh. I see. Good. That's good."

"Is that what you thought?" Devil asked her.

She shrugged, holding on to the tatters of her composure. Something suspiciously close to relief washed through her.

"It's a fair assumption." Yelena also shrugged. "Given your reputation."

"My reputation would suggest you should both be nicer to me," he muttered. "A little dread would not go amiss."

Yelena laughed. Kitty smiled. Devil leaned against his desk, disgruntled. "I've asked Yelena to chaperone you," he said.

Kitty snorted. "Devil, aging spinsters do not require chaperones. Even when they are betrothed to *you*."

"Not that kind of chaperone," he said. "Do give me a little credit, Miss Caldecott."

"While I am passable at watercolors and waltzing," Yelena said, "I am far better with fencing and fisticuffs."

"That was very poetic," Kitty approved. "Wait. You are?"

Yelena inclined her head. "I know a great many tricks with a hatpin."

"Will you teach me?" Kitty sounded awed, even to her own ears.

Devil raised his eyebrows. "I knew you'd be interested once you learned that little tidbit. And as a lady, Yelena can go with you into places my men cannot follow."

"I doubt Lord Portsmouth would attack me in a ladies' retiring room."

"Do not doubt me," he said darkly. "I mean to keep you safe."

That was nice. So nice her eyes prickled. She blinked rapidly. She had had a trying morning. That must be why she was threatening to turn into a watering pot. *Mortifying.* "Thank you."

Yelena nodded. "I will be in the parlor."

"Do you need something to read?" Kitty pulled two books out of her reticule. It had seen better days, the heaviness of books continuously pulling at the seams she reinforced on a regular basis. "Pirates or Minotaurs?"

"Oh, Minotaurs, definitely. They are Greek like me, and sometimes I am homesick." Yelena took the book and glided away, looking every inch the lady in her sage-green walking dress and not like someone who could murder a man. Kitty thought she might be in love already.

"Do you always carry books when you're out for a walk?" Devil asked.

"Always. Walking, visiting. At the Park."

"You'll start a fashion in the ballroom."

"I am not invited to ballrooms, Devil."

"*Rhys*. And you are now."

"I'm all aflutter."

"I can see that." He grinned, and it changed his face, made him even more tempting. It did not change the dark electricity that crackled around him, though—nothing could temper that. And truthfully, Kitty would not want it to. "You're the one who made a deal with the Devil."

"I did not think it would involve the quadrille." She wrinkled her nose. "I am not sure I can even remember how to dance a quadrille. It has been many, many years. And I only learned because my aunt is delusional."

"I'm not worried about a quadrille."

"Do you think Yelena could teach me?"

"After she teaches you between which ribs to stab a man?"

"Naturally."

"I wonder if I am going to regret this," he said drily.

"Probably." She paused. "Do you think you will?" The question made her feel exposed for some reason.

Devil held her gaze, moss-green eyes glittering. "I will never regret your being able to defend yourself, Kitty."

"I am sure the Spinster Society could teach me a thing or two."

"Good. Learn them all, every technique, every method. Whatever it takes to keep you safe."

Well, that was nice too. She was perilously close to simpering.

And that would not do.

She drew herself up with a brusque nod. Confident. Competent. Not at all swooning inside because the most beautiful man she had ever known wanted to arm her.

Devil read the change in her the way he would read a hand of cards. Calculating, filing it away for later use. "Why did you come here, firecracker?"

"Apparently, I came to scandalize your boot boy. That I could scandalize anyone at the Sins is a wonder, even for me."

"Pierre?"

"He informed me most gravely that women do not visit the Devil. They wait for *him* to visit. No doubt with bated breath." She was, abruptly, mildly peeved and couldn't think why.

He snorted. "Pierre is ten years old."

"Pierre has wisdom beyond his years."

"Why else did you come?"

"I need a favor," she admitted.

He tilted his head. "Do you?"

He was going to make her work for it. She should have known. This man was like a prism, all complicated angles and light. And unexpected colors. "I need to look through Lord Tadworth's library."

"Tadworth? The recluse with the whiskers and the toad collection?"

"He also collects books. But I wouldn't mind a peek at a toad collection either, actually. More importantly, he recently purchased a trunk of books from Portsmouth."

"Ah." He raised an eyebrow. She deeply mistrusted the glint in his eye. "Are you asking for my permission?"

"Bollocks to that, Lord Birmingham."

Devil laughed. It was like melted chocolate. Fine whiskey. A new book. It was everything.

To her.

Not to his brother, clearly.

"Good God, are you laughing?" Tom called from somewhere down the hall. "Terrifying. Don't do it again. Think of the children."

"There are no children."

"Think of *me*, then."

"Go away," Devil said mildly, before pushing off the desk and nudging the door closed.

"Lord Tadworth has invited us for a tour," Kitty elaborated. "Well, *you*. Seeing as you asked him."

"Did I, now?"

"He won't talk to *me*." Devil's eyes narrowed at that. She shrugged, well used to it. "He's expecting us shortly."

"Today?"

"Within the hour."

"Ah." He strolled back to his desk, diabolically indifference to the time constraints.

"Devil."

He only looked at her.

She rolled her eyes. "*Rhys.*"

"Yes?"

"We have to go. Now."

"Ask me nicely."

CHAPTER EIGHTEEN

KITTY NARROWED HER eyes back at him. "We are going to be late."

"That's not asking me nicely," he drawled.

"You're very accustomed to getting your own way."

"Yes."

"I'm sure it's not good for you," she said.

"And yet."

The game shivered between them. The thread that seemed to bind her to him, her body to his presence. Despite it—or because of it—she shrugged and turned, tossing him a glance over her shoulder. "Then I suppose I shall visit Lord Tadworth on my own."

He caught up to her in a single step. It did things to her ability to breathe normally.

"The hell you will." So did that thrilling, unyielding tone.

"Well, if *you're* not interested…" She fluttered her eyelashes.

He very deliberately leaned a palm against the door behind her, caging her in. Just a bit. Just enough. Every part of her longed to arch closer, or better yet, to press back against the door to see if he would follow. "Is this you asking me nicely?" he said, deep voice both soft and rough.

She lifted her chin defiantly, even as her heart picked up speed and her thigh muscles quivered. Something he could never know. His effect on her was already too powerful. Too danger-ous. Too delicious. "If I said please and flattered your ego and told you were handsome, you'd die of boredom."

"True." His mouth quirked. "Are you saying I'm not hand-some?"

She licked her lower lip. He tracked the movement, green eyes flaring hungrily. He was so close that she could see the flecks of silver in his irises. He had forest eyes. Oak-leaf eyes. "You're passable, I suppose."

He grinned. A true, amused grin. Not a sardonic smile, or a wry quirk of his perfect mouth. A *grin*. And it was devastating. His scent wrapped around her, amber and wood smoke. And then his voice followed, a rough caress over her skin. "Are you at least going to say please?"

He trailed his free hand up her arm, along her neckline, just a tease to raise the gooseflesh. It was successful.

Exceedingly successful.

And then he closed his fingers very carefully around the base of her throat and tipped her head back.

Every thought in her head incinerated.

He applied no pressure, no hint of menace. Only a light hold on her, as though she was precious. Delicate.

His.

It was a promise. A foretelling. A claiming.

She whimpered, heat building in her chest, between her legs, streaking down her spine. He smiled slowly, hungrily. "I'm going to make you make that sound again and again."

She leaned forward until his fingertips dug into her flesh. If he didn't kiss her, she might expire on the spot. He tightened his grip infinitesimally, only enough to pin her back to the door. She nearly growled in frustration. His tone was soft but demanding. Utterly in control.

Even as he gave her that same control.

"Just as soon as you say please."

She felt wild with the need to have him touch her. To touch

him. He made her feel things she had never felt before. And ever since their interrupted moment, she had been tense with need and want and unfulfilled desires. His breathing was harsh, not quite as polished as the rest of him appeared. It snapped whatever resembled restraint in her.

"Please," she begged softly. "Please."

"Thank God," he murmured before yanking her forward. Their mouths met, tongues tangling, soft moans fueling the heat between them. The need to chase and be chased, the need to taste and be tasted. A hunger only he could sate.

He was already pulling up her skirts, using his boot to urge her feet apart, widening her stance. Opening her for his touch. He stroked up her inner thigh, slowly. "So soft."

She squirmed, trying to get closer.

"What do you need, firecracker?" She reached for him blindly, but he pinned her again. "Say it."

Their eyes met and there was a brief, brief moment where some unfathomable, unknowable fork in the road was taken.

"You."

And then he was on his knees and pressing his mouth to her. Licking at her, flattening his tongue over her bud, sucking it into his mouth like a delicacy. She nearly screamed, her entire body quivering.

And then he pulled away. Again.

"Not here," he said hoarsely.

"*Rhys.*" Why was he still pulling away, torturing her, making her wild? Did he want her to beg again? She would beg. Pleasure coiled too tightly in her center, denied a release.

He licked her again, as though he couldn't help himself. Then he rose, eyes just wild enough to make her feel better.

"Not with everyone waiting for us on the other side of this door." He kissed her again deeply, reverently. "I'm going to take my time with you." The whisper tickled her ear and had her nipples tightening in anticipation. "I'm going to make you whimper my name and then I'm going to make you come until your legs give out."

They might give out right here and now. Her knees were decidedly weak.

She had read about lovers who brought each other to the edge again and again, only to deny the final release. Stretching out the sensations, building toward the climax. She had never experienced it before. It was invigorating. Painful. Frustration. Amazing.

She hated it.

She *loved* it.

And because she had no intention of burning with need alone—and because she was desperate for one more forbidden touch—she stroked him once through his breeches, and then again, gripping tighter. He cursed, bucking into her hand. "Oh, you'll pay for that, little firecracker."

"Promise?"

His laugh was soft with just a hint of menace. "Oh, I promise."

"When?" she taunted.

"Tonight."

KITTY LEFT THE study knowing she was flushed, as pink as the inside of a seashell. She was half convinced Pan winked at her. She had never been so aware of her body, of her legs, of her quim swollen and fluttering with every step she took. She was grounded to every sensation. And yet oddly felt as though she might float away.

Devil followed behind her after a gratifying pause to adjust himself. She could see the fun in it, since she wasn't suffering alone.

Yelena waited on a bench set under a mirror the length of a swimming pond. Shelby greeted Devil while Tom brushed sawdust off his beaver-crowned hat in a stunning dark green.

"What are you doing here?" Devil asked him. "I sent you down for ice for your eye."

"I'm on my way." Tom did not look the least bit intimidated by his brother. Interesting. He winked at Kitty again. "A pleasure, as always, Miss Caldecott."

Devil's eyes sharpened. "You two know each other?"

"We are old friends," Tom said lightly, accepting a swan-headed walking stick from Shelby. His grin faded, turned serious. "She saved my life."

Kitty shook her head. "Not really."

"Absolutely you did."

"Explain," Devil said.

"Kitty was the one who threw paint at the blighters who followed me from…there."

"That was you?" Devil asked softly. "I should have guessed."

Tom smirked. "Barnabus still has gold paint in his hair."

"Good," Kitty said. "I hope it got up his nose too."

They grinned at each other.

Devil groaned. "I've never known two people more prone to attracting trouble. London is not safe if you two are friendly."

"London could do with a bit of shaking up," Tom said dismissively. "We can't let *you* have all the fun."

"Oh, am I having fun?"

"The Devil always has fun." Tom bowed smartly. "Miss Caldecott, do call on us anytime. I am much more entertaining than my brother."

"I will keep that in mind."

"The hell you will," Devil said mildly. "Tom?"

"Yes?"

"Be careful."

Tom waved a hand negligently. Devil gestured to a footman, who materialized like magic. He bowed and hurried after Tom. There was a dagger in his boot.

"Do you have everyone followed?" Kitty asked.

"Only when it's necessary." Devil scowled. "As to that, where the hell is Wulf?"

"He followed me very carefully," Kitty assured him.

"Good."

"About that."

He accepted his own hat from Shelby. "You're never going to convince me to let you jump headfirst into danger without an armed escort. When I'm not with you, they are."

Something warm bloomed inside her chest. She tried to ignore it. "I was only going to say that they can hover just as effectively *inside* the shop when it's raining. They'll catch their death."

"A little rain won't hurt them."

"Neither will a little dry," she pointed out. "*And* they have to let me give them tea."

"It's not a damn picnic."

"I know you did not just curse in front of a lady," Shelby said, disapproval all but shooting from him like darts.

"I don't mind." Kitty grinned. "I know he's a little *sensitive*. His moods, you know."

The workers in the vicinity froze, waiting for his reaction. Shelby was the first to break, and his laugh boomed like a cannon.

"*You* are the real devil here," Devil said. His expression stayed stern, disapproving. But his eyes glinted, faintly amused.

"I'll stop teasing you if you give me a tour." She was itching to see the rest of the pleasure hall.

Devil's mouth was very close to her ear. "Perhaps I'll tease you instead."

"You already have."

"Oh, just you wait, firecracker." He laughed softly.

It took every ounce of self-control not to squirm. Not to press her thighs together.

"Lust is on the top floor," he said as if he knew exactly how she was struggling. His half-smile was wicked, a flash of lightning. "Selene is in charge of the brothel." Kitty remembered Selene from the Devil's Night. She was stunning and clever and could easily run an empire. "We will just bust heads when necessary. And you've seen Pride, which is the entrance hall. Tom's domain, memberships, guest lists, and the like."

Devil had given him the power to close the door in the faces of those who would close every door in his. It was brilliant. Perceptive.

"Envy and Gluttony are nearly finished." He led her up the stairs. "And this is Greed."

Greed took up the entire floor, with rows of card tables and billiard tables, three roulette wheels, and a sharp-eyed man keeping an eye on the proceedings. The excitement was palpable—the entire building thrummed with it. The pause before the storm broke.

Sloth was a series of rooms with luxurious carpets, soft chairs, even beds piled high with pillows. Candles burned and a silver carafe of coffee waited on a low table, more chairs clustered together where drinks would be served. "A place to rest, a moment between floors," Devil explained. "But it needs something."

Kitty tilted her head. "It needs books."

He paused, then nodded. "Of course it does."

"Naughty ones."

"Naturally. You are brilliant, Miss Caldecott."

Oil lamps had been lit, and they lent a softness to the dark and dramatic décor. The red stained glass, the gilded scrollwork, the pediments in the shape of leaping goats. Mayfair called Rhys the devil, and he had obliged. Perhaps it ought to make her nervous, but it was quite the opposite. She had read too many stories where the monster was not the real monster. And where the darkness held only pleasure.

This line of thought was not exactly quelling the electricity running through her.

She skirted around a tin of paint that shimmered like silver and coveted it deeply. No detail was too small to matter. It was obvious in the care taken from the ceiling to the floor. "This place is magnificent, Rhys. Even Vauxhall does not compare."

"Vauxhall probably has not had the threats we've already

received."

"No to worry. I can teach you how to duck a flying cabbage."

"It's always best to have an expert on hand."

"I've counted six sins," she pointed out. "Where is Wrath?"

"In the lowest level. The boxing rings are already set up. Not nearly as fine as the rest of it."

"I want to see it." She squeezed his arm. "You should be proud of this, you know."

"It's a pleasure hall."

"It's a safe place for your men," she said. She could see that much, even if she did not know the story that bound them.

"With a brothel on the top floor and Wrath on the lowest level because it's easier to clean away the blood?"

"Safe places don't all look the same," she said.

"Aye, Devil," the sharp-eyed man from the gaming floor said from behind them. "Introduce her to Granny Brutus."

"That sounds lovely. Who is Granny Brutus?"

Devil sighed. "Miss Caldecott, may I present MacLeod."

"How do you, Mr. MacLeod?" She had always assumed someone like Devil led a solitary life, but she was clearly mistaken. There were workers everywhere, of course, but other men who looked to him for direction. With respect, not just fear.

"Just MacLeod," he said, Scottish accent thick as butter on toast. She could not remember the last time she'd had fresh butter. "There's only one of me left, you ken?"

"Suitably mysterious for an assassin."

Devil raised his brows. "He's not an assassin."

"He works for you, doesn't he? And assassin sounds much fiercer than… What's your actual title?"

MacLeod grinned. "I don't have one."

"Pain in my ass," Devil supplied.

"I keep him alive," MacLeod countered.

"Well done, you." Kitty nodded. "I imagine it is a full-time occupation."

"People do tend to react somewhat violently to his presence."

"It's the scowl."

"I don't scowl," Devil muttered. Scowling.

Kitty was suddenly enjoying herself immensely. Especially when he almost smiled. His almost-smile was her favorite. Even though she should not even *have* a favorite.

He led her back to Pride, with its mirrors reflecting dozens of Devils back at her, each more mysterious than the last. "Let's get this visit over with," he grumbled. "Tadworth and his bloody toads."

"Oh dear, are you afraid of toads?" Kitty pushed because it was the most fun she had all week. And because she was still considering biting all along the muscles of his shoulders. His hips. His thighs.

"No."

"Ah," she said, innocence floating off her like dandelion fluff. "Is it your arm? Does it pain you very much?" She knew it didn't—he had gripped her with too much delicious strength in the study. "If you are too weak to accompany me, I do understand."

"Just get in the carriage, firecracker," he growled.

She giggled all the way down the walkway.

And she was quite sure she had never giggled a day in her life.

CHAPTER NINETEEN

TADWORTH HOUSE WAS on the edge of St. James's Square and did not stand out from the rest in any noticeable fashion.

Until you stepped inside.

Kitty had never seen so much green, from the glass chandelier to the lime velvet curtains to the embroidered cushions all sporting toads of one type or another. The paintings were also on theme: mostly ponds and fens. The footman's livery was in the same eye-watering shade of lime. The butler's shoes were green.

It was a lot to take in. And this was from a woman who had snuck through Sir Reginald's House of a Hundred Cabbages.

Kitty smiled up at Devil, who watched her expectantly as they waited for Lord Tadworth to join them. "I love it."

"I shall summon a doctor posthaste," he said drily.

For a man who terrified all of London, he was surprisingly funny and considerate. Considerate even despite the unsated arousal still pulsing between her thighs. The Devil had many tricks.

One of those tricks had gotten them through the front door and into Lord Tadworth's spectacular library. Two stories of books soared around them, the oak polished to a smooth, warm finish underfoot. There were soft grooves worked into the wood, betraying Lord Tadworth's regular path strolling through his beloved collection. Reading chairs sat near the hearth, padded and welcoming. A line of tables dissected the center, set with oil lamps between large terrariums filled with sand and dirt and greenery.

"Welcome, welcome," Lord Tadworth bellowed from the doorway.

Kitty liked him immediately. His whiskers were as wild as promised, the same white as his bushy eyebrows. He wore spectacles and a waistcoat of faded green damask. He blinked at Kitty. "A lady, eh? Can't remember the last time I had a lady in my library."

Kitty curtsied. "Lord Tadworth."

"Miss Caldecott is my fiancée," Devil said, with more than a hint of warning.

"Eh?" Lord Tadworth said.

"I said Miss Caldecott is my fiancée," Devil repeated, a touch louder.

Lord Tadworth blinked at him and then turned slightly to wink at Kitty. Kitty instantly wanted to trade in her angry, blustering grandfather for this eccentric old man who loved toads and teased the devil. "Want some tea?" he barked. "Of course you do." He pulled the bell, not waiting for a response.

"You have an impressive library," Kitty said. The bulk of his collection had been bound in leather, all dyed his signature green and with gold lettering.

Very helpful of him, actually. It would be simple enough to see which books were newly purchased from another library.

He frowned at her. A peridot pin flashed from the folds of his green cravat. "Miss Caldecott, did you say?"

"Yes."

"You own that bookstore."

Devil's stance turned threatening with barely a muscle twitch. "And?"

"I'm not selling any of my books," Lord Tadworth said stubbornly. "I don't care if the Devil himself demands it. Call in my debt early if you must."

"No one is forcing you to sell your books," Kitty said fiercely. "Who would do that?"

"Every single one of my children," he muttered. "Think the estate is already theirs, don't they? Bah."

Kitty realized his debt must have been incurred by purchasing new books or marble statues of toads. She shook her head. "I'm not here to take your books," she promised. "Only to look at them, if I may. It's rare to find another collector as avid as I am." Avid. Obsessive. Fanatical. Close enough.

"Well, if that's the truth, then."

"It is, I promise."

"I like you."

"I like you too, Lord Tadworth."

Devil cleared his throat, amused.

"Settle down," Lord Tadworth muttered. "I'm too old for her. But you're lucky, young man. I had the best calves in town in my youth. And I still have most of my teeth."

Kitty grinned at him. "I believe it. May I walk around?"

"Go ahead, go ahead, then. Start in the top-right corner— that's where the nature guides are. Did you know toads can puff themselves up to appear threatening?" He peered into one of the terrariums. "And they don't drink water. They absorb it through their skin. Fascinating creatures."

"I confess I've never really considered them."

"Well, come over here, girl," Lord Tadworth said. "They tend to hide during the day, but we'll see if we can lure one out with some crickets. You're not squeamish, are you?"

Kitty thought of the state of the pavement outside her door before Devil sent his men to lurk about menacingly. "Not anymore."

"Good, good."

He dug through the grit inside the terrarium like a proud father about to show off his newborn baby. He might be a recluse for reasons Kitty did not know, but he was also lonely. She wondered if she could conjure up a reason to visit him again.

Perhaps bring him a book of poetry about toads. Had anyone written such a thing? She would have to ask around.

"Here's one," he said, booming with excitement. He immediately lowered his impressive voice. "Oh, pardon, my darling. Didn't mean to shout at you."

The toad in his palm did not look particularly concerned. Nor particularly impressed. He was mottled with several shades of green and brown, round eyes bulging. The curve of his mouth made him look grumpy. "Oh, he's lovely," Kitty said. "Very expressive."

"I've named him King Arthur."

"My sister has a hedgehog named Galahad."

"Ha! Clever girl. Is she older than you?"

"Younger by a great many years, I'm afraid."

"Ah well. Hedgehogs eat frogs. Not sure about toads. Best not risk it." He lifted King Arthur with a twinkle in his eye. "Do you want to hold him?"

He clearly thought it was a good jest, that she would flinch away.

"Certainly," she said instead. She would have kissed the damned toad if it meant having a proper look through his books. Evie was worth kissing a dozen toads.

She flattened her hand and encouraged the toad to slide into her palm. His skin was bumpy and drier than she would have thought. His toes were long and tickled as he stretched, considering the climb up her arm. He tottered like a milk-drunk child.

Lord Tadworth positively beamed at her.

When King Arthur started to get a little too jumpy, Lord Tadworth reclaimed him and set him carefully back into his terrarium. Devil passed her his handkerchief before she could wipe her hands on her skirt. She scrubbed her palms as Lord Tadworth led her to a washbasin.

"You've got to scrub up better than that and dry well if you're going to touch my books," he said.

She did as she was bidden as he continued to rattle off more facts about toads. He would keep her here talking about them for the rest of the visit if she let him. She would never find Lady Caroline's books.

And she knew Lord Tadworth's type of reader. Books were cared for like delicate flowers, barely opened even to read them. Kept from sunlight and dust and fingertips. Kitty on the other hand, preferred to devour her books. She liked them to be well loved, the pages softened, with creases where a beloved passage was read and reread. It was a map left behind by the reader. A love letter of sorts.

Clearly, this particular opinion would get her booted right out on her backside into the street. Even if she had held a toad. He would hover, wincing every time she flipped through pages a little too quickly.

"Lord Birmingham was just telling me he was keen to learn about toads," she said. "Perhaps you might show him more while I look at your books?"

"Well, come along, then, my boy. Lots to see."

"He gets bored in libraries," Kitty called down as she darted up the staircase. She had no idea if that was true.

"Blasphemy," Lord Tadworth muttered. "You'll never get her to marry you like that."

Devil's gaze tracked her, pinned her. Promised retribution.

She just grinned at him.

He shook his head and turned politely to Lord Tadworth.

"It's my name, you see," the elderly earl said. "They called me Toadworth when I was a boy and snuck toads and frogs into my shoes and my bed and even my supper bowl at Eton. It backfired, of course. I don't mind being called Toad at all now."

Kitty ignored the rows of matching green books, though the sheer number of them tempted her to linger. It was difficult not to reach for them, to read a few pages. She forced herself past rows of poetry and plays and more books on natural history than she could have even guessed existed in London. All of England. There were novels, too, she was gratified to see. The critics said novels were bad for the female brain, that they caused anxiety and headaches. Poppycock. Novels were good for the soul. They were simply another way to make friends, to see the world. To *rest.*

And here they were. Shelves of novels, none of them in matching leather bindings. She searched, finding nothing but prose and poetry.

And then: *The Delights of the Duchess,* volume six.

She had found Lady Caroline's note and scrawled symbol in another volume of the same series. Anticipation caught in her throat as she reached for it. Lord Tadworth was still talking to Devil about toad habitats. He had forgotten all about her. She bent over the book, shielding it as she thumbed through the pages. *Please, please let there be something. Anything.*

In this volume, the duchess explored her very wicked desires for the duke's valet.

Lady Caroline had dog-eared a few pages.

And she'd also scrawled a note.

This is my favorite of the series thus far. I point you to chapter fifty-five. I'm sending this copy with Agnes. I would hate for your maman to open it accidentally!

Who was Agnes? Did Lady Caroline merely enjoy reading about being trapped in an artist's studio in a snowstorm with a handsome man, or was there some other clue to the chapter?

Kitty dropped the book into her reticule, vowing to return it as soon as Evie was safe from Lord Portsmouth.

Whenever that might be.

CHAPTER TWENTY

I T WOULD HAVE done Kitty a great service if the author of *Pride and Prejudice* had set any of her books in London.

Kitty's walking tours were popular enough, but they would surely have showered her in gold coins were Mr. Darcy said to have strolled along Piccadilly or stopped at Fortnum and Masons.

Never mind—her customers still wanted to see where fictional characters were said to have hidden from vampire hunters or met lovers for secret trysts. They only condescended to stop at the very ordinary if lovely Gunter's Ices because of a scene in which very wicked things were done with lemon ices.

Very wicked.

There had been a run on lemon ices for several weeks after publication, which had bewildered the chefs. She had taken to warning them when she led her tours now so they might lay in a supply of the fruit.

All to say that Kitty's customers were an odd bunch and she adored them.

Her walking tours met just before dusk at Montagu House, where an intrepid antiquarian wallflower was swept off her feet by an adventurer who had stolen a jewel from one of the pyramids. According to the gothic novel, at any rate.

There was a respectable number of customers today: a couple who mostly stared at each other, two young girls with their father, who was already bored but patient, two dandies who were out on a lark, and a family just arrived from Nottingham and in London for the first time. And, as always, Miss Peridot with her raw onion in hand. She never missed a tour. She claimed it was the only way she could tolerate calisthenics. Also Miss Hastings, whom Kitty was glad to see the Ladies' Novel Society had not scared off. The same could not be said for many an intrepid soul.

There was also a very tall Viking strolling along as though this was his idea in the first place.

And not Devil's idea.

Wulf grinned at her, then at the two young girls who were gaping at him like he had walked out of a novel. One they liked very much.

"Did you lose a wager?" Kitty murmured.

He shrugged. "I like books."

Montagu House was open to the public for tours of their collection of marbles, for the first mummy displayed in Britain, though that had been some time ago. There were also treasures from Captain Cook's Pacific voyages, Saxon coins, and the Rosetta Stone.

It was all quite fascinating, but Kitty remained out front with her guests. She had learned her lesson. Particularly avid fans of a certain novel had lingered for an hour over the Rosetta Stone alone, whispering about the hero who broke a mummy's curse for his antiquarian love. Two ladies had vanished altogether, only to be escorted out by two gentlemen blushing to the roots of their hair. Kitty had been *encouraged* to remain in the garden after that.

Which was mildly unjust. There were many ways to appreciate history, surely. But at least she was not outright banned.

Carriages trundled behind her, the sound of the horses' hooves on the road a comforting heartbeat. The smells of coal smoke, the shouts of hawkers—all lent itself to the tales she told of a magical London lurking beneath this one.

An ancient mummy's curse in the British Museum. A siren

singing in a pub in Covent Garden across from St. Paul's church.

The pub did not exist, but the church did, which was good enough. It had a stone façade, a round window over the door, and a somewhat perplexed clergyman when readers began leaving seashells painted gold outside the church. The siren was said to leave them to communicate with her lover, a dashing sea captain she'd accidentally drowned. Twice.

Gothic novels were simply the very best.

The Theatre Royal was naturally home to a ghost searching for a woman to love more than he loved music.

They passed another tour on their way from Covent Garden to Berkely Square. Miss Macallister nodded at Kitty curtly, like they were two soldiers on the battlefield. Sometimes their groups crossed paths; sometimes they even shared an audience. Miss Macallister's tended to weeping throngs of ladies desperate for a glimpse of the poet Byron. There was a great deal of screaming if he was spotted. Sometimes swooning. It seemed rather a lot of work to Kitty for a syphilitic poet who treated women with contempt.

Next was Gunter's, where they stopped for lemon ices, of course.

It was a short walk to Brook Street, where a handsome vampire hid from hungers and hunters and sunlight in very luxurious rooms at the Claridge Hotel. He drank a lot of wine.

Also lingering near the hotel was a certain Devil, leaning against a column.

"And he has dark, windswept hair," Kitty said pointedly, altering her description of the notorious vampire. "And green eyes, of course."

Devil tilted his head in that way of his, green eyes finding her.

"He's very dashing, of course." She grinned. "But also *quite* maddening. All that power and prestige. It's not good for the character, I'm sure."

He bowed. No one else noticed him. She could not help *but* notice him. And then he moved, just barely, and the air changed.

Gazes snapped toward him, transfixed. Or skittered away, scared. She heard more than one murmur of "About that club of yours…"

She felt his eyes on her all the way to St. George Church in Hanover Square, where the forbidden love of a dairymaid and a duke was celebrated. And where a side gate to a rose garden formed an iron oak tree with black leaves.

This corner of London was not only the purview of a duke and his dairymaid—a certain duchess had also visited. In volume seven of *The Delights of the Duchess*. It was a simple gate tucked away and unnoticed. But a strapping coachman had once pressed the duchess against it under the stars. Several times.

Meet me at the oak tree.

Was this what Lady Caroline had meant? The duchess had called it her favorite oak tree in England.

Kitty ought to have realized it sooner. It felt possible. Right, even.

Lady Caroline was not here now, of course. But she knew the place. Maybe she returned once in a while?

It was worth a try.

Books really did save lives.

THE LAST STOP was the Golden Griffin Bookshop, where Godric stood outside, arms crossed, window shining clean behind him.

"I'll wait for you," Devil said to Kitty, nodding to his carriage waiting at the corner. "I'm taking you home."

She tried not to feel warm inside. Failed.

But she also sold three copies of *Desires of a Duchess* volume one, and four copies of *The Curse of the Mummy*, which she'd had specially bound with Egyptian hieroglyphs. No one knew what they meant yet, but they were very popular nonetheless. There was happy chatter, favorite books recommended to other readers.

In short, it was perfect. The tour had centered her, made her feel more like herself and less like she was running in circles. She felt better. Calmer. Ready to do whatever needed doing.

Which, of course, meant everything fell spectacularly to pieces.

Almost immediately.

She found the culprit behind her father asking why the shop smelled like soup. Someone had managed to wedge a turnip under the corner of a bookcase. It must have been several weeks ago, judging by the state of it. She popped it loose and went to the back to toss it into the alley, so as not to have to carry it past any lingering customers. It squelched as it hit the ground and rolled away. "Vile thing."

As if summoned, another vile thing emerged.

From behind her, tucked into the shadows of the alley. Before she could react, before she could punch or kick or scream, a hand slapped over her mouth. "Someone wants a word," a man grunted in her ear. He stank of cheroot smoke.

She struggled even though she knew it was in vain. He picked her up like she was a rag doll, forcing her down the alley and out the side to a hackney. Her screams were muffled, barely loud enough to be heard over the fiddle from a pub down the way.

Her captor forced her closer to the carriage, ripping the door open. She managed to clip him in the kneecap with her heel when he hauled her off her feet. It was enough for him to swear at her, not enough to drop her. She scratched at the hand stealing her breath but to no avail. It was becoming difficult to breathe. He shoved her into the carriage.

Where was everyone?

A useless question. Pedestrians didn't venture back here, and the one person watching from a balcony two buildings down turned away. Her customers were inside. Devil was waiting for her out front.

And then he wasn't.

There was a soft grunt of pain before her captor went flying into a heap on the pavement. Another sound, this time of something cracking. A nose? A bone?

Devil appeared in the carriage opening, eyes chillingly furious. They roamed over her. "Did he hurt you?"

She shook her head as he pulled her out. Her ankle protested the weight of the rest of her leg, buckling. Devil caught her. It gave her captor just enough time to crawl into the street and scramble to his feet, into a dead run. Devil swore, loud and vicious.

"Wulf," he barked as the man in question came around the corner, dagger in hand. "I want him caught."

Wulf nodded and took off in pursuit. Devil glared at the hackney's coachman, who reached for the reins. "You don't move, understand?"

Something in Devil's expression had him gulping and nodding. That expression softened, if only briefly, when Devil glanced down at Kitty. Her teeth chattered as she tried to catch her breath. "He did hurt you. I'll kill him."

"I hurt myself kicking him," she admitted. "Not very heroic of me, I'm afraid."

Miss Peridot poked her head around the side of the building. Kitty smiled at her as though her heart wasn't still fluttering in her throat. She turned and tried to hop back into the alley. Devil frowned, slipping his arms under her and picking her up. Right up off the ground.

"What are you doing?" he demanded, like hauling around booksellers was all perfectly normal.

"I don't want them to make a fuss," she said. "I hate fussing. I can walk, you know." She said it even as she snuggled closer. His scent of wood smoke and amber was almost as good as the smell of books. Almost better.

Maybe she had hit her head when tossed into that carriage.

Devil ducked into the back room but did not set her down just yet, as if he did not want to. The cords of his neck were taut, his pulse thrumming under the skin. His arms were firm but surprisingly gentle around her. She could get used to this.

She should *not* get used to this.

"You can put me down now," she said.

"No."

"I'm—"

"Just give me a moment."

There was something else under the rage, the clench of his jaw. Concern? Worry? Was it merely pride? A man like Devil could not afford to let his name be associated with anything but authority and fear. He would protect his betrothed. That had to be it.

He finally put her down, very carefully in the rickety chair. It creaked and wobbled. He scowled at it.

"It always does that," she said, refusing to be embarrassed because she was certain not a single chair in his Mayfair townhouse would dare wobble.

"I need to talk to that coachman," he said. "Don't move." He looked at her for a long moment, eyes narrowed. "On second thought—Godric!"

Godric hurried through the shop. "Yes, Devil?"

"Don't let anyone steal her."

Godric nodded, looking far less like the helpful giant who let her sneak him frosted cakes shaped like ducks and much more like a proper Viking.

Devil stalked out. Kitty tried to smile. She felt strange: full of lightning but also exhausted. Rain began to fall outside, pattering at the windows. "Would you like some tea?" she asked. Her grate was small and smoky and she had a shockingly small amount of coal, but she would make do. She couldn't just sit here.

Godric snorted. "If you stand up to make me tea, Devil will murder us both."

"I think my ankle is already much better."

"Please, don't," Godric begged when she stood up. He would never even consider shoving her back into her chair. Devil would, as attested to by his reaction when he came back to find her testing her weight. Her ankle ached but the pain no longer lanced up the back of her calf. An improvement.

"I've locked up the front—I told you not to move," he

growled.

"It's feeling better already," she said. She put her full weight on that leg, decided not to do that anymore, and leaned a little to the other side.

"You are a terrible patient." Devil glared.

"*You* got stabbed and wouldn't even see a doctor!"

"*You* nearly got kidnapped and won't sit down!" He sounded half wild, very unlike the chillingly composed Devil she knew. He scrubbed a hand over his face. His voice turned quiet. "Godric, I've got this."

Godric nodded and left. Quickly. *Very* quickly for a man who'd looked like a brutal warrior not five minutes ago.

"That was an inexcusable mistake," Devil said. "No one should have gotten that close to you. It won't happen again."

"None of that was your fault."

"I should have been more careful."

"You saved me," she pointed out. She had not thought it possible that he would have heard her struggling or wondered where she had got to. It made her want to cry. A little. Merely an aftereffect of an eventful evening, surely. "That was careful enough, surely."

"Not nearly enough. I don't suppose he very conveniently explained just who the hell sent him and what the bloody hell he wanted?"

"I'm afraid not. Very rude of him."

Devil used his knuckles to tilt her chin up. They look bruised. "Are you sure you are all right?"

She nodded, feeling weepy, which would not do. "Thanks to you. He just said someone wanted a word."

"I'm going to find Portsmouth."

"You can't."

"I promise you, I can."

"We can't be sure he was behind this." Devil just waited patiently until she wrinkled her nose. "Oh, very well," she muttered. She could not imagine who else would bother to have her snatched off the street. "But you still cannot just go off and terrorize him."

He scoffed.

"You *can*," she allowed. "But you *shouldn't*."

"Why the hell not?"

"Because it will not help my sister."

"We are not trading your safety for your sister's."

She shrugged one shoulder. "A fair trade."

"No." Uncompromising, stern. Furious.

"Yes." Just as uncompromising.

"I can save you both, damn it."

Her eyes widened. She had not expected *that*, and certainly not so empathically. Something warm and unfamiliar bloomed behind the breastbone, but softly, not the way it usually burned. She rubbed it, but just to make sure she was not imagining it. Her ankle throbbed. She almost didn't notice.

"The others have all gone," he said. "I'll take you home and we can argue about it some more until you admit I am right." That almost-smile was a brief candlelight against the wild storm of him. "Where I will also be sending for a doctor."

"I just need a bit of ice," she said, as if ice was something she could afford. "Or better yet, a comfrey poultice." She still had some comfrey salve in her kit.

"A doctor," Devil insisted.

She wrinkled her nose. "The only doctor I know will want to apply leeches, and I really hate leeches."

"No leeches," Devil promised solemnly. "And I have a doctor of my own."

"Hmph. That might have been helpful when you were *stabbed*."

"Barely grazed." He reached for her.

"I'm sure I can make it to the carriage. I was very good at hopscotch when I was a child."

"Humor me."

CHAPTER TWENTY-ONE

T HE RIDE TO the house was short and quiet. Kitty was not sure what to say. Should she make idle chatter? Should she discuss the extraterrestrial band of blue-skinned warriors from a popular chapbook series? Or Malcolm, a ship's captain turned pirate? None of her usual topics of conversation were appropriate. Which was not to imply they had ever been appropriate to begin with. But this was something different.

Devil sat quietly watching her as though she were worth watching. As though he *saw* her. And still meant to keep her safe.

He did not know what she was capable of, what she had nearly done to her closest friend. This would all go away when he truly knew her.

"Does it hurt?" he asked softly.

How she had treated Clara? How angry she was with her father? She opened her mouth, snapped it shut. He meant her ankle, of course. "It's fine."

"Mm-hmm."

The carriage pulled up to her house, a single window soft with lamplight. The rain continued to fall, gilding the glass, the puddles on the road. Devil insisted on carrying her to the door, setting her gently down only when no one answered his imperious knock.

"Where's your butler?" Devil asked when she opened the

door and still no one came to greet her.

Kitty laughed. "We haven't had a butler for years now."

"Footmen?"

She shook her head, smiling at him like he was being ridiculous.

"Not a one?" He finally sounded shocked, he who was shocked by nothing. He ran an actual, literal den of iniquity, but *this* had him scandalized. It was endearing. "You're alone in there?"

"There's my father and my aunt." She had the sudden feeling she was going to wake up with half a dozen more Winchesters on her front stair by morning. She was tired, achy. Vulnerable. She could not withstand any more kindness from him. She might shatter. "Good night, Devil."

He gripped the door handle, keeping her from going inside. He raised a brow expectantly. Patiently.

"Good night, *Rhys*," she amended.

"Good girl," he murmured in her hair. "I'll be right back. You've had a long night, but I haven't forgotten my promise," he added roughly.

"What promise is that?"

"To make you come until your legs give out."

And just like that, she was on fire from the top of her head straight down her spine. Her nipples puckered in response. She grew wet right there standing on her front step.

He really would have to follow through on his promise soon, or she would never get anything done. This kind of attraction was distracting.

"Lock the door, firecracker."

The floaty-sparkly feeling lasted all of three minutes. And then her aunt charged out of the parlor. "Was that Lord Birmingham?"

"Yes, Aunt Priscilla."

"Did you not invite him in?"

"He is a busy man." And Kitty could not think of many things she wanted less than Devil in her house with her father and her aunt buzzing around him like wasps.

"He has yet to ask your father's permission, you know."

"As I am laughably beyond my age of majority and have no dowry, Father is not involved in this."

"Don't be ridiculous. The least you can do is have him forgive your father's debt."

"It doesn't work that way." If he even held a debt of her father's. She had not asked directly. Part of her did not want to know. There were already too many tangled, complicated threads between them. And because she didn't *want* to know. Even if that made her a terrible daughter.

And any debt her father owed to Devil would, frankly, not make a difference. There were too many of them owed to too many men. He hadn't a considerable sum available for him to lose in a long time. It was all dripping away like rainwater through a crack in the roof.

That was not a metaphor, unfortunately.

"Ask him for pin money, then," Aunt Priscilla said.

"We aren't even married yet," Kitty pointed out. Nor would they be. And then any favors asked would sit oddly, chafing. One disaster at a time. If she said it often enough, maybe some benevolent spirit would indulge her.

"Useless, as always. Bewitch him if you must, though I can see how that might pose a problem." She shook her head. "You are starting to look like a street urchin. Ladies do not go about with ink on their fingers and mud on their hems."

Walking through London, literary tour notwithstanding, was messy business. Walking anywhere in London was generally messy business.

Nearly getting abducted was not much better for one's sartorial splendor.

Her dress was dusty, her hair coming loose of its pins, as it always did at the end of a long day. She was not fit for a drawing room. It did not appear to bother Devil any at present, but surely he would change his mind. At the moment, she was a unique taste of something different, not a full meal. And he had every banquet and feast available to him.

"Catherine, are you listening to me?"

She was suddenly so very, very tired.

She glanced at the door longingly, wondering if it was worth walking back to the shop on her sore ankle in the rain in order to sleep in the one comfortable chair in her reading room.

The door swung open as if by magic.

And it was not an angel come to save her.

IT FELT WRONG to leave Kitty, even for a moment. Not even here across the river in Lambeth, on Hercules Street, with terraced brick houses overgrown with ivy. But he had caught the movement in the shadows across the street when he set her down.

He knew when someone was lurking.

And he knew when it was not one of his men. They would never be so sloppy. They had learned their tricks on battlefields and hidden camps from Spain to Waterloo. A rainy street in London was nothing.

He paused behind his carriage to retrieve his walking stick, the one with the silver swan head his brother insisted on stealing at every opportunity. He nodded to Dean, who had also spotted the man lurking in view of Kitty's front window and was ready. His brother Michael was perched at the back of the carriage, as usual, armed to the teeth.

The brothers Winchester had been on the Continent with him as well, and as they preferred riding through the night on temperamental horses even then, they chose the mews instead of the Sins. But they were both trusted and well trained and vicious enough to watch over Kitty for a quarter of an hour.

That was all the time he estimated he would need to fix this particular problem.

He waited for another carriage to pass, using it to hide until he was safely across the street. And then he was on the man in moments, driving him back further into the darkness. One solid, brutal punch to the nose had him reeling back, smashing his head on the brick wall in the process. He grunted, spat blood, and was slow to react. Devil got in another strike to the stomach. A blow glanced his jaw, not close enough for any real damage. Another hit before he had to duck a fist the size of a Christmas goose.

As he was spoiling for a proper fight, it made him smile.

Even the flash of the pistol aimed at him did not make his smile falter. He brought his walking stick down, smashing it over the man's wrist. There was a crack that could be heard even with the rain falling on them. The pistol hit the ground.

The man's eyes widened when he recognized Devil, saw the infamously ruthless green eyes. "Devil," he said. "Ain't got no beef with you. No trouble."

"You're lurking outside the house of my betrothed. So I can assure you, there is, indeed, trouble." Devil knew what he sounded like: chillingly, icily merciless. He felt worse. He felt unmoored with the fury inside his chest over even the suggestion of danger to Kitty. He pressed the walking stick across the man's throat until he choked. "Did Portsmouth send you?"

"He'll kill me."

"*I'll* kill you," Devil said. He increased the pressure of the walking stick across his windpipe. "Die today or die tomorrow. Roll the dice."

The man shivered at whatever he saw in Devil's face. "I never saw him, but yeah. I get messages and payment through the Blue Lion. That's all I know, I swear."

Devil contemplated another threat, decided it wasn't needed. As he had no intention of leaving Kitty here, Portsmouth could send as many men as he liked.

This one, though…

"Were you at the Golden Griffin tonight? Did you put your hands on her?"

He shook his head, going pale. "No! I never touched her! I've been here since morning. Ask the lamplighters."

"Who, then?"

"There's three of us meet at the Lion. But we stay on this side of the river. The others I don't know. Fancy ones, from your part of London."

"You don't work for them anymore," Devil said. "Am I making myself clear?"

The man gulped, nodded.

"I'll know everything there is to know about you within the hour," Devil added. "Don't cross me."

Another nod, and then a grunt when Devil knocked the out cold. He slid down the brick wall with a satisfying thud.

Devil crossed the street, heedless of the rain and the puddles and everything that was not Kitty and her safety. "Follow him when he wakes up," he called to Michael, who jumped off his perch. "When you know enough about him, let him see you."

Michael nodded with a grim, glittering smile. Memories of army encampments, muddy battlefields. Blood. *Nothing's forgotten. Nothing is ever forgotten.*

Devil's temper was not improved by overhearing Mrs. Bartley's strident voice, which carried with all the subtlety of a rain of bullets through the open window. Her words were just as bad. Worse. That Kitty had to listen to vitriol daily at her shop and then again in her home where her family ought to be caring for her infuriated… The tired droop of her shoulders through the glass and the way she favored her twisted ankle filled him with incandescent rage. The kind that no one walked away from unscathed. He had already knocked a man out tonight. He could do so much more.

Although Kitty might not thank him for burning this house to ash as punishment.

It was still tempting. Too tempting.

The door was locked, as he'd ordered. He didn't have the patience to wait for it to be opened or the composure to watch Kitty limp with pain because no one else would answer it.

So he kicked it in.

That *did* help his temper. Enormously.

He stalked into the house, knowing that his expression was stone and iron, the one even his brother did not try to tease him out of. It was a warning. The only one he was going to give.

Kitty'd aunt shrieked. He speared her with a glare that had once made a grown man wet himself. "Quiet."

She swallowed thickly. "Lord Birmingham."

"You do not talk to her that way," he said, very clearly, with every word like the slice of a sword. She had called Kitty stupid. Useless. Blood should have been pooling at his feet in retribution. There were consequences when someone came for one of his own. "Ever."

"It's fine," Kitty said haltingly. *Haltingly.* His *firecracker*.

"It is *not* fine." He didn't take his eyes off Priscilla. "Where's the baron?"

"He..." She was flustered, unaccustomed to this kind of command. Or the front door hanging off its hinges, letting in the rain. "That is..."

"You wanted me to speak to him," he said. "Fetch him."

She hurried away, and Kitty sent him a dry smile. "I've never seen her move that fast, even the time a rat got into the carriage."

"Are you hurt? Did she hurt you?"

She was taken aback. A simple question over her wellbeing bewildered her. The rage sharpened. Her family had a lot to answer for. By his estimation, they should be weeping with gratitude for the care she took of them. He noticed the hole in the wall behind her head, only partially covered by a watercolor sketch of a hedgehog. The illustrious Galahad.

He knew exactly what it looked like when someone punched through a wall with fist or pipe. And why such a someone might do so in the front hall of the house of this particular baron.

"Send your maid to pack your things," he told her.

She rolled her eyes, even though she was still pale with the kind of fatigue that itched at his bones. The soul-deep weariness that had no business touching her. He wanted to bring her tea again. Why was he obsessed with giving her tea? "I don't have a maid, Rhys."

Rhys.

She might not know it yet, but she had just welcomed him into her life in a way that had nothing to do with stolen wagers or pretend betrothals or her sister. In a way he had not realized he needed until he had it. And now he would not give it back.

She had given ground to him, and he would not lose it.

"Get your things," he said softly. "You're not staying here."

"I live here."

"She's not staying here." Devil raised his voice, turning to spear the baron and his sister as they scurried down the hall.

"You can't just take her," Kitty's aunt blustered. "It's not done."

"Why not?" Kitty asked quietly. "You tried to do it to Evie."

"Don't be so stupid. You—"

"I told you not to speak to her that way." Devil interrupted coldly. He was through with warnings. "It would be a shame if Society's doors all closed to you. Every one."

Priscilla's mouth worked like a fish. She nudged her brother, but everyone in London knew the baron was a weak man, never mind everyone in this particular house.

"Kitty will be staying with me from now on."

"But the gossip…"

"I have a chaperone in Mrs. Dimitriou, as well as my brother in residence. I will invite as many guests as make Kitty comfortable. But she's not staying here with you two for one more night. You'll have to make your own supper."

The baron gave a start, as if that was something so very difficult to figure out. "Kitty is a fine girl. She does her duty."

"Yes, and it's time you did yours."

"She—"

"Should anyone ask, you will be enthusiastic in your support of our betrothal. Am I being understood?" Devil paused. "I know exactly what you owe, and to whom."

The baron blinked, hovering between selfishness and fatherhood. "As to that, Birmingham, perhaps you could talk to that hell on the Strand for me? I only owe a—"

"Father, please." Kitty closed her eyes with barely concealed mortification. Something else glinted in them when she lifted her lids: hurt, anger, sorrow.

Devil hated it.

"The money you stole from my shop today should be enough to buy food for the week."

Devil thought he had felt all the variations of anger there were to be felt. If not in the last hour, then certainly in the last decade. Napoleon, the ineptitude of officers in the army who did not care for their own men. His brother dragging himself home with blood in his mouth.

Someone trying to shove Kitty into a carriage. The brittle way she had smiled earlier this evening; the way she held herself as though she were full of needles and knives. Because of her father.

"You stole from her?" Devil asked evenly. So evenly that everyone flinched.

"I..." the baron blustered. "She's my daughter. She should—"

"You're right." Devil cut him off, because if the man said anything else, he might actually murder Kitty's own father right in front of her. "She's your *daughter.*"

"I have every right—"

"For God's sake, Francis," Priscilla snapped. "Shut your mouth."

"Excellent advice," Devil said. "I suggest you take it. Immediately." He glanced at Kitty, her damp hair curling around her wide gray eyes. "Evie's not here," Devil murmured to her. "You don't have to protect her from them. Not tonight."

He saw the moment Kitty realized it, the real moment it dawned on her. Some battles were not worth fighting when you had too many other fronts to protect.

She nodded, once.

"Get your things," he said again. "Please."

IT WAS THE please that did it.

The ominous commands and power emanating from him might be enough to fire her senses, but it didn't cloud her mind completely. Taking orders from Rhys set a bad precedent. Anyone could see that.

But a simple please? From a man who was seething with anger on her behalf?

That, she could not resist.

Which was how she found herself back inside his plush carriage with a beaten-up trunk stuffed with her clothing and all of her books. Priorities. She didn't own that many dresses anyway. The carriage swayed, the lantern light adding a soft glow as they went from crowded streets across the river to the manicured estates of Mayfair.

She was completely out of place.

She rubbed her breastbone, willing away the burning there, as if she had drunk lemon juice. Evie was facing marriage to Lord Portsmouth, so Kitty could certainly face this. She dropped her hand in her lap.

"Good girl," Devil said as if he knew how she felt. As if he had learned her mannerisms. As if he knew the hot little shiver that bloomed when he said it, despite herself.

"You broke my front door."

"I did."

It should not have been as thrilling as it was. The crack and splinter of the frame, a furious Devil dripping rainwater and rage.

And blood.

She probably ought to be scared of him.

Mostly she wanted to bite his incongruously delicate upper lip. His jawline. The swell of muscles on his forearm.

The carriage drew to a halt before she could embarrass herself. Any more than she already had, that was.

"This is probably a bad idea," she said. "Even I know this sort of thing is not done. My aunt is right, though I will eat your hat before saying that to her."

"*My* hat? Eat your own." That languid drawl, the spark of something underneath it. Not just something. Everything. "I can take you somewhere else if you prefer. Just don't ask me to take you back to that house."

"Why does it bother you so much?" She was genuinely curious. Her family was far from perfect, but they were not the worst in London. They weren't even the worst on their street.

"You don't deserve it."

She thought of Clara and what she had done to her friend. Her smile faltered. "You don't know me, Devil. Not really."

He snorted. "Did you commit murder?"

"No." She paused. He did not look the least bit concerned. "Did *you*? Tonight?" she clarified.

"No, more's the pity."

"Would it matter if *I* had?"

"No." He sounded very sure, very nonchalant about her imaginary violence. "In or out, firecracker?"

She worried at her lower lip, told herself she was being a coward and a fool, and then nodded. "I'm in." She poked him in the knee when his mouth opened to speak. "If you call me a good girl again, I'm going to kick you someplace you will not like."

"Vicious." But when he said it, it sounded like a compliment.

DEVIL'S TOWNHOUSE WAS suitably imposing, clearly the work of several generations' worth of Birmingham earls. It soared five stories high with gleaming white stone and black ironwork. Unlike the more common terraced houses, Birmingham House was bordered by walkways and gardens behind tall fences. Windows gleamed and glittered, not a single one boarded up by his grandparents to save on taxes. The Golden Griffin had several boarded-up windows, as did most of the buildings on the street.

The marble floor was laid out in a black-and-white checkerboard pattern, polished so expertly that her own reflection stared back up at her. She did not need to look at it to know she was woefully underdressed for such a house. A white statue of a Roman lady stood at the bottom of the curved staircase, easily ten feet tall.

Kitty was shown to a bedchamber the size of her entire bookshop by the housekeeper, who did not blink an eye at a spinster moving in so late at night and hobbling on one foot. Until Devil swept Kitty up in his arms again and insisted on carrying her up the stairs.

"I can walk," she whispered against his chest.

"I like carrying you," he said simply.

And there was nothing she could think of to say back to that. Because she liked him carrying her too. A lot. Too much.

Devil summoned a doctor, who confirmed her ankle was not sprained, and when he suggested ice and a comfrey wrap, Kitty smirked at Devil smugly. He also confirmed that the cut on Devil's arm was healed and would not trouble him further, because Kitty refused to present her ankle until Devil presented his arm.

Devil also sent word to Yelena that she should join them as a chaperone. He looked charmingly helpless when he asked Kitty if he should invite anyone else to stay with them in order to safeguard her reputation.

Safeguarding reputations was not exactly what he was known for.

She only shrugged at him just as helplessly. It was not exactly her area of expertise either. She was the daughter of a disgraced minor baron. She was firmly on the shelf. Evie would have known. She'd read all of the etiquette books when she was not devouring volumes on the insects and venomous snakes of Ancient Egypt.

Kitty would rather poke herself in the eye. There were so many other books to read. Decorum made her sleepy.

A slight miscalculation on her part, perhaps.

She limped across the polished floors, dotted with hand-knotted rugs in a rich, dark blue that matched the curtains and the bedspread. Porcelain candlesticks painted with white roses stood on the mantel and on the table by the chair. A bench draped with lace sat next to the bed with another candle and a dish of sugared violets. The ceiling was a mural of the sky swirling with stars, a glowing moon overlooking it all. The whole chamber was like a still, dark winter's night.

She loved it. It was peaceful. Dark in a way that was more comforting than froth and sunshine.

She still could not sleep.

The idea was laughable. She felt as though she had drunk the equivalent of the Thames in tea and then added a trough of coffee. Devil was just across the hall, doing whatever it was devils did when night fell. He had promised to do lovely, filthy things to her, but that was before the attempted abduction, before he broke down her door, before her family. Before the scramble to find a chaperone, which she still found ridiculous. Not only was she nearly thirty years old, but chaperones had to sleep like everyone else. It was laughably easy to work around them and sneak from bed to bed if one so wished. She would never understand Mayfair.

And she would not have to.

She was not really marrying Devil.

That was the entire point of not ruining her. So he would not be forced to marry her. She did not blame him. And so she would not fight the occult rules of the *ton*.

As if staying even one hour under the Devil's roof was not enough to thoroughly ruin her.

In fact, she looked forward to it. If nothing else, she would have delicious memories that were just for her. It would have to be enough when Evie was safe and settled and Kitty went back to being a spinster who ducked rotting fruit professionally.

And anyway, she had more pressing problems, surely. Such as Lady Carolie. Or at least Agnes. Was it really only this morning that she had stolen a book from Lord Tadworth?

When it all threatened to overwhelm her, she left her rooms in favor of lurking about the house. A walk would do her good. It would siphon off some of the jagged energy swimming under her skin. Her ankle already felt much better. She was barely hobbling.

She headed for the library, because she always headed for the library.

It did not disappoint: it was filled with books and marble busts of Roman emperors. It smelled like wood smoke and roses and the sweet vanilla scent of paper.

And it was presided over by its king.

"I've been waiting for you," Devil said quietly from the shadows of a leather armchair. The candle burning at his elbow cast him into suitable relief, like a carved Hades. He wore a black dressing gown. His damp hair curled, slightly too long and entirely perfect. She wanted to feel it between her fingers.

"Devil," she said uselessly. She could not call him Rhys, not when he was so thoroughly *Devil*, from the shadows to the glint of his otherworldly eyes. She could easily imagine his ruling over hell. Or as a faery king. Didn't some people consider the fairy folk to be just fallen angels under a different name?

"I thought you'd end up here eventually."

"I can't sleep," she admitted.

"Is the chamber not to your liking?"

She sent him a dry look. There was no point in answering such an absurd question.

"Then you should go to bed," he warned in a silky, whiskey-rough voice that made her swallow.

"Why?"

"Because I very much want to keep my promise to you."

Chapter Twenty-Two

"WHAT IF I want that too?" Kitty asked because she wanted it so much. Desperately. More than she might want her next breath.

He half smiled and it was a dark smile. It was a forest at night, a storm approaching. "Then lock the door, Kitty."

She reached behind her and locked it without dropping her gaze. It was impossible to look away. He was seduction and hunger and wicked promise incarnate. And he was so beautiful—the crooked tilt to his smile, that sculpted dip in his upper lip. The sharp line of his jaw.

When he gestured for her to come to him, she briefly considered defying him, just to see what he might do. But tonight she would much rather see what he would do if she joined him. She was wearing a simple day dress, nothing silky or frilly or fashionable, but it did not matter. He looked at her as though she were dressed in whispers and moonlight. As if she belonged here. With him.

It made her feel a little drunk. A little wild. Exhilarated.

It was remarkably difficult to walk normally, to not run and throw herself at him. He spread his legs and leaned back in his chair like it was a throne. He tapped his knee. Autocratic. Impatient.

He made her feel pampered and like prey, all in the same

heartbeat.

She faltered a moment once she reached him. What was she supposed to do now? Make a sophisticated remark? She only knew how to make irreverent and shockingly inappropriate quips. How to calculate ledgers, and how to hide people. How to hide herself.

He watched her, waiting.

A challenge.

But also power. It was entirely up to her. He wasn't giving it to her, only acknowledging that it was already hers. She licked her lower lip.

"Are you teasing me, firecracker?"

"Maybe." She was teasing herself. Teasing them both. She wanted this. Any hesitation had more to do with her pride than anything else. And pride would not make her climax until her legs shook. But Rhys absolutely would. Devil might make the powerful men of London shake with fear, but she knew *Rhys* would make her shake with pleasure.

"Careful," he warned softly, expression forbidding in a way that sent hot shivers up her thighs. She stepped closer, between his knees. "So you've decided?" he asked.

She didn't pretend to misunderstand. "Yes."

"And?"

"Yes," she said again, anticipation washing through her, chasing away the nervousness.

He smiled, smug, satisfied, wanting her. She could see as much. The muscles in his jaw, the tendons in his neck flexing. The demanding tap on his knee. "Then what are you waiting for, love?"

He was pure seduction. She had thought so before, but this was overwhelming. Her senses reeled, clamoring for attention. She perched lightly. Too lightly. As if she were taking tea with a dowager.

"I think we can do better than that," he growled, pulling her sharply against him and angling his knee so that it widened her thighs. He dragged an open-mouthed kiss along her jawline, back and forth until she melted. She turned her head so their mouths met, and the kiss was like drowning, softly, deeply, inexorably. His tongue slid against hers as he gripped the back of her head to angle her. To drink from her, never letting her retreat. It was dizzying.

Perfect.

She gripped the front of his dressing gown in response, and the soft rasp of his chest hair peeking through the opening tickled. He closed his other hand around her thigh, firmly, as if anchoring himself to her, and her to him. She bit back a whimper. "Those noises are *mine*," he said against her mouth. "Don't you dare keep them from me."

He shoved her skirts up, claiming the soft, warm skin behind her knee, on the inside of her thigh, and finally, *finally* her quim. She was already desperate for his touch. He stroked between her lips, gathering her wetness before stroking deep. She arched against him, moaning. "More," he demanded, which was the same word echoing through her head, through every corner of her body: *more, more, more.*

He circled her bud gently, then, with more pressure, plunged his fingers inside her, and back to her bud, a maddening rhythm that had her whimpering and panting.

And then he moved his hand away. She clutched at his arm.

"It will be so much better if you wait." He kissed her, and it was slowly and beautifully carnal.

She squirmed in his lap, eager for friction, any kind of contact. She was so *close.*

"Ah ah," he murmured just firm enough to have her intimate muscles quivering. "You'll wait until I give you permission and not before."

She pouted. She was fairly certain she had never pouted in her life. "*Rhys.*"

He only laughed softly.

Want and need shivered through her, and she struggled to

stem the sparks shooting off each other deep inside. "Then I want to touch *you*," she very nearly whined.

Very well, she *did* whine. She wasn't proud of it, but he was making her feral.

He grabbed her wrist in a stern grip when she reached for him. "When I say so."

"Then say so."

"Not yet. Stand up."

She stood up even though her legs already felt weak.

"Now turn around."

He brushed the nape of her neck, trailing his fingertips down to the little button at the top of her dress. Then he undid the laces that closed at the side, and her skirts fell to the floor. He pulled the bodice down slowly, so slowly, until she stood in her stays and chemise.

There was a pause, then he stroked down her spine. "How the devil do these stays come off?"

She laughed, turning around. The laugh died in her throat. His green eyes raked over her hungrily. "They lace at the front," she whispered. "I don't have a lady's maid, remember?"

"Right." He tugged at the laces until they slipped free. She tried not to wish, once again, that she was not wearing something silkier, frothier. "Perfect," he said. "I like opening presents, but too much frippery just gets in the way."

She stifled a groan. "I thought that out loud, didn't I?"

"Shh," he said, tightening his grip on her waist. "I'm working."

The candlelight played over his dark, tousled hair, over his strong fingers as he guided her gaping stays down over her hips, pulling her stockings with them until they joined her dress on the floor. "Kitty?"

"Yes?"

"I will buy you new undergarments."

"Why w—"

His big hands closed around the material already worn thin

and pulled. Her shift ripped, the sound shocking in the quiet library. He had literally torn it from her body. Her bud pulsed with awareness. Her nipples pebbled at the brush of air.

She stood wearing nothing but his ring, gleaming on her finger. He was still fully clothed, though his cravat was undone and his sleeves rolled up, coat discarded. It was a simple thing to picture him ruling the Underworld. She was exposed before him, vulnerable. Trying not to squirm with desire. Waiting for his next command.

She ought to be bristling with defiance.

That might be fun too.

But tonight, it was so nice just to *be*. Not to have to make every decision, to constantly adjust plans or make hard, imperfect choices. There was no strategy here, and it was freeing—soothing, even as it excited every nerve ending until every brush against her skin felt positively wanton. His breath ghosting over her had tension sparking deep inside again.

"Oh, not yet, firecracker," he breathed against her belly.

"I need—"

"I know what you need."

"Only because you are withholding it from me," she grumbled.

"Poor firecracker," he said with false sympathy and a smile that made the hairs on the back of her neck prickle. "Are you suffering?"

She raked her fingers through his hair and tightened her hold. "Yes."

His eyes flared, as green as the dancing lights in the north that she had only read about. She twisted slightly, pulling his hair. His breath caught, low and harsh. Like music. She understood now why he wanted to claim all of the noises she made.

He surged up, catching her off her feet. She squeaked, and he spun her around, laying her gently in the chair. "Didn't anyone ever warn you not to taunt the Devil?"

She couldn't answer. His mouth was already on her and he

was feasting with obscene sounds that proved he wanted to be nowhere else. He wedged his broad shoulders between her knees, widening her for his pleasure. She was already half mad with her own pleasure. He sucked and licked at her until she was squirming and gasping, trying to get away, trying to get closer. He slipped two fingers into her glistening heat, rolling her bud into his warm mouth. She jerked—too many sensations, too much tension building. "Not yet," he said. "I could do this all night."

"Please," she babbled. "Please, *please*."

"I suppose," he finally relented. "Since you asked so nicely." He did not alter the pattern of his ministrations, only went deeper, sucked harder. "Now," he growled. "Come *now*."

Her climax finally slipped its leash and bore down on her, all soft silk and teeth. It was almost too much, just this side of pain, demanding everything from her. She *keened*. There was no other word for it. And then she went limp, blinking. There was such luxury to this kind of exhaustion.

"I think I'm seeing stars," she murmured.

"Good." Rhys shrugged out of his dressing gown and used it to wipe his face, before tossing it away. His cheekbones were flushed. The rest of him was gloriously naked as he knelt before her—muscles shifting, an intriguing line that cut from his hip and lower, one she wanted to bite. He thickened as she watched, cock growing even harder, the tip engorged and glistening. For her. She scraped her nails lightly down his chest. She wanted to purr. Actually purr.

"Your turn to stand up," she ordered him.

He rose slowly, as if he were doing her a favor by obeying. *This man.* She wanted to grin, even as her quim pulsed at the way he looked down at her. As if she were beautiful; as if he might die if she didn't take him in her hand or in her mouth. She had to clench her legs together. She stroked him lightly, once, twice, then bent her head to explore, first with a kiss, then by licking the length of him. He shuddered. She glanced up at him through her lashes, and he groaned. "I've never done this before," she admitted. "I don't want to hurt you."

"You won't hurt me," he assured her, even as he sounded like he was in pain. She gathered it was the good kind, the kind that tickled and teased. "Do what feels right, firecracker. What feels good. I can guarantee it will also feel goo—" he broke off with a gasp because she had taken his words to heart and closed her mouth around his cock. "Jesus," he growled.

She swirled her tongue around him as she tried to suck him deeper.

"Jesus," he said again. "You feel fucking perfect."

She did feel rather perfect, like a queen, even though she was on her knees. He tasted clean and warm, faintly of salt. She licked and sucked until her cheeks hollowed and her jaw ached in the best way. She used her hands after that, gripping him hard even as she licked the tip of his cock almost delicately. His thighs tensed. They were so thick, so strong. And shaking. She smiled around him.

"You are the only devil here," Rhys said, pulling free of her, only to press her back into the thick rug, The soft light of the oil lamps cocooned them, glinting off the gilded titles of the books, the swirls of a sunset painted behind tree branches on the ceiling. Of *course* it would be in a library surrounded by books. The rightness of it had her reaching for him as her thighs opened and he surged between them.

He entered her slowly, teasing again, but with a darker, sweeter edge of passion. She arched to meet every thrust, demanding more. She tightened around him too soon, intimate muscles fluttering as her pleasure crested again. And again. He panted roughly in her ear and his hips stuttered. He pulled out and spent himself into his dressing gown crumpled beside her, his tendons and muscles straining, teeth bared.

He finally turned his head and kissed her, sweat gleaming on his shoulders. He lowered himself and pulled her on top of him. "The floor is hard," he muttered.

She snuggled into him, comfortable and happy even as worry

began to nibble at her. What if—

"Kitty." Rhys said her name both sternly and fondly, and she loved it. He gently ran his fingers through her tangled hair. It was soothing. "The worries will be there tomorrow."

"I didn't say anything."

"You are a loud thinker." He continued to stroke her hair, wrapping his other arm tighter around her. "Rest now, firecracker."

DAWN FOUND DEVIL in his study, examining a package with sapphire earrings, a collar of more sapphires with diamonds, and a tiara fit for a queen. They sparkled under the light of the candle on his desk.

He intended to see Kitty wearing them.

Nothing *but* them.

Just as soon as he could convince her to accept them. She was skittish, mule headed.

Perfect.

He'd never had to *convince* anyone to accept gifts before. To beg to let him spoil them. Because he *was* going to pamper her, however covertly he had to do it. It was a primal need. A demand inside his blood and bones.

Protect. Pamper.

Keep.

Whatever that means.

He'd have better luck intimidating the stars from the sky.

He loved that about her too, damn it—her strength, her determination. The freckles on her lower back. The way she moaned. Tasted.

It was too damn early to be this hard. To know she was upstairs right now, soft and warm in her bed. But she needed rest, despite what she might have to say on the matter. She needed care.

Stealing from her house was such a good decision that he was only sorry he had not done so before. She was at war with the world with no one at her back. No more. Not ever again.

At the knock at the study door, he tucked the jewelry away. "Come."

It wasn't Kitty, unfortunately.

"Shipment was taken again," Macleod said. "Bastards stole it barely ten feet from the docks."

"Which one?" Devil asked.

"The bourbon from America." Macleod narrowed his eyes. "You don't look upset."

"Do I ever?"

"Your left eye twitches."

Devil leaned back in his chair. "The bourbon was delivered to Yelena's house. You can have it picked up and taken to the Sins. The gin coming in from Holland will go to Soho Square and the chocolate goes to the modiste on Oxford Street. Knock twice at the back door or she'll set her dog on you."

"You cagey bastard."

Devil shrugged. "Sabotage is boring. And Portsmouth doesn't get to talk about the Sins, never mind get in the way." He smiled, and it was his smile from the Continent. "And you might want to tell the nearest magistrate that he just received a trunk of smuggled wine. He can't afford the tax, seeing as he owes me a fortune. How embarrassing for him."

"I don't recall a debt."

"Neither will he, but who will believe him?"

"A hit to his reputation and sense of power will hurt more than any monetary debt." Macleod whistled. "You did always tell us to know the enemy better than they know themselves."

"I know he's hiding something," Devil said. "Three dead wives is a lot even for his cronies to overlook. Something else is going on. He's an earl, not a duke or a prince."

"We'll get our man. We always do."

Devil thought of Kitty.

"Damn right we will."

CHAPTER TWENTY-THREE

DUE TO HER extensive and varied reading material, Kitty knew what to expect after a night of torrid lovemaking with a vampire, say. Or a Minotaur, or a kraken. An *actual* devil.

She did *not* know what to expect this morning, however. Never mind devils—earls were even more mythical than monsters.

For one thing, she woke in her bed knowing full well that she had not fallen asleep there. She had fallen asleep in Rhys's arms, her bones soft and warm as melted wax. Had he carried her all the way up to her chamber? Was he the one who had tucked the coverlet around her? Had she snored? Murmured sleepy poems about his thighs? The way she thought about him being properly betrothed to someone else and bared her teeth?

She buried her face into her pillow. He wasn't for her.

But oh, a woman could dream. She had never felt anything akin to what he made her feel. Even when she wasn't naked.

It was extremely inconvenient.

And no one's problem but her own. She could handle pontificating vicars, disparaging ladies, any number of flying vegetables. She could handle violent men shouting at her because they could not find their wives. Her family. Disdain.

So she could certainly handle her own self.

She washed with cold water from the basin and pulled on one

of the dresses she had packed. It was her favorite one, the one with the pretty gathers at the capped sleeves. She pinned up her hair. Took it down, brushed it, pinned it up again. Wiped her damp palms on her skirt. Called herself a fool and a coward and marched herself down the stairs like a soldier going to battle.

Shelby met her with a smile. "The breakfast room is just this way."

"Thank you, Shelby."

She was shown to a room painted with murals of a country hillside, complete with shining rivers where nymphs gathered. The table was long enough to seat twenty people. The sideboard glittered with crystal bowls of sugar and marmalade and spiced honeys, as well as mountains of potatoes, rashers of bacon, coddled eggs, fried trout, and baskets of pastries. There was enough food for a dozen people. For an army.

Devil sat with a cup of steaming coffee and a folded newspaper. Across from him, Macleod drank tea. Yelena was beside him, eating raspberries with a gold fork. "Good morning," she said, smiling.

"Good morning." Kitty smiled back. This was a lot of smiling for someone who generally communicated with grimaces before noon.

"Good morning, Miss Caldecott," Devil murmured.

His deep voice had the same effect it always did: it shot straight through her body like mulled wine on a cold day. She swallowed and tried not to look like she needed to fan herself. Did women really swoon at his feet? Probably.

Had he really carried her up to her bed in his arms? And she had slept through it like a cabbagehead?

She turned to the sideboard so her blush would not give her away entirely, but then could only hover there uncertainly. Could she serve herself? Was she supposed to sit down and wait for a footman? That did not seem expeditious. Her arms worked perfectly well. She could scoop up her own eggs. But she swore her aunt had once gone on a tirade about being served breakfast properly, and now she did not know what to do.

That was too many decisions to make before even a single cup of tea.

"Angus, make a plate for Miss Caldecott with some of everything," Devil said calmly. "So she may decide what she likes."

Kitty turned back to the table in relief. She sat in the nearest chair, probably a little too abruptly to be considered perfectly genteel. Something about the way Macleod also sat in his chair, alert and as though he had a claymore hiding under the table, as well as the way the footmen stood at attention. Even Shelby had the same wary stance. And they shared quite the collection of scars between them.

Something clicked in her head, like puzzle pieces. Everyone knew Devil had his own soldiers, but she had not realized before now that it might be literal. "You fought in the war together," she murmured, one of the many mysteries of Devil coming to the light. "On the Continent. Didn't you? All of you?"

"Aye, well spotted." MacLeod nodded.

She turned to Devil, searching for new clues, new stories. He sat so still and expressionless that she knew she had hit a nerve. "I'm sorry."

"He was our commanding officer. Saw us through Waterloo. And the years before."

"Macleod." Devil said it softly, but it reverberated like a command across a battlefield.

The men who had returned from the war with France had not returned the same. That much she knew for herself, though she had not thought many earls went fighting overseas, and certainly not through the blood and mud of Waterloo.

"Have a crumpet," Yelena said lightly into the silence. Her black hair gleamed, coiled in perfect curls.

Kitty helped herself to a crumpet. A cup of strong tea was placed before her, with a dish of sugar and a crystal swan that poured milk from its beak. "Tom thinks he has good taste," Devil said drily. Kitty did not miss the way the others relaxed their posture when it was clear he was changing the subject of the conversation.

Kitty poured herself some milk and smiled. It was such an odd, sweet thing to find in a house dripping with velvet and gold. Not to mention assassins. Footmen-turned-bodyguards. Soldiers home from war. She drank her tea, unsurprised to find it was the best she had drunk in her entire life, with hints of bergamot and vanilla. "I want to swim in this."

"Shelby, make sure this tea is available to Miss Caldecott whenever she wants it."

The butler bowed. He was standing near the door in case he was needed, with three of those footmen-turned-bodyguards in their livery. What a strange thing to have people standing about watching you eat. Especially with so many daggers gleaming on their persons. Now she knew what to look for: at the top of the boot, inside the lining of a coat, in the small of the back.

Kitty ate eggs and toasted bread with butter and honey and something green and salty that she loved but could not have named on pain of death. There was sweet custard topped with stewed raspberries. First thing in the morning, on a random, ordinary day. Maybe there *was* something to this ludicrously decadent lifestyle.

But she could not let it distract her. She could not let *Devil* distract her.

Even if he had carried her in his arms, even when he insisted she was supplied with tea. Even if he had saved her from abduction—she absolutely, positively, could *not* fall in love with him.

Too late.

She was in love with Devil. Lord Birmingham. Rhys. All the parts that made him who he was.

The knowledge of it flooded through her, and she would be as successful fighting it as she would have been fighting the tide.

It wasn't just inconvenient. It was a bloody *disaster*.

"Miss Caldecott, are you well?" MacLeod asked. "You've

turned green."

She forced a smile. "Perfectly well."

She was not at all in love. With the wrong man.

Liar.

"I would like to find Lady Caroline's lady's maid and speak to her," she said instead. "Servants always know more than anyone else in a household. I assume she is the Agnes mentioned in the book." The book she'd stolen. "It's as good a place as any to start, anyway."

"Very well. I'll go with you," Devil said. He was darkly and impeccably dressed as always, wearing power and menace as easily as other people wore perfume. His green eyes were sharp and otherworldly. His handsomeness made others feel awkward, as if they had too many hands, not enough feet. An extra nose. She could attest to it personally, even if his glance now made her only think of bare skin and fingers gripping her hips.

"You can't come with us," Kitty blurted out.

He looked mildly insulted. "Why not?"

"No lady's maid is going to tell the truth with you looming over her."

"I do not *loom.*"

"You are the Lord of Looming. And brooding."

"Arc you quitc finishcd?"

She tilted her head. "The Daunting Devil. Harrowing Hades." She flashed a grin. "*Now* I'm finished. Maybe."

"Oh, please say you aren't," Tom interrupted, dragging himself toward the silver carafe of coffee. It was shaped like a bear rearing up on its back legs, clearly another one of his purchases. She loved it. "What time is it?"

"Half past ten."

He shuddered. His hair was not quite tamed and he wore a dressing gown and no slippers. There was lipstick on his neck. "We aren't becoming morning people, are we?"

"The Dastardly Devil?" Kitty asked. "Perish the thought."

"I really do like you," Tom yawned at her over his cup.

"I like you too."

Devil sat back in his chair, faintly amused and also exasperated. "The lady's maid?" he asked, steering back to the matter at hand.

"Oh, right," Kitty said. She licked a crumb off her finger, realized it was probably a terribly gauche thing to do, contemplated fretting over it, caught the flare in Devil's eyes, and decided right then and there that Mayfair manners were not going to interfere with her fun. "Um."

"A lady's maid will be too scared of repercussions to speak freely if you are there," Yelena explained as Kitty tried to herd her thoughts back together. It was as successful as herding cats toward the sea.

"Yes," she said. "That. Especially if she has been around the likes of Portsmouth for any length of time at all. She'll be scared."

Devil looked disgruntled. It was endearing.

Kitty did not have time to be endeared.

"Right, we're off, then," she declared.

Devil frowned. "Take Brutus." Brutus was his most fearsome footman, for lack of a better term. Man-at-arms? Captain? Soldier. He was not as big as the Viking brothers, but everything about him screamed a slow and bloody death. He probably made rampaging bulls cry with fear. Kitty adored him. But he was not right for the task.

"He is not going to make a maid feel any more at ease." She rolled her eyes. "Leave the spinsters and the maids to me, if you please."

"That's why you hired me," Yelena pointed out. "To protect Miss Caldecott."

Devil nodded. "Fine."

Kitty curtsied before him, as low as she knew how, as though he were an emperor. But also: mockingly. "I wasn't asking for your permission," she said tartly.

The word *permission* sizzled between them, rife with memories of sweaty whimpers, desperate hands.

"Brat," he said softly.

She sent him one last taunting smile and then hurried out of the breakfast room before she could lose her momentary victory.

THANKS TO PRIYA'S folder on Lady Caroline, it was not too difficult to discover that "Agnes" was a Miss Agnes Jones, and she now worked for a dowager who liked to sit in the sun by the Serpentine of an afternoon and doze. Agnes sat next to her on the bench, watching the ducks and glaring at any pickpockets who dared stray too near, thinking an old woman and her middle-aged companion easy pickings. The dowager snored on, blissfully unaware.

Kitty would not have wanted to face off against Agnes either. She looked formidable. It was not likely that either Brutus *or* Devil would have put her off. That would be helpful.

Probably.

"Miss Agnes Jones?"

Agnes's mouth flattened suspiciously. "Yes."

"I'm Kitty Cald—"

"I know who you are."

Kitty blinked at her. "You do?"

"You own that shop."

"I do. Perhaps I ought to change the name to That Shop, since that is all anyone ever calls it."

Agnes shrugged. "I like it there, whatever you call it."

"You do? Thank you."

"Don't read much, but it feels nice."

Kitty beamed at her. "That might be the nicest thing anyone has ever said to me."

Agnes snorted. "Your man needs lessons, then."

Kitty grinned. She couldn't help it. "I will tell him you said so."

Agnes sat back, the sunshine playing over the cap pinned to her fair hair. She looked strong, tired. Sad. "I doubt that's why you sought me out."

"No," Kitty admitted. "No, it's not." She took Lord Tadworth's *Delights of the Duchess*, volume seven, from her reticule. Agnes's gaze darted around, landing on the water, the trees, a nursemaid with a pram, a dog slipping its leash, then finally, *finally* on the book in Kitty's hands. Kitty opened it to the page with the neat handwriting. "This belonged to Lady Caroline, didn't it?"

"Why do you want to know?" Agnes asked flatly. "Did Lord Portsmouth send you?"

"Definitely not." Kitty decided it would be more expedient to just tell her the truth. "I want to know because if I don't do something, my sister will be his next bride."

"If that's true, don't just do something, do *anything*."

Kitty shivered. "This was her book, wasn't it?"

"Yes, she was a great reader. Went to *your* shop often enough."

"She did?"

"Yes. She and Miss Campbell would send books back and forth to each other. They grew up together, you see. And Lady Caro would not disdain the friendship even when she became a countess and Lord Portsmouth forbade her from the association."

Miss Campbell. Kitty stored the name away for later. "Do you know what their plan was?"

Agnes shook her head.

Kitty rubbed her breastbone. "Blast. Can you tell me about her? Lady Caroline?"

"She was young, barely twenty-two, when she married. Her parents were ecstatic. They chose to look the other way on the fate of his previous wives as soon as Lord Portsmouth told them he did not need Lady Caro's dowry."

"Sounds familiar." Kitty grimaced. And Lord Portsmouth was in his early forties. She already knew his other wives were in their early twenties as well. Evie was only nineteen. "Did she love him?"

Agnes snorted. "That man is unlovable, though he puts on a

good mask, as long as he gets his way. As long as he gets exactly what he wants."

"And what did he want?"

"A male heir," Agnes replied bluntly.

"That's why his wives…do not last?" Kitty said. "Why he keeps marrying younger and younger."

"He's obsessed. Controlling. Desperate." Agnes sighed. "Lady Caro knew it was going to get even worse. We had a plan, you see. But in the end, she just vanished."

"Do you think she ran away? Could she be safe somewhere?"

"I hope so," Agnes said. "I pray for that every day."

Yelena handed her a handkerchief because she was the type to carry such a thing, while Kitty had two books, the key to her shop, and a wrinkled, empty packet of headache powder in her reticule. "Lady Caro sounds resourceful," she said comfortingly.

"She was clever as ten cats." Agnes nodded. "I hope your sister Evangeline is the same, Miss Caldecott."

"How do you know her name?"

Agnes pulled the newspaper from her employers' slack hands. "The dowager loves the gossip pages. She likes to predict who will have a falling out." Agnes unfolded the paper to the section she was searching for. "Your sister's engagement is mentioned here. And here. And again here."

Kitty went cold. "Bollocks."

Agnes smiled briefly, as if finally trusting her. Her smile died. "If Lord Portsmouth has made the announcement public, there's no stopping him."

"*I* will stop him."

"I wish you luck, Miss Caldecott. I truly do."

"Thank you," Kitty said. She would take all the luck she could find.

They were running out of time.

CHAPTER TWENTY-FOUR

"THAT WAS NOT as successful as I was hoping it would be," Kitty muttered to Yelena as they walked back to the carriage with the waiting brothers Winchester.

"Bu now you know for certain that Lady Caroline is more likely to be on the run than killed by Portsmouth."

"I do?" She hoped so.

"If Lord Portsmouth murdered her, he would not be asking her lady's maid anything about her whereabouts. And if he thought she saw something she should not have seen, I doubt she would be alive right now."

Kitty nodded slowly. "That's true." It wasn't much to pin her hopes on, but she would take anything. Both for Evie's sake and for "Lady Caro." She was feeling quite protective of the young woman she had never met. "I wish she had gone to the Spinster Society for help."

"I suppose the society will have to go to *her* instead."

"Are you acquainted with Lady Priya?"

Yelena smiled. "Lady Priya knows everyone."

"Well, she knows everyone's secrets, at any rate."

"That too."

"I wish I could talk to her." But it was too risky to Evie. Lord Portsmouth would know immediately were Kitty to go anywhere near the Spinster Society house. She was lucky he did not know already, to be honest. "I guess I will settle for talking to Miss Campbell instead. Perhaps she still has some of the *Duchess* books and I can piece the rest of the letter together. *Someone* has to know where Lady Caro is if she doesn't."

She worried at it as the carriage was expertly handled around street sweepers, carts overfilled with wares, shouting hackney drivers. And when thinking and more thinking did not produce any miraculous results, Kitty let herself think about something else. Just for a moment. She had overheard a customer once say that the best way to solve a puzzle was to let yourself forget about it for just a moment. To walk somewhere new, bake a loaf of bread. Embroider a cushion. Anything.

Kitty was not sure if thinking about Devil counted, since he was a puzzle himself.

"Have you known Devil long?" She probably should not ask personal questions. It would make no difference whatsoever. Devil was Devil and she was…Kitty. None of that had changed, no matter how often she found herself thinking about his forearms, or his thighs, or the way he almost smiled. Mostly at her.

Yelena nodded. She was lovely in her walking dress, the ribbons matching the flowers on her bonnet. Kitty did not have a bonnet. And she knew she was already wrinkled from the day. "Lord Birmingham was friends with my husband," Yelena replied.

"On the Continent?" Kitty asked tentatively.

"Yes. They saved each other's lives more than once. But even Devil could not save him from a wound gone to rot. Lord knows he tried."

"I'm sorry."

"It was a few years ago. At least I was there to hold him."

"Is that where you learned your hatpin tricks? The army."

Yelena smiled. "The British Army is not keen on teaching women to fight. Especially women from another country. But my grandfather was as vicious as a cornered dog. He taught me what he could, and then my *yaya* taught me the rest. She was the only one who could best him. What of your family?"

Kitty snorted. "My grandfather likes to throw wet cabbages at my shop."

Yelena frowned. "Why?"

"Because I am a disgrace."

"Is that all?" she scoffed.

"But he's also scared of my grandmother, and sometimes she writes him very long letters and he magically leaves London for a few weeks."

"I think I would like your grandmother."

"She is a termagant. I adore her."

"And your sister?"

"Not a termagant. But I adore her as well. Enough to take on Devil and force him to help me."

"Devil cannot be forced to do anything he does not wish to do."

It was not much longer before they arrived at their destination, Yelena's words still ringing in Kitty's head.

They knocked at the door of a small house with a brass knocker in the shape of a fish. A man answered, pale, wearing a waistcoat slightly too large for his frame. He scowled at them.

"Hello," Kitty said with her best shopkeeper smile, the one that did not dim even in the face of insults, arguments over prices, or the same questions repeated over and over again. "I am Miss Caldecott and this is Mrs. Dimitriou. We are here to see Miss Campbell."

"She's not here."

"Oh dear," Kitty said. "Do you know when she might be accepting callers? We have an appointment, you see."

"Not anymore, you don't, young lady."

"Erm." Kitty blinked. Did he recognize her from the bookshop? Was he insulted by her very presence? What a nuisance. "Why is that?"

"Because my daughter is missing and has been missing for the last two weeks."

Kitty could only stare at him for too long a moment. With every step forward she managed on this investigation, she was yanked back another two steps.

Poor Evie. Poor Lady Caroline. And poor Miss Campbell. If they were waiting for her to save them, they would be sorely disappointed.

No. None of that. There was no time for wallowing and whinging. Only war. Target: Lord Portsmouth.

There were no defeats, only minor setbacks.

Still, she lowered her gaze so Mr. Campbell would not be alarmed by the martial gleam he would no doubt find there. She added a wobble to her voice for good measure. "I'm terribly sorry, you've shocked me. Missing?" She knew she went red then pale. She always did, at the least provocation. It was rather helpful this time. "Might I trouble you for a glass of water? I feel a bit faint."

He took her arm and helped her to the nearest chair in the parlor. It was small and tidy, with a basket of knitting on the floor and a row of books on the windowsill behind her. She slid them a sidelong glance as Mr. Campbell called for his wife. She bustled down the stairs, snapping, "Shout at me again, old man."

Mr. Campbell cleared his throat. Mrs. Campbell noticed Yelena, then Kitty, who did her best to look feeble. Unassuming. Wan.

"This lady needs some water. And some smelling salts?"

Gah. No, thank you.

Mrs. Campbell marched away, returning with a glass of water.

"I'm sorry to be such a bother," Kitty murmured.

"This is Miss Caldecott, a friend of Elspeth," Mr. Campbell said.

Mrs. Campbell pressed her lips together as if forcing herself not to cry at the sound of her daughter's name. Then she narrowed her eyes. "I knew all of Elspeth's friends."

Kitty nodded. "We were not close friends." A truth followed

by a lie. "I run a bookshop, and she often visited with her friend. Lady Caroline, Countess Portsmouth? Perhaps you know her?" *Also missing, incidentally.* "I enjoyed our conversations very much."

"She loved books."

"*Loves* books," Mrs. Campbell corrected her husband fiercely.

"Of course, of course."

"We haven't seen her in over a month," Mrs. Campbell continued, mostly, Kitty thought, because someone was listening to her. "We hired a Bow Street runner, but he's found nothing. Poor Caro is gone too."

"Are they together, do you think?"

"They always were. But…that man…her *husband*." She spat the word. Kitty did not blame her.

"Hush, Mrs. Campbell."

"I *won't* hush."

"We are not friendly with Lord Portsmouth," Kitty assured them. "What of Lady Portsmouth's parents?"

"They left the country altogether barely a week after she married. They might not even know she is dead." A strangled sob. "Poor Caro. They are in Italy. Or Istanbul. Somewhere it does not rain." The disdain coating Mrs. Campbell's words could have tarred every boat in the Thames.

"I don't wish to presume," Kitty said, "but you might try talking to Lady Priya Langdon. She might be able to help."

"Another aristocrat?" More disdain, in heaps and heaps.

"She is more than a dowager countess," Kitty said. "Please, believe me."

"Can't hurt, Mrs. Campbell," Mr. Campbell said.

Kitty looked at Yelena, meeting her gaze. She widened her eyes in a way she hoped conveyed clear instructions.

If Yelena's slight frown was anything to go by, it did not, in fact, convey any instructions whatsoever.

Kitty finished her water and set the glass down, deliberately too near the edge of the table. It toppled and hit the floor with a crack. Kitty scrambled back as though the shards had cut her, exclaiming all the while. "Oh, I'm so clumsy! My apologies!"

Yelena rushed in to help, giving Kitty the time she needed to once again prove the Ladies' Association for Moral Standards right.

She *was* a Menace to All Good Society.

She had a reputation to uphold, after all.

"I SHOULD HAVE hired a Bow Street Runner as well," Kitty said as they stepped once more into the carriage after rushing out in a flurry of apologies. It would have normally taken her most of the day to walk this route across London. "They must be expensive."

"Devil works with them," Yelena said, unpinning her bonnet and tossing it aside. She massaged her scalp. "I cannot abide English hats, even all of these years later. The Runners come to Devil as often as he goes to them. If they knew anything, you would know it."

"Oh. I suppose that makes sense, with all of the wagers and whatnot." And he had mentioned it once. She had been suddenly desperate to know where the Bow Street Runners met and what she could sell in order to be able to afford their services. She swallowed, her throat itchy. "They must be together? Lady Caro and Miss Campbell? Two friends going missing around the same time cannot be a coincidence."

"I would be very surprised if it were," Yelena agreed.

"Well, the Runners might have a fancy office and an earl and actual skills, but I have something they do not," Kitty declared.

"Aplomb?"

"Better." She pulled three books from various parts of her person from her stays to her reticule. "I have these."

She should probably stop stealing soon. It was not good *ton*. And it might get her in gaol, if not outright hanged.

On the other hand, a life of criminal pursuits might also help her find Lady Caroline and her friend and save her sister. With apologies to Lord Tadworth and the Campbells, she would carry on for the moment.

The Delights of the Duchess, volumes three, four, and five, papered in a very inoffensive concealing print of flowers that Kitty sold for just this purpose—hiding your naughty books in plain sight.

"However did you manage it?" Yelena asked. "Is that why you asked to sit down?"

"I was feeling faint," Kitty said primly.

Yelena laughed. "Even I believed you were overcome for a moment there. Well done."

"I'll return them," Kitty felt the need to clarify. "Eventually. With a little gift. And a new glass."

Yelena shrugged, supremely unbothered with a spot of thievery.

Kitty requested they stop at St. George's, where she tucked a note into the oak tree gate. *Please help my sister. Please let me help you. K.C. Golden Griffin Bookshop.*

When they reached the bookshop, Wulf was in his usual guard position but also eating a raspberry tart—mostly because a very diminutive lady insisted upon it as a thank you for carrying her packages to a hackney.

Inside, a large box had been delivered from Fortnum & Mason for Kitty: the tea she had enjoyed so much just this morning, sent by Devil.

Kitty stood clutching a tin of tea leaves to her chest for an embarrassingly long time.

CHAPTER TWENTY-FIVE

Dinner at Rochester House was like nothing Kitty had ever experienced.

She was accustomed to her distracted father drifting in and out between high-stakes games, her aunt's pointed lectures, Evie's attempts to keep the peace. More often than not, Kitty remained at the shop for a quick meal of bread and cheese and then felt guilty for abandoning her sister.

She missed her sister terribly, but she did not miss her father or her aunt. She wondered if that made her a bad person. If she cared.

The cutlery was silver and a single fork cost more than her wardrobe. The goblets were cut crystal, the tablecloth cream-colored lace. It was a crime to eat on it. Some old woman had likely spent months working on it by the light of a single, awful-smelling tallow candle, her fingers gnarled and aching.

"Daphne Penderghast is half my age and suggested I soak my head in a pail of slop when I asked her if she would rather I find her other work," Devil said drily, as if Kitty amused him deeply.

She closed her eyes briefly. She really had to learn how to keep her every thought inside her head.

"That sounds dull," he said.

"Stop it."

"Stop what?"

"Reading my mind. I am sure I didn't say that last part out loud."

"Are you?"

"Mostly sure." She made a face. "Probably."

Tom sat across the table watching them as if they were the most fascinating play ever to grace Drury Lane. Beside him was Yelena, and Macleod, Brutus, and Godric had joined them as well. None of them wore silks or brocades or diamond buckles. It made her feel better about her simple dress, the one she had borrowed from the Spinster Society house. It was nicer than all of hers, with nary an ink stain on the sleeve or bodice. Yet.

"Are you very shocked to be eating with simple soldiers?" Tom grinned at her. He wore diamond buckles and a brocade vest, but it did not make her feel smaller. It only made him happy. She was too used to diamonds and pearls being used as weapons, subtly or otherwise.

Godric looked up, pained. "We can eat in the kitchen. I didn't think."

"You'll do no such thing," Kitty said sharply. "Godric, you are aware by now, I am sure, of the sorts of books I mostly sell and lend?" His cheeks turned ruddy. She took that as an affirmative. "So you see, *I* should be the one eating in the kitchen."

"No one is eating in the kitchen," Devil said in that mild way of his, which was not mild at all.

Kitty liked this table and this room and this group of people eating together. She liked this man. And as she was very aware that their time together was limited, she did not bring up the kitchen again. Except to offer her firstborn child for another serving of the best strawberry trifle she had eaten in her entire life.

"How is your ankle?" Devil asked her as they rose from their chairs to move to the drawing room.

"Barely hurts at all," she assured him.

"Bet it feels better than that blighter's ankle does after trying to snatch you away," Tom said with a vengeful glee.

"Tom…" Devil said.

"What do you mean?" Kitty asked.

Tom grinned. "Look at the time. I'm late to…be somewhere else." He took off with a jaunty wave.

Kitty narrowed her eyes. "What did he mean? About the man who tried to abduct me?"

Devil shrugged. "He hurt your ankle. So I broke his."

She gaped at him. "You can't just—"

He raised an eyebrow. "He hurt you."

"But—"

"Now he knows better. So does everyone else."

He shrugged again as if that was the matter settled.

SHE FOUND HERSELF in the garden some time later wondering what was wrong with her that Devil's violence on her behalf did not upset her. No one had ever done anything like that for her before.

It was unacceptable, of course. Inappropriate. She should be shocked.

She should be feeling a great many things she was not feeling, and *not* feeling a great many things she *was* feeling.

She should *not* be fighting a secret smile. Not here in this beautiful Mayfair garden where she could only smell mint and roses and not a hint of the Thames. Mayfair did not escape the ubiquitous yellow fog completely, but it hung in wisps, allowing starlight to peek through. She knew in the later weeks of summer the stink of the Thames would reach even here, and the neighborhood would pack up for their country estates. She imagined patchwork hills, stone walls, clear rivers frothing through groves of trees. It would be lovely. But this garden lit by candles with white gravel footpaths and benches tucked under rose arbors was even lovelier.

Because it belonged to Devil. And he was here sharing it with her.

She knew he was there before he made a sound. Her body

recognized his nearness. The amber and wood smoke smell of him. Her pulse thrummed in her wrists and throat and belly. He stepped out of the shadows, looming over her.

"I should have guessed that you would not sit on one of the perfectly good benches."

She had found a soft corner of grass tucked under an arch of red roses. "I like it here."

"I like you here too," he said softly, sitting next to her.

She flushed, feeling suddenly shy. She was not used to compliments. His gaze tracked her blush, the heat of it traveling up her throat. She was not used to feeling shy, either. She generally had no time for it.

"Are you planning on sleeping out here?" he asked. "With the grasshoppers and the nightingales?"

"Maybe. I have never slept outside before. You must have done during the war."

"Yes."

"Do you ever miss it?"

"No."

"Will I shock the neighbors?" she asked wryly. "It's a talent of mine, after all."

"Don't worry, I have thoroughly shocked them already. They know not to bother us back here."

"The *neighbors* might," she scoffed. "But I am quite certain you have any number of ladies still trying to climb over the garden wall to catch a glimpse of the Devil himself." When he shifted uncomfortably, she turned to grin at him. "I'm right, aren't I?"

"Certainly not."

"I am! I knew it." The tiny triumph at catching him out was swiftly replaced with an odd sense of discomfort. Why would he be here with her when debutantes and widows from the length and breadth of England probably daydreamed about him on a regular basis? In fact, there was more than one novel in her circulating library with a dark devil of a hero, usually named something like Hades or Sebastian or Maximillian, who was uncannily similar to Devil, right down to his chilling green eyes. Not that she found them chilling anymore.

At all.

"Do they leave you tokens?" she asked, wondering why she was torturing herself with details that did not matter. "They must be very beautiful," she added before he could answer, and she sounded a little more wistful than she meant to.

"*You* are beautiful."

Now he was mocking her. She was not long and lithe and beautiful. She did not have fortune or connections or land. She did not even have a proper set of stays that did such interesting things to a woman's decolletage. She had red hair and freckles and an upper lip that was too big for the rest of her mouth.

And debt. Mustn't forget that.

When she shifted to move away, his fingers closed around her wrist. "Why do you do that?"

She stilled. "Do what?"

"Doubt me."

"I...don't."

"Have I lied to you?" he asked. He still had not let go of her wrist. He must surely feel her pulse wild under his thumb.

"No," she admitted reluctantly. She was the one who had lied. And stolen.

"Then why not believe me when I tell you that you are beautiful?"

She swallowed. "I suppose it's myself I doubt." She hated acknowledging it out loud. It was embarrassing. Inconsequential.

"Hmm."

"Hmm?"

He nodded solemnly. "I suppose I shall just have to convince you."

His hold tightened abruptly and he tugged, sliding her toward him. His leg pressed between hers, pinning her in place. Had anyone else tried anything similar, she would have kicked them.

Hard.

With Devil, she could only stare up at him, her entire body tingling hotly.

"Well, firecracker?" he asked against her mouth. "Are you going to let me convince you?"

She nodded.

"I can't hear you," he said, tone hardening. Her quim softened and quivered in response. How dare he have this effect on her with just his voice, his words? "Answer me, Catherine."

The sound of her name, rarely used, in his mouth.

She swallowed. "Y-yes."

She wanted to feel the weight of his body pressing into her, but he was looming maddeningly above, so close and yet nowhere close enough. His thigh brushed the heat between her legs.

"Yes, what?" he demanded.

She tried to arch closer. "Yes, you can convince me."

"Not quite."

She stroked her hand down his strong chest, toward the hardening bulge behind the placket of his breeches. He caught her hand and pinned it beside her in the cool grass. She was surprised steam did not come off her. Surely she had melted clean away by now.

"Yes, *you are beautiful*," he corrected her. "Say it."

She gave a little laugh. "I'm not saying *that*."

"Oh, I think you will." He nipped at her bottom lip, and she gasped.

She shook her head mutely.

"Defiant," he murmured, dragging his open mouth along her neck, sucking at the spot under her ear that made her shiver. Again and again.

When his hardness rubbed the spot between her legs that ached fiercely, she moaned.

"Well?"

"I will concede that *you* think I'm beautiful," she said. She could not help adding, "For some reason."

His eyes flared at her continued defiance, both exasperated and amused. "I've said it before and I'll say it again—*you're* the real devil here."

He finally lowered himself onto her, pressing her into the grass. She smelled flowers and mint and rich, deep earth. She was cocooned beneath him, suddenly safe enough to give into her own wildness. Protected.

Her eyes stung, and she pulled him down closer to kiss him because it was all she wanted and because she did not want to explain why she was being weepy and ridiculous. No one had ever made her feel protected. And she was very much afraid she would crave it for the rest of her life, the way she knew she would crave his touch. His body. The way he looked at her, like she was a curiosity he meant to keep for himself. And she was equally afraid—*more* afraid—that if she said any of it out loud, he would feel obligated in some way. And that might actually break her, far quicker than her family, than her sister, than Portsmouth and his men.

"If you are thinking that hard right now, I must be doing something wrong," Devil said. She shook her head, wrapping her leg around his. He kissed her deeply, slowly, before pulling back. "What's going on in that little busy head of yours?"

"Nothing."

He tilted his head. "Now, I know *that's* not true, little liar."

She glanced away. "I do lie."

"Kitty?"

"Yes?"

"I don't care. As long as you don't lie to *me*."

"I've done worse," she admitted even as the building heat inside her body shrieked at her to *stop talking. Immediately.*

Devil's smile quirked, flashing that single, tiny dimple so few people had the privilege of seeing. "Kitty?"

"Yes?"

"I've done much worse than lying too."

She nearly smiled back. "That's different."

"Why?"

"I don't know," she admitted. "It just is. I've never heard of you attacking someone who did not deserve it. They break faith and you punish them. It's different."

His eyes flared, his voice dropping to a hoarse whisper in her ear. "And do you want to be punished?"

"No!" *Yes. Maybe.*

He laughed softly and it did things to her, loosened the muscles in her thighs, tightened the muscles inside her quim until it fluttered.

"I'm trying to tell you something," she said.

"I'm not your confessor, love. But I'll hear anything you want to tell me." He wove the fingers of his free hand into her hair and tightened, pulling her head back. "Go on."

There was no sympathy in his face, no pity.

It helped. It was exactly what she needed.

Even the hint of softness hidden under the stern patience.

"I...blackmailed my only real friend." She had never said so out loud before. Had never looked at it so starkly.

He searched her face, and she couldn't tell if he was surprised or disgusted or bored. Or if he already knew about it. "Tell me."

"I thought she had money to spare and I wanted to take Evie away. I was desperate. Stupid. Selfish."

"Also loving, loyal. Protective."

She shook her head. "That's no excuse. I scared her. I didn't mean to." Clara always seemed so self-possessed. Sharp. "I really thought... Well, I guess we all hide parts of ourselves. And I didn't go through with it," she rushed to add. She never even went to the spot where she had told Clara to leave the money in exchange for keeping her secret that she was the infamous author known as the Nightingale. "Not in the end. I couldn't."

"When was this?"

"At your Devil's Night."

"Let me guess, right before you stole from me?"

She nodded, feeling wretched. Lighter for having spoken it, but also wretched. "My aunt had just pushed my sister in front of a carriage to gain the attention of a single gentleman. She damaged her knee, I think permanently, but it could have been so much worse. And then Lord Portsmouth started to pay her calls and I knew it *would* get so much worse. I was running out of places to hide her. I'm sorry," she said. "For what it's worth."

"Would you do it again?"

She sighed. "I don't know."

"To save your sister?"

"Probably," she said. "Do you see? I'm not a good person, Rhys."

He kept her pinned when she tried to look away. "You're a good sister."

"Not a good friend."

"You made a mistake," he said. "I've made a hundred."

"Are you admitting that you're not perfect?"

"I'll deny it if you tell anyone."

"I...I'll understand if that...changes things between us. I forced your hand as it was."

He smiled again, dark and indulgent. "Is that what you think? That you forced my hand?"

"I blackmailed *you* as well, if you'll recall." He made a scoffing sound. She stared at him, a needle of outrage piercing through her guilt. "Are you mocking my blackmail?"

"Sweetheart, if I didn't want to help you, I wouldn't have."

She scowled. "Excuse me, I stole from the *Devil*. No one else has managed that, thank you very much."

"That's true. It did get my attention." His eyes hardened. "And I suppose you owe me an apology."

"I'm...sorry?"

"Oh, I think we can do better than that." He bit her earlobe.

"Rhys."

"Yes?"

"I... How can you still..."

He caught her gaze, kept it. She felt naked, exposed. "Kitty, I was on the Continent for too many years. My men and I didn't march with the others. We didn't fight on the battlefield; we didn't wear gold braid and medals. We did the things no gentleman would consider doing. And we did it in exchange for thousands *not* being lost in battles that might not need to be fought. Was it right? Fair? Just?" He didn't look away. She stroked down his spine as he talked, wanting to touch him. To offer comfort. "I couldn't tell you. I lost men, but I kept more alive than I lost, and in the end it had to be enough. We were unprepared, untrained. The officers in charge were gentlemen with titles, like me, who didn't know a maneuver from their own arse. I just wanted to get people home."

She kept touching him, down his back, the hair at his nape. "I'm sorry you went through that. I'm sorry for all of you."

"I chose my fate," he said. "I was young and stupid and only wanted to infuriate my father. After a particularly bad quarrel, I purchased a commission. And I left my brother behind."

Kitty swallowed. "Your father…"

"Was not a good man. The Rochesters are not easy men. I knew, but even I underestimated it. I was at war, but so was Tom, at thirteen, and he received no medals for it. So I know about feeling remorse," he added. "Regret. And I also know that if you let it eat at you, it will never be satisfied until it has swallowed you whole. The only thing you can do is do better." He raised an eyebrow. "Or open a gaming hell."

"Will a naughty bookshop do?"

"Might. But you still want to be punished," he said. "And I just want you to have everything you need. Let me take care of you."

"Why?"

"Because no one else does," he said severely. "And because it would be my fucking privilege."

CHAPTER TWENTY-SIX

KITTY COULD ONLY blink at the raw need, the brutal power of his honesty. The way he looked at her had not changed since before she confessed. Everything was a whirlwind inside of her, but it no longer felt like it was going to sweep her away or toss her about or pull her under the water. "You don't think less of me," she said, awed.

"I think less of every single person in your life who allowed you to be in that position in the first place."

"Oh." She had not anticipated that.

"I won't punish you for that," he said. "But I *will* punish you for refusing to admit that you are beautiful. Resilient. If you want me to."

"Yes, please."

"You could at least *pretend* to act intimidated. A *little* bit sorry for disobeying me." He bit her lower lip again, harder this time. "No one else dares, you know."

But she *wasn't* scared of him. And although admitting what she had done had not magically taken away the consequences of her choices, she did feel lighter, less murky inside, like a pond too overgrown to thrive. She felt seen. Accepted. Not alone.

It was powerful. Heady.

"Oh no," she teased in a faintly mocking tone, all while rubbing against him. "The Devil's got me now. Whatever shall I do?"

"Oh, that's it," he growled, dragging her arms above her head. He curled her fingers around the base of a tree. "You're mine now. You hold on to this. Understand?

"Yes, Rhys."

He raised an eyebrow. "Better, but you're not fooling anyone."

She arched against him again. He grabbed her hips, stilling her. The suddenness of it made her gasp. Made her moan. He kept her there even as he settled between her legs, widening them, teasing, promising. Slowly. Making her wait.

"I thought I told you to keep your hands on that tree?" he asked, deceptively mild.

"I...forgot?" She needed to touch him. Needed him to touch her. Now.

He looked down at her, at his most dominating and stern.

She loved it. She bloody well *loved* it.

And he knew it.

"Do you know something?" he said silkily. "I'm not sure I can trust you to follow orders."

"Probably not," she admitted happily. Probably a little *too* happily.

He unknotted his cravat and wound it around her wrists, securing them above her head to the tree. She was properly bound, just like a maiden sacrifice to the Devil. "Better," he said when she tested the knot but could not get free. The gleam in his eyes was predatory. "Much better."

And then he just sat back on his heels and let his gaze roam over her.

But not his hands. Or his mouth. Or his teeth.

"Rhys, *please*."

He smiled as if she weren't writhing in the grass, already begging for him when he had barely touched her. "Such pretty manners when you want something," he said. "Tell me, firecracker. What is it you want?"

"You."

"I'm right here."

"Rhys, I swear to God I'm going to—"

A disapproving click of his tongue. A correction.

Infuriating.

She subsided, trying to be patient. The grass was touching the back of her legs but he wasn't. It was touching her ankles, her arms. Her neck. But he wasn't.

And he wouldn't.

She swallowed back another demand.

He closed his hand around her calf, fingers warm and strong. "Good girl." He stroked up her leg, thumb digging into the softness of her inner thigh. "You've carried everything for too long. This time I'm in charge." He shoved her skirts higher, brushing her quim lightly. Again. And again. He bent his head to kiss along her collarbone, to dip his tongue under her bodice.

He moved lower and lower, his breath warm on her belly, stirring the hair below. He licked at her opening, then around her bud. He used the tip of his tongue, then the flat of it, applied more pressure, less pressure. Used his fingers to part her folds, slick with her need. There was a rhythm to his attention that she had not noticed until the pressure mounted inside her, sparking through her core. *"Rhys."*

"Not yet."

"But…" She couldn't stop it, did not want to. *Why* would she want to?

"I said not yet." He eased back, and she whimpered, chasing the sparks, the crest. "Didn't I tell you not to interrupt me?" he asked with false regret. "Now I have to start all over again."

"Rhys!"

"Hush."

She was not going to survive this. It was torture.

It was perfect.

He continued to nibble and suck and lick up and down her body, to slide his fingers into her, first one then two, but always pulling back when she neared her climax—when her gasps tore from her, when she dug her fingers into his hair and he chuckled, clearly pleased. Another lick, a deeper thrust. And then he pulled her entire bud into his mouth and worked it gently, relentlessly. She bucked against his mouth. "Please. *Please, please, please.*" Was she begging? Demanding? She had no idea. "Please, Rhys."

"I do so love it when you beg," he growled against her swollen, pulsing bud. "Come, Kitty. *Now.*"

She had never followed orders in her life. She had never wanted to.

"Don't keep me waiting."

Whatever he did with his mouth sent her careering over the edge. Her climax washed through her so abruptly, so deeply, that it stole her breath, her ability to think. There were only the waves of sensations claiming her. Devil smiling against her most private parts. She jerked when he kissed her, she was that sensitive.

"Do you really want to know that I think of you?" he asked, reaching up to release the cravat that bound her.

She nodded mutely. She was boneless, wordless, floating.

"I think you're too damned good to lie on the cold ground."

He flipped her so suddenly that she squeaked a laugh. It was no surprise to her that Devil was incredibly skilled with his mouth and his hands and his entre sculpted, beautiful body. No surprise that he would pull pleasure from her like he was merely claiming something that already belonged to him. It *was* still a surprise, though, how much she enjoyed being with him. How they could grin at each other, even now, half naked and half spent in the back garden, her secrets and her body bared to the starlight.

She straddled him, her knees in the grass. His cock pushed at his breeches until she freed him, gripping him tight enough that he bucked in her hand. She dragged the tip between her folds, once twice.

"Are you teasing me, firecracker?" he asked between clenched teeth, gripping her hips.

"You deserve it."

"Probably."

He did deserve it. And she would happily oblige. Next time. Should there be a next time.

Please let there be a next time.

But he was so hard it looked painful, and she wanted to feel him inside of her *right now*. She rubbed against him just because she could, because it made his green eyes go glassy. And then she fit the tip of him inside of her and lowered, down, down, inch by glorious inch until he was swearing and she was moaning. She was stretched and filled; every thrust made her see stars.

He ran his hands up her ribcage and teased her breasts free over the top of her bodice. "Perfect," he grunted. She felt positively wanton, in the most delicious way, her skirts pulled up, her dress pulled down, undulating over Devil, pulling him deeper until the sparks built again, pressure building and mounting, until her hips stuttered and he surged up, coming hard.

She fell forward, catching her breath, her thighs trembling. He pulled her down to his chest, running his fingers through her hair until she purred. "All right?"

"Better than all right," she murmured. "You?"

"Better than all right." He kissed her forehead. "You should go to sleep."

"I don't want to sleep." She shook her head, accidentally nuzzling his neck. Then she did it again because it made him tighten his arms around her.

The threads linking them together seemed stronger. Brighter.

She felt stronger. Brighter.

She *felt* beautiful.

KITTY DID NOT fall asleep, but she drifted, the most comfortable she had ever been, until Devil shifted to clean them up. She protested, because he was so warm and solid beneath her. And then he promised her tea and cake and she begrudgingly slid off his chest. Very begrudgingly. He tucked her into his coat even though the night was not cold. Music drifted from some other house, blazing with light and people dancing. She preferred the dark secret corner tucked into the roses with the tea tray and the devil.

She inhaled the sweet aroma of bergamot and lavender and was well into her second cup before breaking the soft, companionable silence. "Devil?"

"Who?"

She smiled. "Rhys?"

"Yes?"

"Thank you for the tea today."

"What tea?"

"This tea. The exact same you had delivered to the shop."

"I'm sure that wasn't me."

"Must have been my other fiancé."

He scowled. "Stop that."

"I am thinking of starting a collection."

"Sounds like a lot of work."

"True. And I am rather busy."

"Best leave it, then."

"I suppose." She heaved a false sigh and then grinned at him. "Is that strawberry cake?" He had brought a tray to her so they could eat among the rose petals.

"Of course."

"It's my favorite."

"I know."

"You do?"

He smiled. "You threatened to stab me just this afternoon if I took the last slice."

"Oh. Right." She licked strawberry jam off her thumb. "I'm not sorry."

He watched her, throat working as he swallowed. "Neither am I," he said hoarsely.

"Can I ask you a question?"

"You might be the only one who dares."

She knew that wasn't true. Mayfair might tremble before him, but it wasn't fear he inspired in the men of the house behind her. It was loyalty.

"I've never seen you gamble. Godric and Wulf sometimes play dice outside the shop to pass the time, and your brother talks about cards and horse racing. But you never do. And you didn't play during the Devil's Night, not once."

"I don't care for cards." He shrugged. "Have more cake."

"I've had a slice already."

"Have another."

She dipped her finger into the bowl of clotted cream and licked it off. He watched her. "Absolute devil," he murmured appreciatively.

"If you don't care for cards or dice, why a gaming hell? Why open the Seven Deadly Sins? Why bother with the biggest gaming hell London has ever dreamt of?"

"It's not for me," he said quietly.

"It's not?"

He scrubbed a hand over his jaw. "No. It's for them."

"Them? Ah. Macleod and Brutus and the brothers Winchester."

"And Tom."

"How?"

"When we came back to England, it was…an adjustment."

She reached for his hand, and he turned his palm up to let her. It was as intimate as anything they had done to each other's bodies. More.

"I had the estate, my title," he continued. "But the other men had very little, mostly scars and nightmares. And my brother… Well, you've seen what it can be like for him."

She nodded. "I'm going to buy more gold paint, the kind that burns."

His mouth quirked. "The Sins is not just a place for them to work and support themselves. Especially with some of the injuries we collected between us."

"It's not?"

"It's power."

She thought of the women who came to the shop in the dead of night. The ones she sent to the Spinster Society or the house in Covent Garden. She thought of her sister, powerless and sold to someone like Portsmouth. "I understand."

"Holding the bank for Devil's Nights gave me access to secrets, as much as it made obscene amounts of money."

"And the Sins will do the same?"

"For my men, it will. They will have employment and, better than that, power to protect themselves."

"Your brother."

"He was alone when I was gone," he said tightly, jaw clenching. "He won't be vulnerable like that again. No one will dare touch him, not when he's a partner in the Sins."

"Tell me about it."

"I won the house on a wager."

"Naturally. I would expect nothing less. From what I've already seen, it's going to be brilliant."

"The Ladies' Association for Moral Standards do not hold the same opinion."

Kitty snorted. "They really do need to take up a more enjoyable hobby. Decoupage. Or watercolors. Lawn bowls."

"Agreed."

"Who knew the Devil was such a champion?"

"Hush."

Kitty grinned. "You can't take a compliment any better than I can."

"I am always ready to admit that I am clever and handsome, sweetheart."

She snorted. "Admit you're a good man."

He nearly squirmed. She raised an eyebrow.

"Have more cake," he muttered.

"I ate it all."

"I'll get you more."

"See? A good man."

He grumbled some more until the dew began to gather on

the roses and the grass and he led them to his study for a warming draft of whiskey. Kitty sputtered around her mouthful. "This is just awful."

"Philistine," he said, but it was affectionate. Indulgent.

She wanted to eat it like that strawberry cake.

Dawn was starting to lighten the sky, a wash of pearly gray, a hint of pink. It would be daylight soon.

"We really need to get inside Portsmouth's house again," she said, loath to release the night and its dark and beautiful moments but knowing she must.

She had gone through all of the notes in the stolen volumes, most inked right on the page, which would no doubt have made Lord Tadworth scream incoherently. The messages between two very dear friends were like a second story overlaying the first. She knew their favorite scenes, their least favorite characters, the things they wanted to do with the duke. *To* the duke.

But she was no closer to finding out where Lady Caroline had gone, or if Miss Campbell had followed her, or even if their plan had been carried through. Caroline knew she needed to get away, but Kitty was no closer to finding out where she might be now.

"I assume Portsmouth has an army of men like you? Minus the fellow with the broken ankle, of course."

"His men are nothing like mine," Devil said dismissively, eyebrow arched.

"Of course not." She had not known Godric and Wulf, Macleod, or Shelby long, but she was also offended on their behalf. "I was not implying otherwise."

"And he's arrogant. That will work to our advantage."

Kitty shivered. "Please don't underestimate him. He makes my skin crawl."

"He's not going to touch you," Devil said, expression turning hard. "Nor your sister."

The fact that he had mentioned her sister would have made her tumble into love with him right then and there. If she wasn't already in love.

Oh, this was going to be a problem.

Devil did not look remotely concerned. Or like a man in love.

Because he wasn't. This was a means to an end. She had blackmailed him into helping. She was briefly tempted to give him back his stolen vowel.

Briefly.

But her sister's life was at stake, and she would not risk it over sentimentality. Devil would probably help her regardless, but she would be an idiot to rely on that. Her emotions were her own problem to deal with.

Blissfully unaware that she was tying herself up in knots, Devil set his glass down. The soft dawn light caught the whiskey, turning it to gold.

"I have an idea."

CHAPTER TWENTY-SEVEN

"**T**HIS IS A *terrible* idea," Kitty blurted out.

"You wanted to search Portsmouth's house." Devil shrugged as if Kitty was not gaping at him in abject horror.

"I do want that," she said. "But not *this*."

"*This* is how you get *that*."

"Surely there's another way."

That crooked smile, swift as a swallow at dusk. "It's just a party."

"*Celebrating our betrothal*." Which was temporary. She tried not to shout, she really did. "With every duke and earl in London! There are three marquises on this list. The bloody Prince of Wales is on this guest list." She jabbed an accusatory finger at it, then at a sample invitation on thick paper with red and gold trim.

You are cordially invited to join Lord Birmingham in celebration of his betrothal to Miss Catherine Caldecott, Rochester House, Thursday evening.

Even reading it made her break out into a cold sweat.

"That's *tomorrow*."

He would expect her to know the rules of Polite Society beyond the obvious ones. To know how to waltz. Or speak French or Italian. To make scintillating small talk as if she was not sweating through her stays. Worse, he would expect his guests to attend despite her reputation and standing in Society. And they would attend, because he was Devil. Were he anyone else, they would snub him for his supposed marriage to an infamous bookseller.

"You don't know what you're asking." She rubbed at her breastbone. "You're insane. Clearly. I always knew it."

"I'm asking you to stand in an abysmally boring receiving line for half an hour and then sneak out the side door with me so we can rifle through Portsmouth's house while he is drinking my very expensive champagne."

"Oh." She perked up. "*That*, I can do."

"Don't let them scare you."

"I'm not scared of them." She wrinkled her nose. "I'm scared one of them will sneak in a rotten cabbage and hurl it at my head."

"Believe me, that is not going to happen."

"I think you underestimate them, Polite Society or not." After all, she had helped secrete away more than one of their wives.

Devil's eyes were hot, his tone cold. The combination should not have made her lightheaded with sudden desire. "I think you underestimate *me*."

KITTY DID NOT know the first thing about planning a dinner party for nearly one hundred of the highest-ranking members of the *Ton* at the best of times, never mind *these* times, which were very much not the best. This was supposed to be a spectacle, a message to the *Ton*. A way to keep Portsmouth occupied.

The prince had declined, thank God. Her family had not been invited, thank the Devil.

And she had no idea what sauce partridges should be cooked in or if was to be served on silver platters, à la Russe or in the French style.

The housekeeper might as well have been speaking *actual* French. Kitty had no intention of eating pigeon in jelly. There was also mushrooms in white sauce, baked artichokes, fricasseed hare, roasted lamb, mackerel in fennel and mint. White soup.

What *was* white soup?

Kitty stared at the housekeeper while reminding herself that this was not an actual disaster. This was very low on the list. She could withstand public humiliation. She had infinite expertise. She might embarrass Devil, which she did not care to do, but it was his own fault, really.

"I can hear you panicking from down the hall." Tom poked his head into the parlor. "Good afternoon, Mrs. Winter," he said, winking at the housekeeper. He had just come from some errand, likely to the Sins, and wore a lovely lilac top hat to match the fading bruise around his eye. "When are you going to run away with me?"

"Just as soon as you stop leaving your gloves strewn about the place like dandelions," she replied crisply.

Sarcasm. Delightfully inappropriate sarcasm that ignored the proper order of things: i.e. servants and booksellers in an earl's house about to feed three dukes and a marquis. Six earls.

Kitty's spine felt less like it was made of glass that might shatter at any moment. Or at any question regarding dessert forks. She could add columns of numbers in her head and calculate percentages in her sleep. She knew the names of every couple from each of the thirty-book series about blue-skinned warriors.

Tom glanced at the menu prepared by Mrs. Winter. "That looks perfect, Mrs. W," he said. "Perhaps we could substitute the pigeon with pheasant. My brother will want it known that he spares no expense for his bride-to-be."

Kitty goggled at him. "Do you know how many Minerva Press novels I could buy for one pheasant? And they are six shillings apiece!"

Mrs. Winter patted her arm. "It's robbery, plain and simple, but you'll never convince them."

"Certainly not. We'll use the Coalport dishes, the cobalt-blue ones. And the crystal goblets, naturally. Gilded."

Kitty groaned. Tom flicked her a glance. "Take a deep

breath." While she did that, he made half a dozen more decisions with the flare and insouciance of someone who knew exactly what they were doing. "And tell Shelby I've a list of whom he is to turn away at the door. It's the only reason they were invited." Power plays within power plays.

"Of course," Mrs. Winter replied.

Kitty's hands had stopped sweating. "You're very good at that."

He shrugged one shoulder. "I've had more practice. But yes, actually, I am *very* good."

"But you're not supposed to be?"

"I'm supposed to care about horses and shooting pistols and drinking port. Or fashion, if I were a dandy." He tossed his hat onto a chair. "To be clear, I am *very* good at all of those things, too. But I am also good at this. And the pianoforte for some reason."

"Which is why you run Pride at the Sins."

"Yes. I'm a second son, and it beats the hell out of the army or the church. Not that Devil would let me get within a hundred miles of the army."

"I imagine not."

"Even though I am a better shot than him."

"I will remember that. Thank you, by the way."

"You don't have to worry about that sort of thing, you know. Devil doesn't. And Mrs. Winter and I have been making those decisions for ages. It's not a bother."

"I don't want to embarrass him," she admitted. Even if their betrothal would come to an end soon enough and it would not matter who chose between pigeons and pheasants.

Tom grinned, lounging back in the settee and propping his boots on the carved mahogany table in front of him. Kitty squeaked. The furniture in this small family parlor alone could easily grace the palace.

"I am the embarrassment in this family, thank you very much," he said. "You'll have to get your own title."

ON THURSDAY EVENING, Devil stood in the drawing room, impeccably dressed as always. Sophisticated, elegant, but not fussy. As if he knew the names of a hundred different wines, at least half of which he had personally smuggled from France, and also had a dagger in his boot and a pistol inside his coat. A woman waiting in each bedchamber upstairs and one in the unmarked carriage down the lane.

That last woman was Kitty, wearing her simplest, grayest dress and a cap pinned over her hair.

Not remotely right for a celebration dinner at Rochester House, of the marble columns and gold candlesticks. But exceedingly perfect for prowling around Lord Portsmouth's house while pretending to be a housemaid. Just as soon as Devil was finished charming the guests, pouring large quantities of wine, and remarking that ladies had a right to make an entrance and it was their honor to wait.

Devil's hint that invitations to the opening of the Sins might well be handed out as party favors at the end of the evening would be enough to entice Portsmouth to stay, for a little while at least. It was precisely the sort of thing he could not resist: preferential treatment, something to brag about that he would consider his due. Devil had welcomed him personally before sneaking out one of the many hidden doors.

Also, as Portsmouth was still advertising to all and sundry that he was marrying Kitty's sister, it would have been odd indeed had he not attended.

It was probably best that Kitty was waiting in the carriage, as the temptation to poison Portsmouth's soup would have proven too much to resist. But she could not very well welcome guests in a dress better suited to a housemaid.

That was reserved for breaking into Portsmouth's house. Which was minutes away once Devil slipped into the carriage.

Only a few minutes more and they were standing outside another grand Mayfair house. The household staff inside would be taking advantage of a long-awaited rest. The housekeeper would know Kitty was not under her domain, but Kitty did not expect her to be upstairs. The only one who might cause trouble was the valet, but Devil had explained that Portsmouth often traveled with his valet in order to keep the earl's coat looking just right.

The peerage really were an absurd lot.

"Stop grumbling about the peerage," Devil said mildly. "And let's get this done before I change my mind."

"Too late." Kitty tossed him a cheeky grin over her shoulder and darted through the servants' entrance before he could stop her. She would not put it past him to simply haul her over his shoulder.

She refused to consider why the image made her squirm a little. A lot.

Interesting.

Not now, Kitty.

The door led to the servant hall, lit dimly with a single candle in a wall sconce. There were murmurs from the main room where the staff took their meals. The housekeeper's door was shut. If Kitty was very careful, she could sneak up the narrow stairs without anyone noticing her.

Easier to do when one did not trip over the kitchen cat, suddenly interested in the newcomer and whether or not she had treats on her person. Kitty caught herself before she smacked her head into the wall.

She was quite certain Priya would not have stumbled. Nor Yelena.

The cat meowed, insulted.

"Kitty, is that you?

Kitty froze.

The cat padded toward the voice, tail high. "There's a clever cat. Who's a good kitty?"

Kitty hissed out a breath and crept up the stairs as fast as she could. Her heart pounded in her throat as she slipped into a dark drawing room. Devil waited at the window, a stern silhouette.

She unlocked it and pulled the sash open. "Any trouble?"

She smiled. "Of course not."

"You are a terrible liar."

"I am an *excellent* liar."

"You have a tell, Catherine Caldecott."

"I do? What is it?"

He snorted, with clearly no intention of enlightening her. He climbed inside as gracefully as if he did so every day of his life. No cat dared wind around his ankles to trip him up. The floorboards did not even dare to creak. "Hmph," Kitty muttered.

"What was that?"

"Nothing. Hurry."

He stalked behind her like a shadow, silent, unhurried. Graceful. Meanwhile, she felt like she had three left feet and her pulse was a hammer on an anvil, announcing her presence. They ducked through Lady Caroline's chamber, stopping for another quick look around, but found nothing of note.

Kitty wasn't sure what she expected from the earls' chamber: bloody chains suspended from the ceiling, bones piled in the corner? Books burning in the grate instead of coal? Something appropriately awful for someone who murdered his wives.

Instead, it was one more Mayfair chamber that hid its rot behind glittering crystal chandeliers and oil paintings of horses and silk drapery. There was a leather chair by the window, a washstand of carved mahogany, a silver-embroidered coverlet on the bed. No hint that he had had a wife, never mind three. No portraits here, either, or love letters or stray hairpins. Nothing to suggest a woman had ever set foot over the threshold of this bedroom, or the entire house, really. Kitty wasn't sure why, but it felt wrong. Ominous.

She would not let him erase her sister. Nor Lady Caroline. Miss Campbell.

"He has to be hiding something." She was not as calm in her search as Devil. He was methodical, the slight frown beetling his brow the only hint that he was searching for something more than a lost button. He opened the drawers of a decorative table: three enameled snuffboxes, cheroots, matchsticks.

They looked under the mattress, under the bed. Under the cushions. The commode was not spared. Portsmouth's collections of cravat pins and shoe buckles. An astonishing number of hats. Every pocket of every coat.

They only found an original volume of Chaucer's *Decameron*. "He does not deserve this book," Kitty said. She dropped it into the pocket tied around her stays.

Devil's mouth quirked. "You do that a lot."

"What?"

"Steal."

She wrinkled her nose. "You break ankles."

"True. Clearly a match for the ages."

Hope flared in her chest before she trampled it down. He wasn't serious, and she was clever enough to know that. It was getting harder and harder to remind herself that he was not for her. She would not ruin what they had—whatever it was—with unrealistic expectations.

Even if sometimes she thought he looked at her like he might want to keep her.

"There's nothing here," Kitty said softly. Her eyes prickled with frustration.

"We just haven't found it yet," Devil disagreed. "You're not telling me that the Moral Scourge of Ladies' Literature is giving up, are you?"

She scowled. "No."

"I thought not."

The carpet was thick and lush under her shoes as she paced. It was also nicer than he deserved. Everything was nicer than Lord Portsmouth deserved.

But it did remind her of something: the carpet in her own bedroom—a rag rug with horribly clashing colors that Evie had made for her. And that Galahad liked to bite. Also, under which Kitty hid any money she brought into the house. She hid Evie from suitors on the roof and coins from her father under a warped floorboard. She was very sure that none of the floorboards in this house were loose or warped or scratched up by a hedgehog, but even an earl needed a place to hide his secrets. Especially an earl like Portsmouth.

She kicked over the edge of the carpet. Instead of wasting time asking what she was doing, Devil crouched down to help. Then he watched her walk the length of each floorboard, head tilted, listening for the telltale creak or groan.

There.

If one cared to look very, very carefully, one could see the nail head sticking up higher than the others, and a groove in the side of the board. Kitty pried it loose and lifted it just as Devil lowered a candle stub, shielding the flame with his palm so it would not be seen under the door. The warm light fell on pouches of coins, keys, a dagger, and a packet of letters tied with a ribbon.

After a quick glance at the first letter, Kitty knew her smile was smug and sharp and vengeful, and she also knew that Devil would not hold it against her.

In fact, he smiled back.

THEY DID NOT untie the bundle for a proper perusal until they had returned to the carriage. The cat had found them in the bedchamber and was not impressed. It seemed wisest to take what they had found and hope it was enough. Particularly as they had to make a grand and memorable appearance at their own party, and soon.

"Now we know how he keeps getting away with murdering his wives." Devil's mouth was hard as they read the letters.

"He's using blackmail," Kitty said, flipping through the pages. "I've counted a marquis, an archbishop, and one of Queen Charlotte's ladies-in-waiting. A magistrate. A judge. He's blackmailing them all. He's made himself untouchable."

"No longer." Devil leaned back. "Secrets are power, but they aren't the only power."

She forced herself not to grip the letters too tightly, not to crumple them. "This is enough, isn't it?" She was scared to hope. "To stop him from marrying my sister, at the very least?"

Devil smiled grimly. "At the very least. When it comes to blackmail, don't you think we should show him how to do it right?"

She nodded, hope sparking more hope, sparking anticipation, relief. Renewed determination to bury Portsmouth in his own lies. In the ground would be better.

As the carriage rumbled along, Kitty pulled off her gray dress and her shoes and her very sensible stockings. None of which were suitable for the rest of the night that lay before them. And if Lord Portsmouth happened to notice that his belongings were gone, he would remember that Devil had welcomed him personally and that Kitty had greeted him while wearing a glowing gold gown that was impossible to miss.

Assuming she could wiggle her way into it.

She could manage just fine without a lady's maid, but this kind of gown was not easy to handle while inside a moving carriage, especially with her mind whirling with all of the possibilities presented by those letters. In fact, this kind of gown was made by a very skilled modiste and fit Kitty almost perfectly. It had clearly not been pulled from a stack of dresses unpaid for or forgotten.

"Where did you get this gown?" She ought to have asked before. Did it belong to one of Devil's paramours? She didn't want to fuss, but she also had no wish to wear a dress he had peeled off another woman. She was ridiculous, of course. None of that mattered, especially not *now*. But there you had it.

Devil had been watching her wiggle about with great interest. "I had it made."

"Yes, I gathered that. For whom?"

He tilted his head. "For you. Who else?"

"In two days? Without my having visited a modiste?"

He shrugged. "Yelena guessed your measurements, and I have found that if you throw a great deal of money at most problems, they tend to resolve themselves."

Kitty frowned. "How much did you... Never mind, I don't want to know. It will make me queasy."

"Yes," he agreed easily. "It will. And yet it was worth every penny."

She shook her head, wearing only her stays and her chemise. She could argue, she could pretend that she did not feel pleasantly spoiled—later. There simply was no time for it now. Nor the relief that followed his statement that she was not wearing a borrowed dress belonging to someone more suited to marrying an earl.

"Are you cross that I did not let you choose your own dress?" he asked. "I sent Yelena because it seemed expeditious."

She nodded. "It was."

"There are stockings," Devil said, flicking open a small box. They were fine silk, ivory with gold ribbons. She had never seen anything so delicate or so pretty in her life.

"Let me," he added, lifting her foot onto the seat between his knees. He slipped the stocking over her toes and dragged it gently up her bare leg, leaving goosebumps in his wake. He bent his head to tie the ribbon. When he followed with the next stocking, he first brushed his mouth up her calf, over her knee, inside her thigh, until she was biting her lip on a gasp.

He undid the laces of her stays, his gaze never straying from hers until he dragged her chemise down over one shoulder, to bare her breast to him. He sucked at her nipple. The hot, wet heat of his mouth, the stroke of his tongue—all sent pulls of longing straight to her quim. He did not relent, not even when she clutched at his arms, his hair, moaning. He only moved to the other breast and back again until she thought she might come from this alone.

The light from the gas lamps glowed at the windows, behind the curtains. The carriage took a right, jostling them. Devil groaned against her nipple. "Damn the guests." Her chuckle quickly turned to a gasp when he sucked at her breast again, a hot, deep pull that made her squirm. He pulled back reluctantly. His eyes were almost too green, even in the half light.

Her breath was shaky as she reached for the new stays, edged with gold to match her dress. They were soft, structured. Nothing poked through thinning material into her ribs. Devil helped her tie the laces, though he complained about it. "I should be helping you out of this, not into it."

She was grinning when she pulled the gown over her head and it settled down around her like a cloud of fire. It was simple enough in design, with little embellishment, and the gold silk moved like liquid.

"It brings out your freckles," Devil said, satisfied.

"I've been told that is not a good thing."

"Because you've been talking to idiots."

✦

CHAPTER TWENTY-EIGHT

S HE PULLED THE curtains aside to see her reflection in the window. The gown really did *glow*. She certainly looked elegant enough to corner Lord Portsmouth and drown him in a champagne bucket. Beat him about the head with his own blackmail letters.

She rubbed at her breastbone and realized it was not burning in that painful way it usually did, and had not done so for a few days. Long before they had found their secret weapon against Portsmouth.

Who had already left.

"Ladies and gentlemen, I present to you Miss Caldecott, who has condescended to be my wife." Kitty pinched Devil's arm for his dramatic declaration. He smiled down at her, whispering, "Careful—I'll recite a sonnet to your beauty."

She narrowed one eye. "I will jump right out that window."

He chuckled. The guests paused, whispered. Devil frowned. "Why did they always do that?"

"Do what?"

"Act like I've drawn a sword every time I smile."

"Because you're the Devil," she said. "And you're very good at it."

"You don't tremble before me."

Not precisely true. "I happen to prefer a devil," she said. "Now, where's Portsmouth so you can stab him with your pitchfork?"

He looked so fond of her bloodthirsty demands that he brushed his mouth over the top of her head, barely there. A hint of a kiss. Shocking in public, even in one's own drawing room. Kitty blushed. So did three other ladies.

"Honestly," she muttered, "you should not be allowed out in public."

It was almost a relief when, as the guests finally trailed out, Tom came to whisper in his ear to call him away on business at the Sins. She needed a moment to collect herself.

Several moments.

The way he stood by her, looked down at her even when surrounded by the *Ton*, by his own family: as if he wanted to keep her. As if he would *fight* for her. As if he did not care who knew it, in fact insisted everyone acknowledge it or be damned.

It had never felt more real, this little deception of theirs.

And for the first time, it hurt. She wanted so much for it to be real. That he might keep her, that she might keep him. That Evie was safe, and Devil had his stolen wager back and he still wanted to be around her. That he might even miss her when she was not around. Marriage was hardly a thing she expected. But to give him up now seemed a Herculean task.

And there was no one to blame but herself. No one else to make it right. She had read enough books to know that sometimes the Kraken prince could not live on dry land. The dragon queen needed the sky, and her mortal lover was not flameproof.

And she had no right to the doldrums. They were so close to freeing Evie, to getting her life back. Even if that meant finding a way to support them, finding a place to live that would not put them at the mercy of her father and aunt.

She turned her betrothal ring around and around on her finger. Devil had nonchalantly suggested she could sell all of the jewelry he had given her. And the reality was that she would have to. But not her ring. Not the one with the stones that matched her bookshop. Even if she had to wear it on her right hand or not at all, she already knew she would not be able to bring herself to part with it.

It was hers, just as she was Devil's, even if he never knew it.

Kitty changed out of her gold gown and back into her gray dress with the ink stain on the sleeve. Devil might be gone for hours yet, and she knew that if she rattled around his big, fancy house she would only drive herself mad. *Work cures all ills,* or so her grandmother claimed. Mostly to annoy her son-in-law, it had to be said.

It was a strange thing to feel melancholy but also happy, relieved but adrift. Some time spent at the Golden Griffin would put her to rights. It always did.

To his credit, Samuel did not ask questions when he pulled the carriage beside her in the street. She climbed inside because she knew full well that Devil would blame his entire household if she went walking alone at night. Even if it was only Mayfair and only just past midnight. She was hardly alone—there was a flood of carriages bringing people to party after party, to Vauxhall Gardens, to gaming hells. They would all be going in the direction of the Sins soon enough.

When they finally left Mayfair for Piccadilly and St. James and went north to her little shop, Kitty felt calmer. Wulf leaned against the window, eyebrows raised. "Bit late, innit? I thought you had a party."

"We *had* the party," she smiled. Portsmouth might have left before they could corner him, but she knew he was not far. Any one of Devil's men would find him before sunrise.

"And did you dance?"

"I don't dance, Wulf."

"I thought all ladies danced."

Kitty just shrugged and let herself inside, lighting one of the lamps. It was just enough light to make the griffins glow and flicker as if they were flying. She wrapped the peace of it around her like a shawl. She had only been away for a few days, barely that, but it was cheering to be back. It was home. She could do anything here.

Even mend her own broken heart.

If she wasn't careful, she was going to start spouting poetry. The kind she did not care for. Better to turn her attention to the ledgers.

And her strongbox, back on her desk, lock intact. With coins inside, every last one her father had stolen.

And she knew beyond a shadow of a doubt that he had not suddenly found remorse, certainly not enough to return the money. Only one person could have forced his hand like that.

The Devil.

Kitty was smiling as she locked the box back up. She could pay her bills without resorting to unseemly deeds. Such as more stealing.

Probably she did not have the right to be hurt by her father's theft, as someone currently in possession of several books that belonged to other people. Lord Tadworth and the Campbells would get their books back as soon as possible. Portsmouth would not. Ever. His wives were still murdered or missing. Lady Caroline still deserved to be safe, even after Evie was out of Portsmouth's clutches. Kitty would find a way to make it right. With the Spinster Society's help.

Sooner than she would have guessed.

Priya walked through the doors, and Kitty smiled before realizing that was not a good thing. Not a good thing at all.

Her stomach dropped. "Evie?" she asked immediately.

Priya nodded, handing her a folded note. Behind her on the street, Pierce waited for her, ever watchful.

Dear Kitty,

Don't be angry. I had to go with him or he would have hurt you. I love you. Evie.

"No," Kitty said softly, then with more force. The force of the sun searing the sky. *"No."*

"I kept everyone out," Priya said apologetically. "It did not occur to me that I should keep her *in*."

"Portsmouth," Kitty said, her tone perfectly even. "I think I might actually kill him now."

"Oh, do let me help," Priya said grimly.

Kitty ran through her options, her head spinning, her skin prickling painfully with terror for her sister. She could send word to Devil, but even so, she did not have the time to spend waiting for his help. She had Priya, and likely Pierce, as he went where Priya went. Wulf would help. Samuel was outside with the carriage.

It was enough. It would have to be enough.

Please, let it be enough.

If Portsmouth married her sister, he would have absolute authority and control over her. Legally. Kitty would still find a way to hide her, but it would be that much harder.

When a quiet knock sounded at the back door, Kitty ignored it. She crumpled the note in her fist. "We don't even know where they are," she said. "If they are on their way to Gretna Green, I may never catch up in time."

"I know where he is," a soft voice said from the darkness of the back room.

Kitty whirled. She recognized the lady from their last book salon. Her hair was not powdered this time, tucked instead into the hood pulled over her head. She stepped forward. "Miss Hastings?"

"That is not Miss Hastings," Priya said. "That is Lady Caroline Portsmouth."

CHAPTER TWENTY-NINE

KITTY GOGGLED.

She needed to be planning, running, stabbing Portsmouth.

But she still goggled uselessly, wasting a full minute she would berate herself for later. "Lady Portsmouth?"

Caroline nodded.

"Why are—Never mind that now. How do you know where your husband is taking my sister? And will you go with us? We need you. *She* needs you." It was selfish to ask, but Kitty didn't care.

Caroline nodded, though she trembled. "I've hidden long enough. I saw your message at the oak, and I've seen you try to help me even when you did not know me and I was not brave enough to ask for that help. But I will be brave enough to help your sister."

"Thank you," Kitty breathed, nearly lightheaded with relief. "You may be the first to stab him."

"Thank you?"

"Where is he taking her?" Priya asked, motioning to Pierce through the glass. He was striding toward her before her arm dropped back down. "Gretna Green?"

Caroline shook her head. "Not this time, not when he knows you might follow. Gretna Green was to force your sister's hand, to ruin her so she had no choice once they reached Scotland."

"I did not know it was possible to want to stab someone *quite* so much."

"Believe me, I understand."

"I would rather my sister's reputation be ruined than she be murdered. But if not Gretna Green, where? The banns have not been read. I have been checking the papers."

"He wouldn't do it that way, not now that eyes are upon him. Not nearly elegant enough."

"Yes, because abducting women and murdering his wives is very elegant indeed," Kitty said.

They exchanged a cutting, killing glance.

"He's found someone to force into giving him a special license," Caroline continued. "It's what he does."

"So we've discovered." Fat lot of good those secret letters were at the moment.

"I have been following his men. He went to the archbishop's offices at Doctors' Commons and had them procure a special license today."

"There are too many bishops and vicars in London."

"Yes, but only one he is blackmailing. He lives not far from here."

"I have a carriage," Priya said.

"But I have a Winchester brother," Kitty replied. "He'll get us there faster."

Which was how Kitty found herself climbing into a carriage with Priya and Caroline, and Pierce and Wulf acting as outriders.

"We should send for Devil," Wulf said.

"Go ahead," Kitty replied. "But I cannot wait. Not one moment."

Wulf swore under his breath before climbing aboard. "Devil will find us. He'll find *you*."

Kitty could not see how that was even possible, but it did not matter. She had her makeshift army: spinsters and wives on the run and men who did not care about her lack of fortune. Or which dessert spoon to use.

Lord Portsmouth would not have her sister.

"PORTSMOUTH IS A self-important ass," Caroline said a few moments later as the carriage careered down the busy street with very little regard for order.

"Clearly," Priya said. "Well done on surviving him."

"I nearly didn't," Caroline said. "He was courteous enough at first, played the role of suitor well enough. But after we married, each time I got my courses, he flew into a rage. He is *obsessed* with getting an heir." She shook her head. "And then a doctor told him I was barren because it had been a year without a baby."

Priya snorted. "It has been far longer than that for him, including three wives, and I shudder to think of how many other women. Of course, the problem could not possibly lie with *him*."

Caroline pressed her lips together. "The one doctor who suggested that went missing. I decided I should go missing as well shortly after."

The carriage rolled to a stop just down the street from the vicar's house, partially hidden in a line of other carriages waiting outside of a supper party gone late. The stars were very far away, and the moon was barely a suggestion of light. But it was enough for Pierce to nod grimly to a rooftop across from the vicar's house.

"One of Portsmouth's men up there with a rifle," he said. "Don't move until I've dealt with him." He caught Priya's eye. "I mean it."

He was gone before she could reply, melting into the shadows. Kitty knew without looking that he was far more graceful on a rooftop than she was. There was a muffled grunt, the slide of a body on slate tiles. "He's got him," Wulf said.

Priya handed Kitty a dagger.

"Stop giving away your knives, woman," Pierce said, still across the street.

"I have two more," she muttered. "Honestly, if it were up to him, I would be wearing them like jewelry."

"We'll take the others," Wulf said. "There are at least two out front."

It hardly needed to be said that Kitty, Priya, and Caroline did not wait. Not long, at any rate.

Just long enough for Wulf and Pierce to clear a temporary path.

Kitty slipped past them, skirted a spatter of blood, and barreled through the front door.

Not her best plan.

But if she had to throw herself bodily onto the earl to stop him, she would. Stabbing was, of course, a distinct possibility.

The vicar's house was dark, except for the candlelight spilling from a small parlor. Kitty headed straight for it, already knowing what she would find: Lord Portsmouth, a handsome earl of good fortune and tainted soul, standing next to her little sister. Evie's hair glowed gold like a storybook princess's. Her cheeks were pale, her chin at a determined angle.

Until she saw her sister. She closed her eyes briefly. "Kitty, don't."

The vicar and his wife—and the housekeeper and footman serving as the two witnesses—looked on stiffly. Kitty recognized then: the vicar Andover and his wife. Anyone could see this was wrong, even them. Evie was too pale, too young, too alone.

"Evie!" Kitty darted forward, terrified that she was too late.

"Not another step, Miss Caldecott," Portsmouth ordered her. He grabbed Evie by the arm. Hard.

Kitty halted. Evie shook her head once, and Kitty nearly wilted with relief. Not too late, after all. She did not know where Caroline was, or the others, and she dared not look. She was a fox trapped in a foxhole. Let him hunt her and leave the rest.

"You were not invited," Portsmouth said. "But no matter. She's overjoyed to be my countess, aren't you, Miss Evangeline?"

"Yes," Evie whispered, shifting in pain. The bastard had taken away her cane.

"There. You see? Now kindly stop these dramatics, Miss Caldecott."

"She's only marrying you because you threatened me."

He shrugged. And then he smiled. He liked the fear bubbling around him. *Loved* it. Kitty wondered how she was not spitting fire. The rage that filled her was hot as molten iron, just waiting to be formed into a weapon.

In the books she loved, the heroine always felt vindicated. Purposeful. Kitty just felt nervous and sweaty. And furious.

But Portsmouth was out of reach, and she wasn't convinced she could get to her sister before him. No matter how angry she was.

She could, however, punch a vicar right in the mouth.

With no vicar, there was no one able to marry them. It would not solve the problem, but it would buy them time.

Kitty whirled on her heel, closed her fist, and let loose.

The vicar, currently trying to become a part of the furniture along with his wife, yelped. The housekeeper screamed and then fainted. Kitty punched him again even though pain flared through her hand. His teeth cut into his lip with a satisfying rush of blood, and then he too crumpled. She glared at Portsmouth. Even he was shocked that she would dare punch a man of the cloth. She would happily punch anyone trying to hurt her sister. Hopefully not very soon, as her hand hurt more than she would have guessed.

"Well, you can't marry her now," she said more smugly that was wise.

"I can do as I like, you stupid chit." Portsmouth lifted his arm, pistol trained suddenly on Kitty. "Your sister marries me or she watches you die right here. It's simple enough even for you to understand."

"Please don't," Evie begged. "I'm already here. I've already said I'll marry you."

Kitty swallowed. She did not know very much about pistols, but she imagined it would be hard for him to miss entirely at such close quarters.

"I've made the announcement; there are bets in the books at my club. I have the license and the vicar. I've waited long enough—we can wait a bit longer for him to wake up."

"You'll have to wait a long bloody time," Caroline interrupted quietly. "You can't marry her because you're still married to *me*."

Portsmouth frowned at the sound of her voice. "If it isn't my missing wife," he said, eyes narrowing to slits. "You should have stayed missing, my dear."

"Then your heir would be a bastard," Caroline pointed out. "What would all of your exalted ancestors say to that?"

The vein on Portsmouth's temple began to throb. It was an alarming shade of purple. Then he smiled again and Kitty's spine went cold. When the mask slipped, he was truly terrifying. It was suddenly easy to see his soft and pampered hands covered in the blood of his wives.

"This problem I can remedy easily enough, at least," he said.

Kitty saw his shoulder twitch before he moved. A tiny, brief warning.

He released Evie and swung the pistol toward Caroline, pulling the trigger.

Kitty was also swinging out, bringing her bruised hand down onto his forearm with all her might. The bullet fired, an explosion of sound and plaster as it hit the wall. A framed portrait fell from its hook, knocking into a glass vase of carnations. Caroline dropped, as did Priya. Kitty could not tell if either of them had been hit.

The pistol skittered under the settee.

"Evie, run!" Kitty shouted.

Evie, being a Caldecott sister and therefore stubborn to a fault, did not run. She merely backed up a step and grabbed for the fireplace poker. Portsmouth did not immediately notice. His ire was focused on Kitty, who had ruined his plans. With glee. And would happily continue to do so for as long as she lived.

Poor choice of words.

While Kitty was glancing between her sister and Priya and Caroline in a heap, Portsmouth launched himself at her. He grabbed the front of her dress and yanked her off her feet, shaking her like a cat with a mouse. Kitty's head snapped back, disorienting her.

And then she knew exactly where she was, trapped against Portsmouth while he held a dagger to her throat.

He was breathing hard in her ear, furious and frustrated. "This ends now," he seethed. He smelled like cologne, too sweet and too thick. It made her want to sneeze. She did not dare. "No one cares about a spinster, least of all one like you."

"I think that's where you'll find you are wrong."

CHAPTER THIRTY

*D*EVIL.

For a moment, everyone in the room froze.

Kitty's heart leapt in her chest when Devil filled the doorway, pale green eyes cold and sharp. The knife wavered at her throat, pricking her skin.

"Portsmouth, get your goddamn hands off her." The command was a sword at Portsmouth's throat, in exchange for the dagger at hers. Portsmouth's blood was already on the floor, only he had not realized it. He was finished. Kitty's frantic pulse was not quite convinced, but the rest of her knew it. Her bones understood it, her own blood.

She stayed very still while still trying to ease away from the sharp blade. Devil's gaze roamed over her, assessing, reassuring. "You're all right." It was not a question.

"Yes," she whispered. She dared not nod.

"I will slit her throat right now." Portsmouth spat.

Devil's glance might as well have been a cannon ball whistling toward Portsmouth's head. The earl tensed despite himself. "She's bleeding, Portsmouth."

"She'll bleed a lot more if you don't get out of here and take everyone with you."

"There is no scenario where you hurt her in any way that does not end with you choking on your blood right here in this room." It was a promise.

"Evie, you have to run," Kitty said quietly, trying not to move against the blade.

"No."

"Caroline might be hurt. Take her and go—"

She broke off when Portsmouth yanked on her hair. "Shut up."

She wanted to fight back, to bite his hand, incapacitate him in some way. But the galling truth was that he was physically stronger than she was, and he was at an advantage.

"I'm not hurt," Caroline said from somewhere to Kitty's left.

"Oh, thank God," Kitty replied.

"*Everyone shut up.*" Portsmouth was used to being in control of every room he entered. He was not accustomed to being afraid, and anyone could see Devil scared him.

To be fair, Kitty had never seen him look so…bloodcurdling. Vengeful. Ominous.

"All of your men are gone," he informed Portsmouth. "In fact, one of them was so kind as to inform me of your whereabouts. You're alone, Portsmouth."

"I don't need them." But his voice had changed. Kitty heard it, felt it in the way the knife pressed to her neck.

The front door slammed open, echoing down the hall. Devil stopped Pierce, who had been summoned by the gunfire, without taking his eyes off Kitty. "Priya is fine. Don't move."

Pierce subsided, but only barely. His curse blistered the air.

"If you let Kitty go now, you have a chance at getting out of here," Devil said to Portsmouth. "If you don't, you have no chance. Not ever. Not anywhere."

Portsmouth shivered despite having every conceivable advantage. But he did not release Kitty.

"No more chances," Devil said softly.

A sound came from behind Kitty, like a poker hitting the hearthstone. It was just enough to startle Portsmouth, to break his concentration. His gaze flickered to the side.

Devil was on him.

He went for the dagger, prying Portsmouth's hand from Kitty's throat. He slipped between them when Kitty stumbled forward, and then he brought Portsmouth's hand down in a vicious arc, stabbing him in the thigh with his own blade. Portsmouth grunted in pain, blood blooming and dripping down his leg.

And then he grunted again because Evie had brought the poker right down on his head.

He toppled. No one moved to catch him.

"Oh dear," Kitty said above the sound of her own blood rushing in her ears.

Devil caught her by the elbow. "What is it?"

"I promised Caroline she could stab him first."

"My apologies." His eyes were fierce but his hands were gentle as he stroked her cheek, tilted her head back to examine her neck. "Anyone else hurt?" he asked.

"Remarkably little damage, all things considered," Pierce said, helping Priya to her feet, then Caroline.

Devil produced a handkerchief and pressed it to Kitty's small wound, jaw clenched tight. She offered him a wobbly smile. "It doesn't hurt much."

"Much?"

"Stings a little, that's all. My hand aches far more."

"What's wrong with your hand?" He grabbed for them both, sounding panicked and not at all like the sinister, confident Devil of Mayfair.

"She punched a vicar," Evie explained proudly.

Devil raised a brow. "You're punching vicars now?"

"Well, you weren't here to entertain me. I've had a very dull night."

"My fault entirely, then."

"Clearly."

Evie watched them with a startled, considering smile. "No one ever talks to Kitty that way."

"No one talks to Devil that way either," Wulf said, stomping in from outside, shirt torn, cheek bruised. There was a disconcerting amount of blood on his boots. "Told you he would find you."

"Yes, but *how* did you find me?" Kitty asked.

"That wastrel who was watching your house?"

"Yes?"

"He works for me now."

"Of course he does." Kitty turned to Evie, who hovered, eyes wide, as she took in Wulf, Devil, Pierce. "Evie."

Evie threw herself at her sister. Devil only narrowly avoided a fist to the eye. Kitty hugged her hard. She might have been laughing. Crying. Both. "You're safe now. You're safe."

"And you're betrothed!"

"Erm. About that…"

"You're awfully green. Maybe you should sit down."

"I'm fi—" Too late. Devil had plucked her off her feet and deposited her in the nearest chair.

Evie looked very near to swooning.

Kitty looked down at Portsmouth, still sprawled on the carpet, a dagger protruding from his leg. "Well, now what do we do with him?"

Evie scowled. "Can I hit him again?"

"Yes." This was a chorus from everyone in the room. Even the housekeeper, who was helping the vicar sit up.

Kitty narrowed her eyes at Devil, catching his expression. She pointed an accusing finger up at him. "You can't kill an unarmed man."

Devil smiled, amused. "Can't I?"

She rolled her eyes. "You *shouldn't* kill an unarmed man. Even one like him."

"As it happens, I don't have to."

"No?"

"No. I've already sent word to the people he was blackmailing. Some of them are very powerful. Unlike this pathetic excuse for a vicar. And they are rather cross. He'll be on the run.

Probably forever."

"And the evidence? Will you return it to them?"

He snorted. Wulf and Pierce both snorted as well.

"All right," Kitty grumbled. "It's not as if I expected him to."

"What evidence?" Priya demanded.

"Portsmouth was blackmailing a select list of people in order to get away with his murders."

"Who?"

Devil only smirked. Priya muttered something very uncomplimentary under her breath. Then much louder. Twice.

Portsmouth groaned.

"Stay down," Devil snapped, "or Miss Evangeline here will hit you again."

Caroline stepped closer to peer down at her husband. He blinked blearily at her. Her smile was deeply, happily unforgiving. "I will be in charge of your estate while you are running for your pitiful life," she informed him. "I intend to donate most of your money to the family members of your previous wives—the ones who actually loved them. *Not* the one who sold them to you like cows at market. The rest will go to orphanages that care for orphaned girls and aristocratic bastards. And widows." She crossed her arms. "And then I will drive you so deep into debt that creditors will also be hounding you to the ends of the earth, should you escape the others. Your family name will be mud."

He groaned again. She had hit a deeper nerve than Devil's knife.

"You're not leaving him here?" the vicar asked nervously.

"He's your problem until the others find him," Devil replied, shrugging. "Next time don't force girls to marry murderers."

"But—"

"Count yourself very lucky I don't stay here even a moment longer." The threat was clear, sharp. Cold. The vicar shut his mouth.

"You're not going to double back and kill him when we've all gone, are you?" Kitty whispered.

"Probably not," Devil whispered back.

"That is not reassuring."

He just shrugged.

Evie looped her arm through Kitty's. "Let's go home."

Kitty was deeply grateful Evie and the others were safe. That Portsmouth would get justice in one form or another. But there was a thread of uncertainty too.

She did not know where home was anymore.

CHAPTER THIRTY-ONE

As PREDICTED, KITTY could not bring herself to sell her betrothal ring.

She fiddled with it as Devil brought her and Evie to his house, dawn streaking the sky with colors as bold as a tulip field, and then again when they left the next afternoon.

They did not go to their father's house.

They reclaimed Galahad from the Spinster House and then found themselves at the Golden Griffin. Kitty always found herself at the Golden Griffin. Home was books. Home was Evie.

And Devil.

Two out of three wasn't so bad. She had no cause to complain. She had entered this with clear eyes. And though the betrothal had not been called off publicly, it was only a matter of days, surely. Today, maybe.

Or the next.

She checked the papers daily so carefully that Evie bought her a magnifying glass.

It had only been a few days. Exactly six.

Devil was concentrating on the grand opening of the Sins, which was occurring...At this very moment. He did not have time to formally reject her. He was busy. Now that Portsmouth was on the run, as Devil predicted, the sabotage of the club, great and small, had ceased. There were no tea deliveries because she still had masses of tea left. No strawberry cake. No reason to attend the Seven Deadly Sins inaugural evening. There was an invitation on the table in the back room. Evie had pinned it to the wall with a very pointed expression. Not to mention actual pointing.

"Only six days," Kitty reminded herself.

"What was that?" Evie asked from the back room.

"Nothing."

She could wait until tomorrow. One more day was nothing.

Twilight was soft and blue at the windows. Most of Mayfair was no doubt dressing for the Sins, whether or not they had an invitation.

She could not wait until tomorrow.

"Evie, help me with my dress."

MISS PERIDOT MARCHED into the shop not long after, her reticule redolent of raw onion. She blinked at Kitty. "You look like a gold candlestick."

Kitty's gold dress was the only article of clothing she possessed that would not have her turned away at the club doors. "Thank you?" It was not the most encouraging thing Miss Peridot could have said, but also not the worst.

"A very pretty candlestick," she allowed.

Evie grinned, sorting books from one of the boxes that Kitty had finally had a chance to catalogue. Caroline had declined to reclaim any of her belongings. Miss Campbell's parents, being better actors than anyone had credited, had feared for their daughter's life by association and spirited her away before she could meet Caroline at the iron oak. Caroline had kept checking for messages, finding Kitty's note and eventually deciding to respond. Miss Campbell had been in a carriage bound for Galloway for most of the last month, and a message had been sent to bring her back after Portsmouth disappeared. Caroline had invited her friend to move into Portsmouth House in Grosvenor Square, where Evie had already been for tea. She and Caroline had much in common, having evaded a murderer.

Portsmouth had not shown his face since.

Kitty and Evie had moved into the shop's back room until they could find rooms to rent. They might not have a pleasure hall to run, but they had been busy too.

"Where's that big, strapping fellow who usually lurks outside?" Miss Peridot demanded.

"Wulf and Godric are busy elsewhere, I'm afraid."

"No they're not," Evie corrected her. "Wulf is across the street trying to be subtle."

"He is?"

"He's a bit big for subtle," Miss Peridot said. "Delightfully so. I don't care for slender calves, myself."

Kitty felt a wash of affection. She had missed his and his brother scowling at the Ladies' Association for Moral Standards until they fled in a flurry of parasols and offended gasps. Accepting cups of tea, helping ladies with their packages.

It had only been six days, she reminded herself.

"He shouldn't be here, though. I'm sure he's needed at the Sins. Especially tonight."

"*That* place." Miss Peridot sniffed. Paused. "Do you think you can get me an invitation?"

Kitty could not help but smile. "I'll see what I can do."

"Good, good. Now show me a new book. I'm bored. Not all of us have been getting into shenanigans like you."

"Miss Peridot," Evie said, "have you read the one about the duke who turns into a wolf?"

Miss Peridot perked up. "I have not. Would you care for an onion, young lady? It strengthens the blood."

"I've already had one today."

"No, she hasn't." Kitty grinned.

"Yes, I have. I ate *yours*, remember? Kitty has had a very trying time. She should eat this one, don't you think?"

"Must go!" Kitty said hurriedly, grabbing for her reticule. "Can't get any stains on this dress!"

Nothing like the threat of having to eat a raw onion like an apple to put the starch back in one's spine.

She had not walked half a block before the brothers Winchester pulled the carriage to the curb. "Where to, Miss Caldecott?"

She blinked at them. "Surely you can call me Kitty."

"Not if I want to keep my fingers," Samuel said cheerfully. "Where can we take you?"

"I'm happy to walk."

"I really do like my fingers," Michael said from the outrider post. His black hair was wind ruffled, his smile wolfish.

"Did Devil send you?"

"Of course."

"How did he know?" she asked. "*I* didn't know until just now that I was going out."

"We've been here all week," he shrugged. "Just in case."

"An old lady threw an onion at us yesterday," Samuel added. "She thought we were spying on you."

Kitty laughed. "Miss Peridot is not to be trifled with."

"It's about to rain," Samuel pointed out. "Please let us drive you. Anywhere you want to go."

"What if I said Inverness?"

"Then we'd go to Inverness."

"Absurd." She smiled at them, then shook her head. "To the Sins will be fine, thank you."

"Thank God," Samuel muttered. "He's been in a rotten mood. Calm as anything all across the bloody Continent. Didn't flinch at bullets passing by his head. But this... You may be our only hope, Miss Caldecott."

THE SEVEN DEADLY Sins of London burned through the night.

Ladies in diaphanous red gowns sewn all over with spangles stood on marble pedestals in the garden. When they changed their positions, it was an acrobatic feat that drew gasps and murmurs from passersby and the guests waiting to enter. Crowds gathered on the pavement, begging for entry to the opening night. Indecent amounts of money were offered for the privilege. Kitty did not recognize the man stationed at the door, but he bowed to her as he stepped aside. "Miss Caldecott."

Envy was already filled with patrons, music electrifying the air. A balcony presented a woman singing in a voice that belonged to a fairy queen. Dancers whirled below her, eager to see and be seen.

The side doors opened to Gluttony: offering every delicacy, every sweet, every fanciful dessert in the most luxurious of surroundings. Red velvet, gold, and paintings of feasting revelers showcased roasted peacocks and lamb, and tiny potatoes swimming in butter and herbs. Champagne in glasses shaped like lilies. Towers of cheese, biscuits stamped with pitchforks, jellied pâtés molded into Greek temples, castles, swans and songbirds. Pineapples, raspberry trifle, currant cakes dusted with sugar and candied violets. Strawberry cake.

In the entrance hall, Tom smirked at everyone, wearing his best lilac hat to match the faded bruise around his eye. He spotted Kitty immediately. "Thank God," he said, echoing the brothers Winchester.

"About time," Devil said moments later when Kitty walked into his study.

The club bustled with excitement. She had seen an entire boar leaving the kitchen, dressed with apples and yellow lilies. A roasted peacock sewn back into its feathers. Several flower shops had emptied their shelves in every corner of the building. London might well be out of flowers entirely. Courtesans, each more beautiful than the last, floated through the rooms, flirting, laughing, offering champagne. There was music, dance, feasting. Every kind of entertainment, as promised.

And here the devil sat. Brooding.

Not just brooding.

"Are you sulking?" Kitty asked.

"No."

She raised her eyebrows. He was absolutely sulking. "Are you quite certain?"

"Where have you been?" he asked evenly, but the effort clearly cost him. He looked ready to bite into her like fruit. She tried not to like it, but failed.

"I'm sorry, I nearly forgot," she admitted.

"Forgot?" he echoed, tone hardening. He rose to his feet, so slowly and carefully that it was faintly threatening.

Very well, it was *entirely* threatening.

"You forgot where I lived?" he said.

"To bring you the vowel." She hadn't forgotten, of course. She had just been putting it off. But a deal was a deal. Especially a deal with the Devil.

She plucked it out from inside her boot and placed it on the desk.

"You had it in your shoe?" he asked, amused. "This entire time?"

"Mostly." She pushed it closer to him. "Was it very important? This viscount who wagered his house?"

"It's not important in the least."

"It's not?"

"Kitty, do you know how many houses we've collected?"

"No. And don't tell me," she muttered. She frowned. "You put it in your pocket that Devil's Night. I thought it meant something. That's why you gave in to the blackmail."

"I admit it would look bad for business if someone managed to steal from me," he conceded. "My reputation does most of the work for me now."

"Oh. Well, I did promise to give it back when my sister was safe. I should have given it back that night."

He ignored it. "How is your throat?"

She touched the tiny cut, mostly healed and barely visible. "It's fine. As *you* well know."

"How would I know? I haven't seen you in a week."

"You sent three doctors to look at it," she reminded him wryly. "*Three.*"

But *he* hadn't come. Not once.

She swallowed, refusing to read into the easy way they fell into needling each other. *She* might miss it, might find it romantic.

He probably found it annoying.

She had made him wait too long for the stolen vowel, and it had made him cross. No one reneged on a deal with the Devil, not even her. "I'm sorry I made you wait."

He looked mollified.

Until she continued.

"You can cry off the betrothal now," she added. "No one will blame you. They'll only think you've finally come to your senses."

He stalked around the desk. "What did you just say to me?"

She blinked at the intensity rolling off him. The piercing green of his eyes, like the dark forests that hapless fairy tale characters were lost in. Forever.

"You can…" She waved her hand, feeling out of sorts, miserable, just as cross. Why was he making this so difficult? Wasn't it difficult enough?

Well, for her. Obviously not for him.

She waved her hand again. "Cry off. Like we planned." She would not cry. It was ridiculous to cry. Evie was safe. And Kitty had had more time with Devil than could ever have been reasonably expected.

There was silence for a beat. Two.

"Kitty?" he asked silkily, with a hint of danger. Just a hint. Just enough.

"Yes?" Something primal inside her body responded. Aware. Uncertain. Hungry.

"When did I ever say I was going to let you go?"

The air left her lungs, rushed back in. It suddenly felt as though she had not had a proper full breath for the entirety of the last week. "Wh-what?"

"I never said anything about crying off," he replied darkly.

"We agreed to a pretend betrothal."

"*You* said it was pretend," he corrected her. "And I agreed because you needed me to."

"Oh. *Oh.*"

He was closing in, prowling closer. Liquid heat went through her.

Desire.

Hope.

And yet…

"I'm not sure I can be a mistress," she admitted softly. "It would harm Evie's chances for a decent match, and I've already so thoroughly done that."

He scowled. "Who the hell said anything about a mistress?"

She scowled back. "Devil, earls don't marry shopkeepers at whom people throw vegetables."

"First of all, I can assure you no one will ever throw anything at you again. And secondly, I can marry who I want to marry." It was the stubbornness of a man who was used to bending Society to his will.

"What about the ancestral lineage, and all that?" she asked, because someone had to be reasonable, and it obviously was not going to be him.

"The earldom can rot. My brother can be earl. I couldn't care less." He dug his fingers into her hair. "Kitty, there's no one else for me. Ever. Maybe you don't want to marry a devil…"

There was uncertainty under all that confidence. For *her*.

"Marry me, Kitty," he said. "Or don't marry me—whatever you want. Just *be* with me."

"I…" She wanted to. Every part of her wanted to wrap herself around him and not let go. "I really would make a terrible countess. I don't know the first thing about dessert forks."

"We'll use spoons."

"Rhys."

"I was serious. Tom can be earl."

"That's not how that works." Even Devil could not wrestle

primogeniture into submission.

"Don't care. I want *you*, Kitty. Only you."

"I'll embarrass you." She worried at her bottom lip. "Someone will throw a cabbage at your door."

"You are entirely obsessed with vegetables, love. But I'll throw it back. I have very good aim." He stroked his thumb along her collarbone, down between her breasts, where the gnawing, burning hole had somehow filled. "Or we'll make soup."

"You think you're so clever."

"Just in love with you, firecracker." She caught her breath, so he said it again. "*I love you.*" That almost-smile. "I'll find a prince for Evie."

"Oh well, in that case." She smiled back at him, stroking along his strong jaw, until his lids half lowered. She couldn't stop touching him. Did not want to. "I love you too."

His arms tightened around her. "Is that a yes?"

"Yes."

He dropped his brow to hers. "You do make a man work for it," he said, striving to sound unbothered, but she heard the joy in his voice.

"Your brother offered to give me his horse when I got here as a reward for dealing with you. A bribe, I suppose, not a reward. And a goat. Apparently, you are worth a goat? And I thought Shelby was going to outright weep. He says you've been insufferable."

"He's sacked."

"MacLeod stopped me in the hall to wish me luck. He said you were pining."

"He's sacked too. I do not pine. I was being *patient*."

"He was being an ass," Tom shouted as he stalked down the hall, balancing ledgers full of guest lists.

"You can be sacked too," Devil shot back, kicking the door shut with his boot. "Now, where were we?"

"You were being patient."

"Yes, I think I've had enough of that now." He caged her

against the wall, green eyes flaring hotly. Every part of her reacted, like tendrils reaching for the sun. Or, more accurately, jasmine blossoms opening to the moon. There was nothing of the sunshine in him. Thank God.

She frowned, then shoved at his chest. "You!"

"What was that for?"

"You let me stew and worry for days!"

"I was being patient, remember?" He dragged his mouth along her neck. "I'll make it up to you."

"You had better." It would have sounded much fiercer if she hadn't moaned. "If you ever do that to me again, I shall try one of Yelena's hatpin tricks."

"I won't." He kissed her lightly, again and again. "I *am* sorry. I thought I was doing the right thing by waiting for you. I was told empirically that gentlemen do not storm into a lady's bookshop and carry her away."

"Hmmph. Perhaps with prior notice." She couldn't help but melt against him. There was too much happiness inside her, too much want.

"Duly noted." He bit at her pulse point, and she whimpered. "I'm an idiot. But I thought I had scared you away. I didn't want to scare you more."

"I don't scare easily, Devil." She pushed her hips against him, and he groaned.

"I am not a…kind man."

"You've said that before, and it was ridiculous then and it's ridiculous now. You are kind to me," she said. "And to your men. And to your brother."

"I broke that man's ankle. And I'm not sorry about it."

She wrinkled her nose. "Will you think less of me if I said he deserved it? My own grandfather assures me that I am going to hell."

Devil raised an eyebrow. "Hell is my domain, hadn't you heard? You'll be just fine."

"In that case"—she wound her arms around his neck—

"perhaps we could move on to other matters."

"Thank Christ," he said fervently, pinning her more securely to the paneling so that he could taste her, lick into her mouth, growl wonderful, filthy things in her ear. Everything. Everything all at once. And it was almost enough.

She did not think it would ever be enough.

She clawed at his clothing, every bit as desperate. He finally sprang free of his breeches and she wrapped her fingers around his length, hot and hard and silky. She gripped him tight, sliding up and down, and she was already wet and he was shoving her dress up around her hips. He stroked her folds. "So soft and wet," he groaned. "You're ready for me, aren't you, firecracker?"

"Yes," she gasped when he circled her bud, so lightly, then with more pressure, enough that she bucked against him, tension already mounting.

"Ah, ah," he ordered, lifting her up so her legs were around his hips. "Not yet."

"*Devil.*"

"There she is." He kissed her again, and it was a claiming. "Demanding and wicked and needful." He moved so that the tip of his cock parted her folds but went no further. She tried to lower herself onto him but would not allow it. He kept them there, panting and frantic for each other. "You're *mine*, Kitty Caldecott. Lady Birmingham."

She squirmed helplessly, loving it. Wanting more. The tendons on his neck stood out as he forced himself not to let her take him deep. It was the best kind of struggle. "And you're mine."

"Always. Say it properly."

"You're mine, *Rhys.*"

"Better."

But still he kept them just barely touching. Her quim ached. "Rhys." She bit his shoulder. "Is there another name I should call you, you insufferable man? Do you have a middle name? Sebastian? Alfred? Eustace?"

He bit her back, playful but demanding. His growl tightened

her nipples, shot straight to her quim with a flutter. "Call me husband."

She ceased squirming. "Oh." His jaw was so hard, his mouth so soft. She brushed her lips over his. "You're a *romantic*."

"*Countess*." A warning.

"We aren't married, *Lord Birmingham*."

The tip of his cock parted her soft folds, slipping into her wetness. Just the tip and then he stopped again, punishing her. She whimpered, but he was ruthless, merciless. "I'm waiting," he said.

She kissed him once more, then his jaw, her voice soft and hot in his ear. "*Husband*."

He slid into her wetness with a growl that sent shivers and tingles washing through her. He angled himself so that each thrust also dragged against her bud, already swollen and sensitive. It was rough and frantic and perfect. When her moans threatened to turn to screams, he clamped his hand over her mouth.

It was too much.

Her climax swept through her with no warning, washing into every part of her, tightening around his cock until he followed her into blind pleasure. Where there was only his body, his sweat, his harsh breaths in her ear. Only him.

When they came back to themselves, to the wainscotting digging into her back and her left foot tingling numbly, he moved his hand away from her mouth, eyes like green fire.

"Wife."

Author's Note

A part of this book is my love letter to romance novels and fandom communities. It might be a little unusual to find easter eggs in a Regency romance—but I just had the best time putting them there. I hope you have fun collecting them, if you are so inclined.

A Sebastian for Lisa Kleypas's *Devil In Winter*. Robin of Sherwood because it was my first fandom and my first fictional crush. *Firefly, Highlander, Supernatural.* A nod to *Peaky Blinders.* A nod to monster romances. A nod to the romantasy genre through ACOTAR.

I consider my favourite characters to be friends and co-conspirators, at least for the length of a book or a movie, and often much longer.

Stories save us in so many ways. And I am so grateful to you for being part of this story with me.

About the Author

Alyxandra Harvey lives in an old stone house with her husband, multiple dogs, and a few resident ghosts who are allowed to stay as long as they keep company manners. She likes chai lattes, tattoos, and books. Sometimes fueled by literary rage.

Author of The Drake Chronicles, The Witches of London, Haunting Violet, Red, Love Me Love Me Not.

Twitter: AlyxandraH
Instagram: alyxandraharveyauthor